# *The* LAST ORPHAN TRAIN

# *The* LAST ORPHAN TRAIN

*An epic story of despair, rage, hope, and courage*

## MIKE LAPINSKI

*A Novel*

TATE PUBLISHING
AND ENTERPRISES, LLC

Published by Tate Publishing & Enterprises, LLC
127 E. Trade Center Terrace | Mustang, Oklahoma 73064 USA
1.888.361.9473 | www.tatepublishing.com

Tate Publishing is committed to excellence in the publishing industry. The company reflects the philosophy established by the founders, based on Psalm 68:11,
*"The Lord gave the word and great was the company of those who published it."*

Published in the United States of America

ISBN: 978-1-63306-521-5
Fiction / Christian / Suspense
14.07.03

For Tom, Seth, Nathan, Jacob, and Whitney

Come to me, all you who are weary and heavy burdened,
and I will give you rest.

Matthew 11:28

# THE ORPHAN TRAINS

etween the years 1859 and 1929, almost a quarter million youngsters, from babies to teens, were shipped by rail from eastern states to the West. Faced with an overload of orphans and abandoned children in the teeming inner cities of the industrialized East, the New York Children's Aid Society, the New England Home for Little Wanderers and the Chicago Home Society, loaded these young cast-offs onto "orphan trains" to find new homes.

Some children were true orphans, lacking mother and father, but the vast majority were either abandoned or given up. Remarriages were especially bad for casting off children who had fallen out of favor with the new spouse.

Likewise, few families who greeted the trains were childless couples earnestly seeking to adopt and raise a child as their own. Instead, the majority of children were chosen specifically for, or eventually relegated to, servanthood on isolated ranches and farms that dotted the lonely western landscape.

After crossing the Mississippi River, these orphan trains stopped at towns along the rail route where the youngsters were paraded onto depot sidings or community halls to be inspected by the interested and the curious. Depending upon perspective, a few lucky children would be picked out of a lineup. The remainder were herded back onto the train, and the entire routine was repeated at the next scheduled stop.

Though the orphan train movement undoubtedly grew from a sincere desire to help homeless children find loving families, abuses occurred, and by the late 1920s several states threatened to outlaw the orphan trains. To quiet these complaints, orphan train proponents circulated photos of happy children packed into railroad cars. They discovered, too late, that these photos, appearing on the front pages of the nation's newspapers, created the opposite effect.

A storm of protest brought the issue to national attention as concerned citizens decried the dehumanizing effects of herding castoff children into train cars like cattle, then sending them to uncertain futures in a harsh land. In 1929, the U.S. Government finally outlawed the interstate transportation of homeless children, namely the orphan trains.

This is the story of one of the last orphan trains. Though it is a work of fiction, it is based on a chance encounter I had with an old woman named Liz, who told me her father was sent to an orphanage, escaped, and miraculously found his way back home, only to be callously returned to the orphanage. The words in this book are mine; the anguish, rage and hope are his.

# CHAPTER 1

The room reeked of camphor oil and alcohol, just like how his father's room had smelled. It smelled of death.

Fourteen-year-old Bartholomew Henley fought back a rising wave of fear and nausea and put on his best doctor's face as he padded silently across the oak plank floor to an ashen-faced, raven-haired woman lying in bed. Springs creaked as he hesitantly sat next to her. The woman's eyes fluttered open, focused on him, and a weak smile pursed her lips.

He placed a hand on her forehead, surprised to feel it hot and damp. He leaned forward and kissed her cheek before announcing, "Mother, I think you are doing very well today."

Elizabeth Henley brought a thin hand to her son's cheek and spoke in a voice barely above a whisper, "Already you have a better bedside manner than old Doctor Hanes. You are going to make a fine doctor someday."

A sudden coughing spasm engulfed her, and she hacked into a lacy white handkerchief. Bartholomew's eyes widened as dull red splotches soaked through the cloth. His fear surfaced in a panicked rush of words. "Mother, are you going to die?"

"Of course not," she replied breathlessly and lay back on the pillow until her breathing steadied. She studied her son and smiled lovingly. "Oh, what beautiful features you have. My English complexion and high cheekbones, and your father's brown hair and green eyes." Her eyes glazed as she whispered, "My dear, dear Charles."

Bartholomew's eyes widened. He leaned close and corrected her. "Mother, I'm not Poppa. I'm Bartholomew."

Elizabeth Henley's eyes blinked rapidly, then she relaxed and smiled. "Of course you are. You just look so much like your father, God bless his soul." She reached her arms out, and he fell against her breast, squeezing his eyes shut to hold back the tears.

At that moment a chubby, freckled-faced girl with fiery red hair burst into the room. With pigtails flying, Henrietta Henley skidded to a halt at the side of the bed, pecked her mother on the cheek, and announced, "Guess what, Momma? Maura doesn't treat Bar nice!"

Elizabeth Henley sternly corrected her daughter. "Do not call your brother that gutter name. I have given both of you children proper English names so you could maintain some culture in this heathen place. Your brother's name is Bartholomew and you, young lady, will refer to him that way."

Hen, as Bar called her beyond earshot of Momma, curtsied and cast a mischievous glance his way. "I am very sorry, Bartholomew. From now on, I shall always call you Bartholomew."

Bar nodded curtly, but swore vengeance upon his little sister for calling him that detested name—a name the other boys at school teased him about mercilessly. "Now, Bartholomew," Elizabeth's voice rose with gravity. "What is this about Maura not treating you well?"

Bar flushed and dropped his eyes. "Oh, she treats me all right, Momma."

Henrietta stepped forward and volunteered the titillating proof. "This morning she gave me my mid-morning snack of milk and cookies. And she gave Bar, uh, Bartholomew, none."

At that moment Maura swept into the room and flashed a brilliant smile. Both children stiffened, but Elizabeth Henley met her maid squarely, as she had everything else in her adult life.

And that included this hideous, uncivilized place called Windsor, in the state of New York, where she'd come to marry a wealthy American in-law four years ago after her husband's untimely death. Windsor, Elizabeth quickly discovered, was British in name only, being inhabited by unrefined housewives and slovenly farmers.

As for that "rich" American she'd married, Albert Henley turned out to be a beer-bellied lout who thought he had the right to have his way with her. Even worse, his "financial holdings" amounted to a rundown farm house with peeling white paint and sagging roof, and a forty-acre horse and dairy farm that barely supported them.

Thank goodness she'd managed to keep a touch of British refinement within the household, including this impetuous servant girl, Maura, newly arrived from Ireland and willing to work for almost nothing.

Elizabeth Henley turned her full attention to her maid. "Maura have you been treating the children equally well? Henrietta tells me you failed to give Bartholomew his snack this morning," she asked in a voice tinged with her patented petulance

Bar inwardly cringed. Ever since he'd walked into the spare bedroom in the basement and found his stepfather sitting on the bed with her, Maura had not treated him well. Now Henrietta would be in for it, too.

Maura closed her eyes and slapped her forehead with a hand reddened from the caustic Fels Naptha cleaning soap. "Oh, Mrs. Henley, it slipped my mind! I gave Henrietta hers, but then Mr. Henley called me outside to help him, and I forget Bartholomew's snack."

Henrietta opened her mouth to counter the lie, but Bar stopped her with a furious glare. Maura tousled Bar's hair and made a sad face as she cocked her head, allowing her long brown hair to spill over the side of her freckled face. "You will forgive me, won't you, Master Bartholomew?"

Bar glanced up at that smiling face and those cold, dark eyes. He stammered, "I, I didn't complain about it."

Elizabeth Henley erupted in a violent coughing spasm, and Maura quickly herded the children out of the room before attending to their mother.

Later that day, Bar watched Maura stomp out of the house to the corral where short, stout, red-haired Albert Henley stood watching a hired hand work the horses. With hands on hips, Maura gestured back at Bar.

Afterwards, Albert Henley took Bar aside. "Your mother is very sick, Bartholomew," he said in a grave voice while idly twisting a waxed tip of his handlebar mustache. "If you want her to get better, you must not upset her by telling her about anything that happens around here. It just makes her sicker. Do you understand?"

Bar nodded, his face glowing from the rare attention afforded him by Albert Henley. Bar's own father was but a vague memory, so Albert Henley had become the masculine presence that Bar yearned for in a house full of females. On the other hand, Albert Henley frowned whenever Bar called him Poppa.

Bar did as Albert Henley had instructed, and even brow-beat his little sister into quitting her snitching, but Momma got sicker and sicker, and Maura treated them even meaner.

Two weeks later, Bar and Henrietta returned from school and found the doctor's horse and buggy parked in front of the house. A neighbor lady led Henrietta into the kitchen, while a somber-faced Albert Henley took Bar into the parlor and spoke in a low voice, "Your mother is very sick. She wants to talk to you." He looked away and added, "Don't say anything to upset her."

Doc Hanes sighed heavily and placed a stethoscope into his large black leather bag. Slowly shaking his head, he turned to speak to Albert Henley, but stopped when he saw Bar.

Albert nudged Bar forward. With each step, the boy's trepidation increased, until he stood trembling at the side of the bed. His mother lay ashen-faced and still. Bar leaned forward and said in a low, trembling voice, "Momma? Momma, it's me, Bartholomew."

Elizabeth Henley's eyes fluttered open. She labored to raise her hand, and Bar quickly grasped it. She spoke in a halting whisper, "Charles, bring Bartholomew to me."

Bar was about to correct her when her eyes closed. A few seconds later they blinked open, and a faint smile creased her face. "My dear Bartholomew, I…" Her eyes bulged and mouth opened wide as a convulsion ripped through her body. She sucked in a long ragged breath and wheezed, "Take care of your sister." Then her hand fell away.

"I will, Momma! I will!" Bar called back as Albert Henley pulled him away and Doc Hanes rushed forward.

ooooo

The funeral ended Elizabeth Henley's Victorian reign over the household, and brought something far worse to the house afterwards. A week later, after all the well-wishers had stopped coming by to pay their condolences to Albert Henley, Maura moved from the tiny room in the cellar to Albert's bedroom.

Of course, Hen continued to be a pain. She explicitly disobeyed Poppa by crying and asking when Momma was coming back.

She even exasperated Bar. "She's not coming back," Bar would explain, annoyed by his sister's inability to understand their mother's death, and forcing him to confront once more the horrible truth of his words. "Momma's not coming home. She's in heaven. Now stop asking about her."

But what could you expect from a ten-year-old? It had been no one's fault but her own when Maura whirled around during breakfast one morning and cuffed Hen on the back of the head for crying about Momma.

Totally against Momma's instructions for proper behavior, Bar jumped up and pushed Maura backwards. "You leave my sister alone!" he yelled in a quaking voice.

Maura's face contorted into a mask of rage. The hard slap knocked Bar backwards against the table, spilling the breakfast porridge and milk. She stalked out of the room, leaving Bar and Hen trembling in stunned silence. A few seconds later, Albert Henley stormed into the room, grabbed Bar by an ear, and dragged him into the back room. Bar screamed as the leather belt raised welts on his bare bottom.

The next morning before school, Hen urgently beckoned Bar to follow her behind the barn. When they were out of sight, she blurted, "They're gonna send you away, Bar. Far away!" She fell against his chest, wailing.

Bar patted her head and corrected her. "They're not sending me anywhere, Hen. You shouldn't go listening in on other people. You're too young to understand grown-up talk."

"No!" She pulled back, and her eyes widened. "I heard Maura and Poppa talking this morning. Poppa said if you wouldn't mind her, he'd send you away someplace."

Bar dismissed the incident as little-girl hysterics, but a week later Albert Henley took him for a walk in the back pasture to look at a new bull. Bar was elated as he struggled through the high grass to keep up, and the thought occurred to him that they'd probably be doing a lot more things together now that Momma was gone, for she had forbidden Bar from accompanying Albert to the barnyard before he had proper schooling.

Albert Henley stopped at a picket fence and Bar climbed to the top rail. He saw the faraway look in his poppa's eyes and began searching the horizon for whatever he was looking at. "Bartholomew," Albert Henley began, "there comes a time when a boy begins to turn into a young man, and he must strike out to learn about the rest of the world."

He nervously twisted his mustache before continuing. "It had always been the intention of your mother and I to wean you from her when you turned fourteen. This is the way she planned to make you a strong young man, and it is now left to me to continue with this plan. As such, we will be sending you away for a short period of time."

Bar paid respectful attention to his father's words, though his heart beat rapidly. His words rushed out, "Where will I be going, Poppa? Will it be faraway? Will you take me there and make sure they are nice people? Will you come and get me? Will you..."

Albert Henley silenced the boy with an impatient wave of his hand. He cleared his throat and announced. "We will be sending you to spend time with folks who have a farm some distance from here. It won't be for too long. It will make you strong and independent, like me." That said, Albert Henley stomped back to the barn.

For the next three days, Bar went about life in a daze. He desperately wanted to know what the people were like, and if Poppa and Hen would come and visit him, but Albert Henley silenced Bar's questions with narrowed, warning eyes.

Maura seemed to be the only person who was happy. Bar caught her humming a tune as she packed his belongings into a cardboard suitcase. At night, Henrietta slipped into Bar's bed and clung to him, whimpering and trembling. He fought back tears and reminded her, "Geez, Hen. I'm only going away for a little while. I'll be back before you know it."

"No, you won't," came her muffled retort. "She hates us!"

Bar reminded her, "I promised Momma I'd take care of you, and I will."

ooooo

Bar dreaded the morning when he would have to say goodbye to Hen, sure that his little sister would cry and make a scene, but the

17

grown-ups solved that problem. Albert Henley shook him awake before dawn and led him silently past Hen's room. An unsmiling Maura shoved a cold dinner roll into his hand as he was ushered into a waiting buggy. The fear increased within him as the horse plodded through the muddy road in the dark. Though he wasn't hungry, he ate the roll to satiate his nerves, and the bread sat in his belly in a doughy knot.

The gloomy light of dawn fell upon the bustling train station in the nearby city of Binghamton when the buggy lurched to a halt. Albert Henley hopped out and lashed the horse's reins to a hitching post, then checked his pocket watch. "Damn thing's late," he muttered as he grabbed the suitcase from behind the seat. His eyes met Bar's, and he grumbled, "Come on, boy. Get on down from there and get a move on."

While they waited for the train to pull up to the boarding siding, Albert Henley again checked his pocket watch and frowned when he saw Bar's trembling lower lip. "Remember, Bartholomew, you're fourteen now, and young men do not cry." he admonished the teary-eyed boy.

As Bar blinked back the forbidden tears, Albert Henley looked away and spoke in a vague voice, "This journey will strengthen you. Make a man of you."

Bar had doubted those words back at the farm, and he doubted them now. Where he was going, he did not know, and he feared that it was not somewhere nice.

The train chugged slowly to the siding and stopped amidst a swirling, hissing cloud of steam. A loud whistle ripped through the air, followed by the call, "All aboard!"

Albert Henley handed an envelope to a white-jacketed porter and spoke to the man in a hushed voice. The porter nodded and grasped Bar's arm, but he tore free and hugged his stepfather. Albert Henley stood stiffly, hesitantly patting the small shoulders and said, "There, there, now. Go along with the man. He will see you through your journey."

As the porter led Bar away, he turned and called, "Tell Henrietta I'll be back soon!"

But Albert Henley was already gone.

# CHAPTER 2

$\mathcal{T}$oward the front of the lumbering Erie & Lackawanna Railway train, posh Pullman cars, outfitted with stuffed leather booths and red velvet wall coverings, accommodated the first class passengers. A dinner car of polished brass and oak kept the well-to-do satiated with the finest in food. Behind it, a lounge car afforded ample libations to bolster their soaring spirits.

They were mostly bankers and businessmen, speculators, and lawyers who rode the Pullmans—the new rich, riding not only these extravagant railroad cars, but also an unprecedented boom in America's economy. Though it was only April, financial forecasters were expecting the 1929 stock market to outpace even the previous two record-setting years.

Toward the rear of the train, the Pullmans gave way to austere rail cars where the common man rode—farmers who fed the rich, and laborers who built their mansions and sweated in their factories. There was no dinner, or lounge, or sleeping cars. Men, women, and children gritted their teeth and survived nights packed into stiff-back seats. Mothers fed their children milk squeezed from the family cow, bread baked the night before, and jam made from the blackberry patch behind the house.

A conductor entered the last car before the caboose to check tickets, weaving as he walked to counter the train's constant sway. He ignored the urgent eyes and raised hand of the slim boy dressed in short suit and knickers, but an adolescent voice, frightened and pleading, rose above the roar of the train. "Sir, where am I going?"

The conductor continued checking tickets but acknowledged the lad with a shake of his head and the curt reply, "To a place where they will take care of you, boy."

Bar's countenance fell. He slowly sank into the seat and turned toward the window to hide his fear.

It had been his boyhood dream to ride on one of these sleek passenger trains that roared by the farm, but now, with each clickety-clack of massive steel wheels over rails, Bar's trepidation increased. He stared out at a steady parade of farmhouses passing by as the train chugged through New York's fertile Southern Tier farm country. The translucent face that stared back at him on the dirty glass window appeared on the verge of tears. He wrenched his eyes away from the ghostly image, his father's lecture about crying still fresh in his mind.

Twice that first day a porter came by and handed him a sandwich and glass of milk. And his state of shock helped ease the long hours of staring out the window at more fields and lonely farms. During the afternoon of the second day, Bar noticed an increase in towns and roads. The train now made stops more frequently, and the passenger cars became stuffed with people—folks who rarely made eye contact and bustled in and out of the cars without so much as a glance or word to the person seated next to them.

Late morning on the third day, the train rumbled past several steel mills whose smokestacks belched massive gray-black plumes. Gritty, acrid smoke seeped into the car and burned Bar's eyes. On one smokestack was a sign that read: Gary, Illinois Ironworks. Clustered between these mills was a dismal collage of clapboards houses and smaller brick buildings.

A half-hour later, the train slowed as it entered a city. Bar watched, mesmerized, as mile after mile of drab, tightly-packed houses passed by. As the train eased to a halt at a station, a stern-faced porter grabbed his arm and ordered, "Come with me, boy."

Bar felt a mixture of excitement and trepidation as the porter pulled him through a milling crowd of people. He'd formed a mental image of a farmer with weathered face and kind eyes, sitting in his buggy somewhere just ahead, waiting to take Bar to a nice farm.

That dream evaporated when the porter stopped in front of a tall, gaunt man with a pinched face and downturned mouth, wearing a rumpled brown suit. The hard look in the man's eyes made Bar back away.

The porter pushed Bar forward and asked, "You Mr. Johnson?" The man nodded and the porter handed him an envelope, along with Bar's cardboard suitcase, then hurried away.

Mr. Johnson's brows furrowed as he read the letter. He cast a dour glance at Bar and commented, "It says here you have no respect for your elders. I could tell right off you're a troublemaker."

He grabbed Bar's collar and yanked the startled boy forward until they were nose-to-nose. The man's sour breath almost made Bar gag. He drew his head back, eyes wide, and a small cry escaped from his opened mouth.

Shaking Bar like a rag doll, Mr. Johnson growled, "You mind yourself. You hear me, boy?" Bar gulped, blinking back tears, and nodded. He wished Momma were here. She would never allow him to be treated like this.

"Come on, then," Mr. Johnson ordered and yanked Bar along, maintaining his grasp on the stumbling boy's collar. As Mr. Johnson pulled him through a maze of milling humanity, Bar became convinced it was all some kind of mistake. He'd been dropped off at the wrong place.

They arrived at a large black motor coach parked along a paved brick street behind the depot. Mr. Johnson unlocked the door and yanked it open. Bar's eyes fell upon two other boys who sat together with hands on their laps.

Mr. Johnson shoved Bar onto the seat opposite the two boys. "I'll be right back," he said gruffly. "You boys behave, or else." He punctuated the threat by forcing his last words through clenched teeth.

"Yes, sir," the larger of the two boys replied politely. Mr. Johnson glowered at the boy for a second before slamming the door and locking it. The bigger boy's polite demeanor faded with the footfalls. He turned hard eyes on Bar then glanced at the other boy. "You see the way he looked at us, Zeke?"

Zeke stared insolently at Bar and nodded. "I seen it, Charlie."

Charlie leaned forward aggressively. "You lookin' fer trouble, punk?"

Bar's eyes widened and he stammered, "No! I'm…I'm not looking for trouble. I'm on my way to—"

"Shaddup!" Zeke yelled and turned to his cohort. "Charlie, I think he's lookin' fer trouble. See how he talked back at ya?"

Charlie flicked out a hand and knocked Bar's cap off. When he bent down to retrieve it, a hand clamped onto the back of his neck and pushed it down hard. As Bar squealed in pain, Charlie threatened, "You ever talk ta me again like that, punk, I'll smash your face in!"

The cruel hand pulled away, and Bar jumped back, crying in pain and fear as he rubbed his neck. "Aw," Charlie said in a mocking voice, "the little baby is startin' ta cry!"

Bar's whimper turned into a frightened scream when Zeke, sniggering, kicked his shin. "Hold it!" Charlie exclaimed and threw up a cautionary hand. Above Bar's weeping came the sound of approaching footsteps. Both boys assumed a rigid posture, but Charlie snapped a warning look at Bar and hissed, "Stop yer cryin', punk. If we get in trouble, you're dead meat!"

Keys jingled outside the door, and it flew open. Through his tear-blurred eyes, Bar was relieved to see Mr. Johnson with another boy slightly bigger than himself and the other two. The new boy stood sullen and slope-shouldered, with a round face and wide mouth that made him look like a monkey. He carelessly pushed a shock of dark hair off his forehead while defiant eyes scanned the faces of the three boys in the coach.

Mr. Johnson shoved the monkey-faced boy inside, and he flopped down hard beside Bar. The man eyed Bar's sniffling and demanded, "What's going on in here!"

Charlie replied with a shrug, "Nothin', sir. I think the kid's homesick is all."

Mr. Johnson glowered at them and warned, "I'll be right back. Any trouble and there'll be hell to pay." He slammed the door and locked it before hurrying away again.

Charlie and Zeke eyed the new boy like serpents sizing up another meal. Bar stifled a sob, and Charlie snapped, "Shaddup, crybaby!"

The new boy glanced at Bar and asked, "What's a matter with him?"

Charlie nodded at Zeke before turning narrowed eyes on the new boy. "None a yer business," he snapped. "You lookin' fer trouble, too, monkey boy?"

The new boy suddenly jammed his foot into Charlie's crotch and ground his shoe into the screaming boy's groin. Zeke started to rise, but a hand lashed out and clamped onto his face—a thumb rammed up one nostril, with two fingers jammed into the howling boy's eyes. "Nobody talks ta Spike McKovitch like that!" the new boy said through clenched teeth. "Ya give?"

Both victims screamed, "I give up! I give! I give!"

Spike McKovitch flopped back in his seat and smirked as his wailing victims writhed in pain. A gloating grin came to his face as he sang, "Cry baby, cry! Stick a finger in yer eye!"

It was a song Bar had mockingly sung to Henrietta when she cried over some real or imagined slight. Struck with a surge of homesickness, he sucked in a loud, ragged breath.

Spike McKovitch misread Bar's sigh as a conspiring smirk. He nudged Bar hard with his shoulder and said, "Don't worry, kid. These two punks ain't gonna bug ya no more."

Footfalls pounded on bricks again, and all four boys snapped to attention as the door flew open. Mr. Johnson studied the two snivelers. "What're you two crying about?" He grabbed Spike McKovitch's arm and demanded, "Did you do anything to them?"

Spike McKovitch vehemently shook his head. "No sir! I, I think they're just a little homesick."

Mr. Johnson brought forward a teary-eyed blond boy much smaller than the others. He was shoved inside and sat trembling next to the two snivelers. Mr. Johnson walked around and got behind the wheel of the motor car. As the vehicle lurched forward, Charlie quit sniffling long enough to elbow the small boy in the ribs.

Mr. Johnson kept an eye on the boys through his rear view mirror, so there was no more talk or shenanigans. The recent brutality had left Bar in a state of shock as the car rumbled along a brick road and then onto a gravel country lane. His young mind was unable to comprehend much of the train trip, and none of the brutality that had just occurred in the back seat of the coach. But of one thing he was certain. Some kind of mistake had been made.

ooooo

A huge brick building loomed ahead, with a half dozen smaller houses nearby, and endless farm fields surrounding them. As the motor car passed through an open wrought-iron gate, a surge of hope filled Bar when he saw the proof that he was indeed in the wrong place. A large sign above the gate read: Chicago Boys State Orphanage.

The motor car rumbled alongside a large field where three dozen boys toiled. Some planted slim cabbage plants, while others cut down weeds with hoes. As the motor car drove by, the boys paused to glare at the occupants.

The car jolted to a stop in front of the brick building. Mr. Johnson unlocked the door and threw it open. "Out!" he barked. Bar was last out, and he scrambled forward to inform Mr. Johnson of his error. "Sir, I believe there has been a mistake. This is an orphanage. I'm supposed to be…"

The next instant Bar was lying on the ground, stunned by the sudden blow. He gingerly brought a finger to his nose, and when his hand came away crimson, he began to wail. Mr. Johnson stood over him and jabbed a finger at Bar's face, his voice harsh and threatening. "Don't you ever talk out of turn again, you understand?"

Spike pulled Bar to his feet and explained, "He'll be all right, Mr. Johnson. He's just a little bit homesick." Spike led Bar toward the large doors and muttered, "What're ya, stupid or sumpin'? That guy'll beat ya ta death if ya pull that trick again."

Bar whimpered, "But, but I'm not an orphan. My father sent me to work on a farm for—"

"Shaddup!" Spike hissed. "And quit yer cryin' all the time. These punks see ya cryin', they'll eat ya alive."

"But…but I'm not an orphan."

Spike smirked. "Ain't hardly nobody in here real orphans. Me, I got sick of the ole man beatin' on me, so I hit him with a board one night when he come home drunk. I been here off an' on ever since."

Spike looked around before adding in a low voice, "But I ain't gonna be here for long. I escaped once, and I'll do it again. You just watch. Couple weeks and I'll be gone."

The new arrivals were herded into a large bare room that held a powerful chemical odor. A slim man, not much taller than Spike, poked his head into the room and yelled, "Strip!" The other boys began to shuck their clothes, but Bar stood uncertainly, embarrassed by the gleaming white naked bodies

An elbow rammed into his side, and Spike urgently whispered, "Shuck 'em quick, kid! They gotta spray us fer lice. And stay outta that Stallings' way. He's a mean one." Numbly, Bar slipped off his knickers and shirt and stood, humiliated, among two dozen other boys. The younger boys, who had not yet reached puberty, covered their smooth private parts. Most of the older boys who had pubic hair, like Spike, stood sullen and defiant, not bothering to hide their budding maleness. Bar fell into the latter group, having recently noticed dark hairs sprouting down there.

Stallings entered the room carrying a galvanized metal garden sprayer. He vigorously pumped air into the sprayer and shouted, "Cover your eyes with one hand and raise your arms!"

Bar did as he was ordered, but peeked to his left as the man advanced from youth to youth, spraying them with a foul smelling liquid. Suddenly, a cold spray hit Bar, and he almost gagged from the putrid chemical odor.

"Bend over!" came the order. Bar peered through burning eyes and watched the other boys lean forward, so he did the same. A wooden stick was wedged between his buttocks, and Bar jumped as the icy spray assaulted his private areas.

The boys were then sent into another room, where three showers spewed steaming hot water. "Three at a time in the showers." Stallings instructed. "Use the soap and rub hard, or I'll get in there and scrub you myself!"

Bar was in the second group who entered the showers. He gasped as the hard yellow soap and chemical mixed with the water and burned his skin. Fortunately, Spike was next to him, and he imitated the hard scrubbing of his newfound friend. The little blond boy who'd ridden in the motor car jumped out of the shower on the other side of Bar and whined, "It burns!"

Stallings strode forward, wrapped an arm around the boy's waist, and turned him upside down. He vigorously rubbed the screaming boy's crotch with soap. Finally, he dropped the sobbing child to the concrete floor and turned to the others. "Anybody else complain, and I'll rub the hide offa ya. Now get moving!"

Spike nodded toward Stallings' back and whispered in Bar's ear, "Queer as a three dollar bill, that one."

The naked mass was herded into a small room piled high with drab brown pants and long sleeved shirts. Stallings threw a set of clothes at each boy as he walked by. Bar's shirt was too big, but he'd already learned the price of speaking up, so he quietly accepted the ill-fitting clothes.

The sun was low on the horizon as the new arrivals left the small brick building. The crew of boys they'd passed on their way in now trudged tiredly past them. Spike grinned and saluted a few of his old buddies, but he stiffened when a red-haired boy even bigger than himself stopped and eyed him coldly before warning, "I'm boss now, Spike."

Spike gulped hard, but stood nose-to-nose with the bigger boy and replied in a hoarse voice, "We'll see about that, Butch."

"Move along there!" the field supervisor ordered.

Butch walked backwards, glaring at Spike, and smashed a fist into his palm. "You're dead meat!" he called. Spike responded by smashing a fist into his palm, but Bar noticed that he again gulped loudly.

Fifteen minutes later, 112 boys ranging in ages from eight to fifteen assembled in front of a set of large double doors at the side of the brick building. Mr. Johnson opened the doors and ordered, "Two lines! No shoving or talking!"

The procession moved forward, with each boy receiving a bowl of cabbage soup and a thick slice of dark bread. Bar followed Spike to a table where several boys nodded at Spike and muttered hellos under their breath. The tables filled quickly, leaving only the small blond boy to wander from table to table, desperately seeking a place to sit, but he was turned away at each table. He finally stood in the middle of the hall with tears streaming down his face, tiny shoulders hunched and trembling. "Hey you!" Mr. Johnson's voice boomed. "Sit down and eat!"

The boy's lower lip began to tremble, and his pleading eyes met Bar's. Bar motioned to the boy next to him to move over, but he refused to budge. Bar grabbed the edge of the table and rammed his body to the right, forcing the kid over. Bar nodded to the narrow space next to him, and the little boy darted for it.

Spike glared, first at the boy, then at Bar. He leaned forward to slurp his soup and whispered, "What'd ya do that fer? We don't need no little kids in with us. Everybody'll be whackin' 'im, and we'll have ta stick up fer 'im."

Bar glanced at the trembling little boy beside him and muttered, "I'll take care of him."

Spike leaned forward and whispered furiously, "Ya can't take care a yerself!" He shook his head in disgust. "Ya don't know nothin' about this place."

A large bell clanged, and the mess hall erupted in a frenzy of activity as the mass of boys rushed to slurp down the remainder of their soup. "New boys over here!" Mr. Johnson ordered and pointed toward Stallings.

Spike slipped to the head of the line, and Bar fell in behind him. He felt a small head bump into his shoulder and turned to see the little blond boy pressed close to him.

Stallings walked past counting heads and paused to affectionately tousle the small boy's head. Bar figured it was Stallings' way of being nice to the boy for hurting him in the shower. The small boy peered up and gave the man a tentative smile, but Bar noticed Spike shaking his head ever so slightly.

Stallings counted out loud to twelve and said, "You boys are in Room Eight." Then he turned to Spike, and a smirk creased his face as he spoke in a loud voice, "Clarence McKovitch. You know where Room Eight is located. Head that way."

A chorus of muffled giggles spread among the boys, and several mockingly muttered, "Oohh, Clarence! Good boy, Clarence!

Momma's little boy, Clarence!" Spike flushed beet-red, and his hands balled into fists as he stomped through the crowd of sniggering boys.

ooooo

The narrow brick room had been white-washed years ago, but most of the cheap paint had peeled off the damp walls and now lay in cockroach-infested piles on the concrete floor. Six double bunk beds lined one wall, and one large chamber pot lay beneath a single light bulb dangling from the cracked plaster ceiling. Spike walked to the far end of the room and sat heavily on the bottom bunk—head down, hands clasped on his knees. "What a dump," he moaned. "What a miserable dump."

He sighed heavily and stood up. "Okay," he said in a loud voice, "everybody around me." The other boys gathered in a circle and Spike addressed them, "Any a you guys ever been in before?"

None responded. "That's what I thought," Spike commented with a smug nod. "Okay then, here's the way it is. Every room has a boss, and I'm the boss a this room. Anybody got a problem with that, step out an we'll have it out." Spike smacked a fist into his palm and surveyed the boys.

All averted his glare. "Okay, in this place everybody's gotta have a nickname or they'll hound ya ta death. I'm Spike. Anybody calls me Clarence eats his teeth. Got it?" He studied the group and muttered, "Geez, what a bunch a pipsqueaks." He turned to Bar and said, "Yer next biggest ta me. What's yer name, kid?"

"Bartholomew Henley."

Spike rolled his eyes. "See what I mean? These punks'll razz ya ta death with that name." Spike rubbed his chin for a few seconds before announcing, "From now on, your name is Clint. That's a good, tough-soundin' name."

He went on to ask each boy's name, then gave them his own personal moniker. By the time he'd finished, Batholomew's,

Ludwig's, Johnathon's, and Peter's had been replaced with nicknames such as Clint, Mugger, Raker, and Bo.

Everyone received a nickname except the small blond boy. Spike finally stood in front of the child, hands on hips, and slowly shook his head. "What's yer name an how old are ya?"

The little boy stepped forward, his almond eyes growing wide with pleasure at being the center of attention. "My name is Jeremy Phillips," he said in a high-pitched voice, "and I'm almost nine, sir."

Spike stamped his foot and snarled, "My name ain't sir! Got that?"

The small boy stumbled backwards at the outburst. "My name is Spike. I'll forgive ya this one time, but next time yer in fer it. Now, I can see yer a runt who's bound ta get picked on, so I think I'll name ya Mugsy cause yer gonna need all the help ya kin get in here."

The small boy beamed as he mouthed his new tough-guy name.

A stocky, dark-haired boy with a permanent scowl, who'd been dubbed Bo, asked, "What about that big kid ya had the run-in with earlier? Is he the big boss?"

The color drained from Spike's face and his lips became a thin line. "Butch McCarthy's a punk. There ain't room in here fer both of us ta be the boss. Used ta be, a guy named Rocky was the big boss, but he turned sixteen an' they turned him loose. I run away right after that, but they caught me sellin' newspapers on Maxwell Street in the city. Now it's between me an' Butch."

Stallings walked into the room and glared at Spike for a moment before barking, "Everybody in bed! Lights out in five minutes." His eyes followed Mugsy as he struggled to reach the top bunk above Clint.

Stallings hurried forward and propped his hand under Mugsy's butt. "Here's a little help for sonny boy," Stallings said with a grin. He stalked to the door and turned back. "Any noise in here after lights out, and there'll be hell to pay."

The hanging light bulb flickered twice and died. Spike's voice floated through the night, "Hey, Clint, you a good scrapper?"

"Uh, yeah," Clint lied, thinking of the spats he'd had with his little sister, which had amounted to him teasing her to tears.

"Good," Spike's voice came again. "That Butch don't fight fair. Back me up if anything happens, okay?"

"Okay," Clint replied, thankful that Spike could not see his face.

A squeaky voice came from the cot above Clint. "I'll, I'll back you up too."

Spike snorted. "Way ta go, Mugsy. Ya c'n bite 'im on the ankle." Giggles filled the room, but Mugsy's eyes darted back and forth.

The snickers faded, replaced by sighs and sniffles, for the darkness reminded each boy how true Spike's assessment had been about their plight. Clint lay on his belly and buried his face in the mattress to stifle his emotions, but it reeked of disinfectant and urine, so he rolled onto his back. He sighed and thought of his mother, recalling the gentle sound of her voice, reassuring and praising him. He squeezed his eyes shut and drove those thoughts from his mind, lest he burst into tears. He thought about his sister and wondered what Henrietta would do without him for a few weeks.

Clint had just wiped tears from his eyes and was slowly drifting to sleep when hurried footfalls echoed in the hall. A flicker of light shone under the door, which slowly creaked open, revealing three figures silhouetted in the weak glow of two kerosene lanterns.

Spike's bunk shook, and a moment later he stepped into the lantern light. "Well, Butch," he said in a gruff, but quavering voice, "ya wanna have it out already, do ya?"

Clint squinted, and as his eyes became accustomed to the dim glow of the lanterns, he recognized the belligerent face of the big red-haired boy from the field crew. Another boy almost as big as Spike stood on Butch's left, while Charlie, the kid who'd hurt Clint in the motor car, stood on his right.

Butch glanced and nodded. "Jonesy, you and Charlie spread those lanterns out so I c'n see ta pummel this punk's face in." Both boys warily circled Spike.

Spike gulped and croaked, "Whatsa matter, Butch? Ya can't fight fair? Ya need ta cheat ta beat me?"

Butch's face contorted into an ugly mask. "I didn't need help last time, and I don't need none now ta beat a punk like you, Spike!"

That terrible recollection sent a wave of trembling through Spike. He balled his fists and mumbled to himself, "Remember what ya' learned on the streets."

In the ghostly glow of the lanterns, the two young gladiators warily circled each other while the other boys formed a circle around them. The boy named Jonesy, hands balled into fists, shouldered Clint aside.

Butch and Spike sprang at each other. Fists pounded against flesh with loud, sickening thuds as they traded punches. The fury and power of the two fighters shocked Clint, who'd witnessed only a few scuffles behind the grade school in Windsor.

The fighters broke off and warily circled each other. Blood flowed from Spike's nose, and Butch's lower lip bled from a deep gash. Spike spat blood and muttered again, "Think. Think what ya' learned."

Butch crept forward and threw a tremendous roundhouse right, but this time Spike ducked as the fist whistled over his head. With Butch off-balance, Spike sprang forward and unloaded three hard punches to Butch's face that sent him careening against the wall, stunned.

Spike stalked forward and brought his right hand back to deliver a haymaker punch, but Jonesy jumped forward and landed a solid blow to the back of Spike's head. Spike howled and staggered against the wall. Butch, now recovered, started pounding

Spike with punches until he stumbled forward and draped his arms around Butch.

While Butch struggled to free himself, Spike's head cleared. He reared his head back, and Butch made the mistake of thinking that Spike was trying to escape. Spike's head shot forward and butted Butch, the loud smacking concussion eliciting a gasp from the crowd. Butch's eyes rolled upward and he collapsed.

As Spike waded in to finish the fight, Jonesy again sneaked up behind him with fist cocked. Clint leaped forward and grabbed the arm. Jonesy literally carried Clint forward with his punch, then turned his fury on Clint and landed an off-balance blow to the back of Clint's head with his other fist. A burst of stars and darkness engulfed him, but through his dim consciousness, Clint felt he and Jonesy floating to the floor.

Jonesy began screaming hysterically. He pushed Clint aside and grabbed at his leg, where a vicious rat terrier by the name of Jeremy Phillips, aka Mugsy, had sunk his teeth into Jonesy's calf.

Spike whirled to face the commotion behind him and saw that his buddies had Jonesy under control. Butch, almost recovered from the head-butt, was rising to his feet when Spike employed another one of his new fighting techniques. He kicked Butch hard between the legs. Butch screamed and dropped, whereupon Spike pounced on him and began pummeling his face with looping lefts and rights. Butch curled into a ball with his hands over his head and howled, "I give! I give!"

Spike left his battered victim and ran over to Jonesy, who was still screaming and kicking at Mugsy. Spike kicked him low in the back, and Jonesy screamed even louder, arching his back and grabbing behind him. Spike pounded his head until he also yelled, "I give! I give!"

Charlie tried to run, but the boys in Room Eight jumped him at the doorway. Spike grabbed the terrified boy by the hair and threw him at the whimpering Butch on the floor. "Grab yer punk buddy and get outta here before I have a go at ya!" Spike stood with legs spread, chest heaving, fists on hips as he watched Charlie drag Butch out the door, with Jonesy hastily limping behind.

Spike turned to face his audience, eyes dancing as he pumped his fists in the air and bellowed, "Aargh! Who's the toughest kid in this place?"

"Spike!" The boys yelled and joyously descended upon their champion, peppering him with congratulatory pats on the back. Flushed with the sweet adrenalin of victory, the boys sat around the kerosene lamps, each enthusiastically recounting some fragment of the fight, much to the delight of Spike, who seemed oblivious to his swollen face and blackening eye.

"Don't you guys worry," he assured them. "Ole Spike'll protect ya. With Butch outta the way, ain't nobody gonna mess with Room Eight."

But then Mugsy ruined everything when he piped up with, "Spike, when's my momma coming for me?"

# CHAPTER 3

*T*he room became deathly silent. Mugsy's simple question had sliced deep into every boy's heart. Indeed, when were their mommas and poppas coming for them?

Spike stood statue-like for several seconds, a baleful glare directed at Mugsy. "You guys are so stupid!" he erupted. "This is a orphanage! Grow up! It's *not* a place where they send kids with no parents! We're here because our ole man an' ole lady don't want us! Grow up, all a ye, already!"

Spike's chest heaved. His hands clenched into fists. Sweat ran down his face. He angrily swung an arm around the room and challenged, "How many a ya ain't got no ma or pa? How many, huh? Raise yer hands if ya ain't got a ma or pa somewhere." Several boys searched for hands, others dropped their eyes.

Spike put his hands on his hips and remarked, "That's what I thought. You're all throwaways! You're here 'cause yer ole man or ole lady don't want ya no more." He gulped and his eyes misted, then a hard look came to his face. "Me, I don't hardly even remember my ma. She just up an' left one day when I was little. My pa got drunk all the time, an then he'd come home and beat me. Finally, I whacked him with a board an' he sent me here."

Clint cautiously spoke up. "My father told me he was sending me here to help me grow up. You might be right about these other kids, but in a month, I'm supposed to be sent back to New York. My father promised."

A smattering of hopeful voices rippled through the crowd. Spike cocked his head and replied with mock wonder, "Are ya stupid or sumpin', Clint? This ain't no boardin' school for rich kids ta learn how ta be tough. Once ya get in here, they don't let ya out till yer sixteen an' a grown-up."

Clint frowned and kicked the floor. Mugsy sniffled, and a few other muffled sobs reverberated through the crowd.

Spike drew himself up to his full height and glared at the boys. "Anybody got a argument with what I just said?" Silence, except for one ragged sigh.

"Okay, ya want a family? Ya got one. We're all family in this here room from now on. An' I'm the boss, an' I got some rules we're gonna live by. First, nobody picks on nobody from Room Eight. We all stick together."

Spike began pacing with brows furrowed. He stopped abruptly and wagged a finger at the group. "Second, no fightin' amongst ourselves. Any two a ya have a problem, we'll have ya duke it out in here in the evenin'." He paused then added, "But I wanna tell ya all one thing. I get ta fight the winner."

All eyes widened at the ramifications of that last statement. "And no rattin'," Spike added.

Clint glanced around then asked, "What's rattin'?"

Spike smirked. "Don't ya know nothin', Clint? Rattin' is squea-lin', snitchin', tellin' on other kids. Anybody do that, an' yer outta this here family."

Spike stared at the floor and thought for a few seconds before his face became grim. "An' one more thing. No screwin' around with each other."

Clint leaned forward and asked in a tentative voice, "What's 'screwin' around' mean?" Snickers rippled through the crowd. The boy next to him whispered in his ear. Clint's eyes bugged out and his jaw dropped.

Spike rolled his eyes. "Any more bright questions, idiot? Want a blow-by-blow description?" Clint flushed and rapidly shook his head.

Spike walked over to Mugsy and placed a consoling hand on the little boy's shoulder. "All right, listen up now. We gotta do sumpin' ta protect Mugsy. Little kids get picked on a lot in here." He patted Mugsy's shoulder, and a sad, troubled look spread across his face. "Especially if they're pretty little blondies. Whoever gets assigned ta the laundry, get some black dye or shoe polish. We gotta change this blond hair ta sumpin' else."

"Why, Spike?" Mugsy asked, his baby face the epitome of innocence.

Spike shook his head, grinning, and playfully rubbed his knuckles on Mugsy's head. "Nothin' ya gotta worry about, tough guy." He turned and addressed the group. "All right, let's hit the hay. An' remember, it's us against them." That said, he turned down the kerosene lamps.

ooooo

The light bulb flickered on in the morning, and the door banged open. Stallings poked his head through the doorway and yelled, "Fifteen minutes 'till mess hall!"

After a quick breakfast of weak tea, mush, and toast, the new boys were assigned chores ranging from housecleaning, to laundry, to field work. Normally, all boys attended school until noon, but it was Saturday, which meant no school, and a full day of work.

Clint, Mugsy, and the boy named Bo were sent with a dozen others to pull weeds from a large cabbage patch. At midday, Stallings pulled up in a small horse-drawn cart, and the boys eagerly lined up for lunch, which consisted of one slice of bread, a cookie and half cup of milk. Stallings, Clint noticed, slipped Mugsy two cookies.

Clint waited for Bo to get his lunch, while Mugsy wandered over to a log and sat down. As Clint and Bo started toward him, a big boy sauntered over and nudged Mugsy hard with his knee, then reached down and snatched the cookies from his hand. The boy walked away, gloating, but froze when a voice called out, "Give them back!"

The boy warily turned, but when he saw it was only Clint, he smirked and challenged, "You talkin' ta me, punk?"

Clint placed his lunch on the ground and folded his arms to hide his trembling hands. "I said give the kid his cookies back," he croaked.

The boy, half a head taller than Clint, stepped forward aggressively. "Why don't ya try ta take 'em from me, punk?"

Clint gulped and took a step back. Out of the corner of his eye, he saw Bo slip around behind the boy and drop to his knees. Clint stepped forward and pushed hard against the boy's chest, barely budging him. But it was enough. The boy pitched backwards over Bo and hit the ground hard, his bread and milk scattering over the dirt. Clint sprang forward and kneeled on one arm, while Bo kneeled on the other. Pinned securely to the ground, the boy whined, "No fair! Two against one!"

Bo countered, "Yeah, well, you're picking on a little kid. Ya wanna keep on with this, me an' Clint here'll pound ya into the ground." Bo cocked his fist, and Clint did the same. The boy's eyes widened and he exclaimed, "I give! I give!"

Clint and Bo stepped back while the boy sheepishly rose and brushed himself off. He groveled for fragments of his bread and cookie, which had been mashed during the scuffle. Near tears, the boy complained, "Now I ain't got nothin' ta eat till supper."

Clint handed the surprised boy his lunch, with the warning, "Just remember to leave the kids in Room Eight alone, or else."

ooooo

Word spread quickly about Room Eight. Those few hardheaded kids who didn't take heed, got their heads softened by Spike.

Spike also instituted a nightly regimen of teaching all the kids in Room Eight how to fight. Clint was embarrassed to discover that, next to the diminutive Mugsy, he was the worst scrapper in the bunch. Spike took it upon himself to help Clint improve his fighting skills. Their half-hour drills became more dangerous and physically demanding for Clint than a day toiling in the fields.

As a matter of survival, Clint learned to duck as Spike sent wave upon wave of half-speed punches at his head. Clint was surprised to discover that he had quick reflexes, allowing him to dart in and land a few shots before Spike nailed him. After just one week of training, the boys of Room Eight had become a force to be reckoned with.

One evening, Spike had Mugsy's sit in front of him. Spike rubbed shoe polish on a comb and carefully ran it through Mugsy's soft blond locks until the sweet little blond boy had been transformed into a sweet little boy with greasy black hair. Spike pronounced his experiment a success, though when Mugsy sweated in the fields, perspiration ran in dark rivulets down his smooth face. Still, everyone agreed that it did make Mugsy look a bit older and less pretty.

But two nights later, while thunderstorms rumbled across the land, it became obvious that Spike's experiment had failed. Room Eight had been dark for a half-hour, but Clint was still awake, thinking of how the boys back at school would be amazed at his new muscles and scrapping skills. And God help that smarty pants, Joey Thompson, the next time he pulled Henrietta's pigtails and made her cry. Oh, how proud Poppa would be when Clint showed up as a strong young man.

Clint's eyes blinked open at the sound of squeaking hinges. He peered through the darkness and spotted a lone figure standing in the doorway. The person padded forward silently and stood within inches of Clint, who lay rigid under his blanket. Harsh whispering and the squeak of bed springs came from the bunk above. The figure padded swiftly toward the door with a small body in his arms.

Clint lay stiffly for several minutes, his mind straining to understand what had just happened. Finally, he whispered, "Spike!"

"Shaddup!" came the terse reply. Eventually, Clint fell into a fitful sleep but awoke when the door hinges again squeaked, and he watched the figure carry Mugsy back to his bunk.

ooooo

Tension hung heavy in Room Eight when the light blinked on in the morning. A few boys who'd slept through the incident giggled and horsed around, but the others dressed quietly. Finally, Mugsy climbed down and stared at the floor for a few seconds before he slowly dressed. Spike was surly for the rest of the day, but when no intruder appeared the next night, Spike woke up joking and jostling as usual.

But an hour after lights out the next night, the door creaked open, and Mugsy was taken again. Eleven boys lay rigid on their bunks, enduring the torture of knowing that one of their own was out there—and there was nothing they could do about it. An hour later the door creaked open again, and the figure carried a whimpering Mugsy back to his bunk.

As the figure shuffled toward the door, Spike called out, "Queer!"

The figure paused, then whirled and ran back to Spike's bunk. Spike grunted as fists pounded against his flesh. "Don't do nothin', guys!" came his tortured plea. "Stay in yer bunks!"

Clint watched in horror as the bent-over figure pummeled Spike's body, finally stepping back and kicking him before stomping out of the room. Someone lit a candle, and the boys rushed to Spike's bunk. Clint gasped when he saw Spike's blood-covered face. "Spike, you're hurt!" he exclaimed. "I'll get Mr. Johnson."

"No!" Spike groaned. "I'm, I'm okay. Somebody get me a wet rag and some water." He gingerly bathed his face in the rapidly reddening water and groaned, "I'm okay. Everybody go ta bed."

Fear permeated the room. Clint lay on his bunk, his heart beating furiously, until he could stand it no longer and whispered, "Spike?"

"Yeah?"

"What are we gonna do?"

Spike moaned, "I'll think a sumpin'."

In the morning, the boys dressed silently, careful to avoid staring at Spike's puffy face. Clint finally glanced over and winced. Spike's left eye was black, his face a mottled red and purple.

Mugsy hadn't yet stirred, so Clint gently nudged the small body under the blanket. "Mugsy, time to go for breakfast."

"I, I can't!" Mugsy cried. "I'm bleeding down there!"

Spike hobbled over and helped Clint lift Mugsy down to the floor. The small boy stood with his legs slightly spread, staring in shock and terror at the dried blood on his thin thighs. "It hurts down there, Spike!" Mugsy whimpered.

Spike brought his hands to his face to hide his shame. "I want my mommy!" Mugsy wailed and burst into tears. Clint put his arms around Mugsy, and the boy sagged against his chest. Spike, tears pouring down his cheeks, patted Mugsy's trembling little shoulders and sobbed, "Don't worry, Mugsy. He won't hurt ya again. I'll protect ya."

Spike ordered two boys to take Mugsy to the infirmary. As the others trudged out of Room Eight, Spike sidled up to Clint and whispered, "Meet me behind the dinner buildin' after supper." The hard look in Spike's eyes sent a chill up Clint's spine.

At supper that evening, Clint and Spike gobbled down their soup. Both raised their hands to go to the latrine while the other boys were assembling for evening choir practice.

ooooo

"What's up?" Clint asked when he found Spike standing between two weathered sheds, which had old windows on one side and served as greenhouses to start plants in early spring. "Here," Spike said and shoved a gunny sack full of chalkboard erasers into Clint's hands.

"What's this for?"

"They're for ya ta clap the chalk outta. Ya gotta act as my look-out while I do this. We get caught, we're dead meat."

"Do what?"

"You'll see," Spike muttered and pulled an empty Vaseline jar from his pocket. He surveyed the area one last time before creak-ing open the door to the first greenhouse. Inside, he dropped to his knees and began scooting around the piles of empty wooden boxes.

Clint stood outside, slowly clapping the chalk from two eras-ers, and becoming more nervous by the second. Spike finally slipped out the door. Clint blurted, "What did you get?"

Spike shook his head and frowned. "Nothin. Ain't none in there."

"What are you looking for?"

"You'll see when I get one." Spike slipped into the next shed.

As boxes scraped over the wooden floor, the back door to the kitchen opened. Clint began whistling loudly, pounding out a cloud of white dust. A man wearing a food-stained white apron stepped outside and threw a large vat of greasy water onto the ground. He glanced at Clint, but said nothing before slamming the door. "All clear," Clint said in a loud whisper, and the creaking and shuffling began again. Suddenly, there was a furious bang-ing and scraping inside the shed, and a few seconds later, Spike emerged with a triumphant grin on his face.

"Got one!" came his excited whisper.

"What?" Clint asked, exasperated.

"You'll see. C'mon, let's get outta here."

Spike led Clint into a wooden building that housed some of the orphanage's staff. "What are we doing here?" Clint asked with rising trepidation. "It's Stallings' place."

A jolt of adrenaline shot through Clint as he furtively glanced around. "Geez, Spike. He'll kill us if he finds us in here."

"Not if we kill him first," came Spike's terse reply as he brought the Vaseline jar within an inch of Clint's nose. He gasped and jerked his head back. A large, wicked-looking black spider with a red hourglass on its underside scrambled frantically up the side of the glass.

Clint stammered, "Is, is that a…"

Spike grinned and nodded. "I almost got bit by one last summer when we was cleanin' out them sheds."

Mesmerized by the spider's agitated actions, Clint asked, "What are you gonna do with it?"

Spike's mouth became a thin line. "You'll find out soon enough. Just keep an eye out for me." He slipped into a room on the right and closed the door.

When Spike emerged a few minutes later, Clint was in a state of near panic "What'd you do?"

"C'mon," Spike said as he hurried past Clint.

ooooo

Both boys slipped unnoticed into the back line of the choir two songs before the assembly was dismissed. Spike whistled as he entered Room Eight and flopped onto his cot. One of the boys led in Mugsy, who walked bow-legged to his bunk. He stopped in front of Spike and managed a weak smile. "I, I told them I fell on a rake."

Spike nodded and smiled gently at Mugsy. "Good boy. And don't worry 'bout nothin'. Ole Spike's gonna protect ya."

44

Just before lights out, loud voices and yelling came from the staff house. Two car engines roared up, and drove away five minutes later. No one entered Room Eight that night.

ooooo

As the boys were finishing breakfast the next morning, Mr. Johnson cleared his throat and addressed the hall full of boys: "Attention everyone! Attention!" With all eyes on him, he continued, "Last night a very serious accident occurred that we should all be aware of. Mr. Stallings was bitten by a black widow spider while dressing in his room." Clint's eyes widened and his mouth dropped open. He turned to Spike, who calmly slurped his mush.

Mr. Johnson added, "He is in serious condition. Before classes begin, all boys will go to their rooms and shake out their mattresses and clothes."

Ten boys in Room Eight frantically shook out their clothes and pounded their mattresses. Clint and Spike sat facing each other; Clint looking guilty, Spike staring smugly back at him. The boys eventually gathered around Spike's bunk, and the boy named Raker said, "Geez, a black widow spider! I bet that hurt."

Bo leaned forward and volunteered, "Somebody said Stallings got bit on the nuts. They had ta cut his nuts off last night ta save his life. The dirty bugger's a eunuch now."

The boy next to Bo covered his groin and pressed his knees together while making exaggerated howling sounds. The room erupted in laughter. Spike's face showed no emotion, except for a triumphant gleam in his eyes.

ooooo

With Stallings gone, relative harmony reigned at the Chicago Boys Orphanage. Spike and Butch called a truce and set up joint management of all the boys. Fights were kept to a minimum, and the younger boys were protected from bullies.

Clint kept track of the time. He'd been at the orphanage for almost three months, and his father had not yet come for him, but he kept reminding himself that there was lots of farm work in the summer. With fall coming, school would be starting. Poppa would be here soon.

After church on Sunday, Spike motioned Clint to follow him into a cluster of bushes beside the barracks. Once out of sight, Spike kicked the ground and announced, "Stallings is comin' back on Wednesday. My spies tell me he's been mutterin' that he knows how that spider got in his underwear. He knows I did it. He gets back here, I'm dead meat."

Clint's voice rose with his anxiety. "What are you gonna do, Spike?"

"I'm outta here."

"When?"

"Tuesday night."

Clint's emotions erupted in a rush of words, "What'll we do without you?"

Spike shrugged. "Do the same thing ya been doin' all along. Stick together. Don't let nobody push Room Eight around."

Clint nodded numbly. "Ya do have a problem, though," Spike remarked. "Stallings'll have it in fer Room Eight 'cause he'll figure you guys musta know'd about the black widda. An' I just know he'll go after little Mugsy first."

Panic gripped Clint. "Geez! What'll we do?"

Spike rubbed his cheek, thinking. "I dunno if it'll work, but I been thinkin' about a plan. Wanna hear it?"

Clint spread his arms. "I'm up for anything."

"Okay, who do we know c'n get in where the pigs get slaughtered?"

Clint chuckled. "Poor Raker and Blade have to clean up the mess every Monday after the butchering."

"Good!" Spike jumped in. "They gotta sneak somethin' out fer me. Here's the plan…"

Clint's eyes bugged out and his jaw dropped as he listened to Spike's excited words. It was either pure genius or madness.

For the next two days, Clint stuck close to Spike, who explained to him how the real world worked. He also showed Clint every dirty trick he knew—using broken glass, nails, spiders, grease—anything to exact a measure of revenge.

When the light went out on Tuesday evening, Clint lay wide-eyed and rigid on his bunk. A few minutes later, a hand touched his arm and Spike whispered, "See ya later, kiddo. If it gets too bad in here, ya know how ta get out an' where ta find me." Then he was gone.

The next morning at breakfast hall, Clint watched Mr. Johnson frown and shake his head as he listened to a staff worker inform him that Spike McKovitch was gone.

As the boys filed out of the hall to go to their classes, Clint slipped away and retrieved a small package hidden under the porch of the staff building. He sneaked into Stallings' room and, as directed by Spike, placed the package on the bed.

After classes, Clint took the erasers out back and had just dumped them onto the ground when a hospital van pulled up. Stallings, sullen and pale, stepped out. Clint furiously pounded two erasers together, hoping the chalk dust would hide his guilty face, but Stallings' eyes remained downcast. Two hospital orderlies helped him up the porch steps. Staff workers came out and hailed Stallings with hearty, "Hellos."

Stallings' reply was a grim nod. As far as he was concerned, his life was over. Without the excitement of his periodic conquests, he could think of no good reason to live. He knew who was responsible for all this, and they'd pay dearly.

He shuffled past the well-wishers into his room. The bed had been freshly made. Lying on a gray woolen blanket was a small flat box with a bow on it. Stallings eyed the package and grumbled, "One lousy gift's all I get for all I done for this place."

He lifted the cover. A note lay on top of something wrapped in tissue paper. Unable to read the tiny printing, he leaned closer. The note read: *Deer Mistur Stalings, I think you lost thees, Spike.*

A frown creased Stallings' brow as he slowly pulled away the wrapping paper. He stared blankly, unable to comprehend what he was looking at. Then his eyes bulged out. The color drained from his face and his chest began to heave. He was gaping at two bloody testicles.

ooooo

Clint was coughing from an overdose of chalk dust when a loud, tortured scream ripped through the air. Staff members charged into the house, and he stood trembling as more tortured yells and loud voices emanated from within. A staff member ran from the house, spotted Clint, and yelled, "Get on out of here!"

Fifteen minutes later, a hospital van arrived and three brawny white-coated men carried away a babbling Stallings in a straight jacket.

That evening while the rest of Room Eight's boys gossiped about Mr. Stallings going crazy, Clint lay on his cot, a smug smile on his face. Spike's plan had worked perfectly.

The next afternoon, Clint whistled merrily as he walked with the other boys to the fields. A hard shove in the back sent him sprawling. He rolled over and saw Jonesy, hands on hips, standing next to him. "Hey!" Clint complained. "What's the big idea?"

Jonesy stepped forward, fists up, and snarled, "I got a bone ta pick with ya. Ya ain't got Spike ta hide behind no more."

Clint scrambled to his feet and retreated, waiting for his faithful Room Eight boys to back him up, but Bo and Raker stayed well back, wanting no part of Jonesy's two pals, who stood nearby eyeing them menacingly. "Come on!" Jonesy challenged. "Put up yer dukes."

Clint raised opened hands and said, "I don't want to fight you, Jonesy. Look, we just got rid of Stallings. We can all have it a lot better around here now. We can—"

The blow caught Clint flush on the left cheek and sent him flying backwards. He rolled over, felt a salty taste in his mouth and spat a glob of blood onto the dirt.

Jonesy jumped up and down, triumphantly pumping his fists into the air. "There ya go!" he exulted. "Spike's second in command is a wimp. Me an' Butch is the bosses now."

Clint struggled to his feet and stumbled backwards, shaking his head.

Jonesy was strutting away with his cohorts when Clint called, "It's not over yet, Jonesy."

Jonesy spun around, surprised. When he saw Clint with upraised fists, a malicious smile creased his face and he pranced forward in a fighter's stance. He lunged forward and put all his strength behind a looping right hand that would surely end it.

Clint executed one of the primary directives of Spike's training. He ducked. Jonesy's murderous blow whizzed over his head. With Jonesy off-balance, Clint threw a handful of dirt into his face. Jonesy howled and pawed at his eyes while Clint stepped forward and kicked him hard in the groin.

Jonesy screamed and dropped to a fetal position. Clint battered him with feet and fists. "I give! I give!" Jonesy cried, cowering on the ground.

Chest heaving, blood pouring from his mouth, Clint turned on Jonesy's pals and challenged, "Any of you want some of what he got?"

Both boys vigorously shook their heads and backed away. "Good job," Bo sheepishly congratulated him. "We was ready ta back ya up, fer sure."

Clint eyed him with disgust and walked away.

ooooo

While the rest of Room Eight championed Clint's feat that evening, he lay sullenly on his bunk, feeling totally alone. After lights out, he silently wept—for a little sister he desperately missed, for a father who hadn't come for him yet, for a mother who would turn over in her grave if she could see what he'd become.

The next morning as breakfast broke up, Clint slipped six leftover slices of toast inside his shirt as he walked by the tables. During the field work he kept to himself and worked hard.

After dinner, he sidled up to Mugsy and whispered, "I'm outta here tonight, Mugsy. I can't take it in here any longer without Spike. I'm heading back home."

Mugsy turned wide-eyed to Clint. His voice was shrill. "If you leave, I got nobody. These other guys are gonna go with the toughest guy, no matter what room. What'll I do, Clint?"

Clint explained the escape route exactly as Spike had explained it to him. Mugsy nodded woodenly, wiped tears from his eyes and stammered, "Will, will I ever see you again, Clint?"

The question sent hot tears streaming down Clint's cheeks, and he hugged the little boy. "Someday," he sobbed, "we'll all be together again."

ooooo

Clint lay trembling on his bunk for almost an hour after lights out. Finally, the staff quit banging and clunking outside and the place became quite. He slipped out of his bunk and started forward, but a small hand grabbed his shoulder. Clint reached up and embraced the frail, quaking body, found a cheek, and kissed it goodbye.

# CHAPTER 4

*N*ight security at the orphanage was unnecessary because its isolated location eleven miles north of the town of Franklin discouraged most boys from running away. Those few boys who did sneak off into the night were usually found the next morning, frightened, and limping on blistered feet along the lone gravel road leading into town.

Clint knew all this from Spike, but he hid in the shadows beside the barracks for a few minutes and surveyed the grounds. Finally, he took a furtive step into the open. He felt exposed, vulnerable, and a wave of hysteria gripped his heart and threatened to squeeze the blood out of it.

He was thankful for the loud chirping of crickets and cicadas wafting through the warm humid night, for those sounds masked the soft crunch of his threadbare shoes tip-toeing across the courtyard.

A feeling of exuberance rippled through Clint as he climbed the eight foot wrought iron gate. He dropped to the ground on the other side and turned back for one last look at the orphanage. The brick building sat like a brooding giant, a single light illuminating its front doors.

If he'd known it would be this easy, he would have brought Mugsy along. Clint felt an unsettling urge to go back for him, but he shook that dangerous thought from his head. No way was he going back there again. He turned and ran into the night, each step putting the temptation farther and farther behind him. Finally, he was on his way home!

Within a few minutes the lights from the orphanage had faded, but the sliver of a new moon provided little light. Twice, he stumbled when he could not see the road ahead.

As Spike had instructed, he trotted along at a casual pace to conserve energy, but sweat quickly soaked his shirt and his body heat attracted hordes of mosquitoes. As an act of self defense, he increased his pace to keep the bloodthirsty insects from alighting on his fevered body. In a grove of trees, a large animal burst from cover and Clint cried out, but then a deer snorted in the distance.

It was spooky running in the dark, but he pushed back the fear by concentrating on his home and family. He chuckled at the thought of sneaking up behind Henrietta and surprising her. And, oh, how surprised Poppa would be when he stepped forward and shook his hand! Poppa would say, "What a fine young man I have here! In just three months he has not only grown up, but he came all the way home on his own and saved me the trouble of coming to get him."

And there were other fantasies—about how he'd finally get the attention of that new girl, Marilyn Sanders, because of his new muscles and maturity. And wouldn't Joey Thompson be surprised next time he tried to pick on Clint!

Two hours later Clint arrived at a small wooden bridge. He slowly backtracked while peering to his right and located a narrow side road leading away from the gravel. According to Spike, the road was a shortcut to town, built when the wooden bridge had washed out a few years ago.

The lane was overgrown with briars and blackberry bushes and not as easy to follow, but after two hours of intermittent running and walking, Clint stumbled back onto the wide gravel road. The town should be only a few miles away.

But now he had a problem. He felt the first raw tinglings of a blister forming on the ball of his right foot, then his left foot started smarting.

His legs were sore and cramped, but he continued at a steady pace, running on the outside edges of his feet to ease the pressure on his blisters. But the blisters grew worse and finally popped, filling his socks with a slippery fluid and increasing the pain until each footfall resulted in a sharp stab shooting up his leg.

An hour later the lights of Franklin sliced through the night. He limped behind a shed at the edge of town and collapsed. Cramps ravaged his aching leg muscles, but he endured their torturous contractions in silent agony, fearful that he might be discovered if he cried out. The cramps finally subsided, and he ate a slice of bread to appease his grumbling belly.

ooooo

A faint glow on the horizon signaled the coming of dawn. He hobbled as best he could along the railroad tracks until he came to the train station at the edge of town. Spike said to take the trains headed toward the rising sun that would be east. "East!" The thought sent a shiver of excitement through him. East meant New York, and Henrietta and Poppa. Heck, he'd even be glad to see Maura.

He moved cautiously, staying in the shadows of an idling freight train to avoid the railroad bulls. That's what Spike had called them—bad men who checked the empty boxcars and beat anyone they found. Steam hissed loudly from hose couplings between the cars. The train suddenly jolted forward with a deafening crash of steel that almost knocked him over.

When he'd recovered his wits, he noticed that the train was creeping forward. Again the jarring crash came, but this time Clint heard it rippling back from the front of the train, though the concussion and noise still knocked him back a step. The cars had doubled their speed, but were still moving slowly. A boxcar with an open door loomed in front of him. He grabbed onto the heavy steel handle alongside the door and swung up and in. "That was simple," Clint muttered as he sat on the floor, watching the ground move faster and faster. A rustling at the rear of the car startled him, and he scrambled to his feet.

A weathered, bony face emerged from the dark and wheezed, "Well, well, if it ain't sonny boy. Come on over here, kiddo. I got lotsa chocolate and a soft bunk fer us."

Spike had warned him about these kinds of men. Clint dove out the open doorway into the black void, arms and legs flailing. The ground suddenly rose up and smashed into him. He tumbled into the bushes and lay there for a minute, stunned and whimpering. His eyes widened in shock when he brought his hands up. They were a bloody mess, as were his knees.

He struggled to his feet and began limping along next to the train, which was now moving swiftly. He glanced back and saw an open car coming, but it passed before he could grab the door handle. He glanced back and gasped when he saw the end of the train coming up. He ran faster, spurred on by a desperation that pushed the pain from his mind. The last car before the caboose was open, and he grabbed the handle, but was dragged along the ground by the swift moving train. He glanced down and yelled in terror when he saw the huge steel wheels grinding against rails just inches from his legs. He mustered every ounce of strength and slowly dragged himself into the car. If someone else was in there, he'd have to live with whatever happened because he was not going to jump again.

Hesitantly, he moved deeper into the car and was relieved to find it empty. He sank to the floor and within seconds was asleep. But even in his fatigued condition, he dreamed of triumphantly walking into his classroom, and his teacher bringing him to the front of the class to relate his experiences out in the big world to his awestruck classmates.

A change in the train's motion awakened him, but he lay there for a few seconds, smiling as he relished the delicious dream. It was light now, and he decided to take a look at where he was, but he cried out when he attempted to sit up. His pants at the knees were torn and bloody, and his hands were a mass of crusted blood and dirt. He could barely close his fingers. He looked like an old man as he dragged his bent, sore body to the door.

When he stuck his head out the door, his face was blasted by sooty smoke and cinders billowing from the locomotive's smoke stack. After blinking the grit from his eyes, he peered out at farm fields separated by narrow strips of trees, with an occasional farmhouse and barn off in the distance. Even through his pain, he felt a nudging in his spirit. Already, it was beginning to look like home.

ooooo

The train stopped with a thudding jar amidst the loud hissing of steam. Clint moaned as he gingerly grabbed the door handle and climbed down, then sucked in a breath through gritted teeth at the searing pain when his blistered feet struck the rocky ground. He hobbled stilt-like on his heels to a clump of elderberry bushes ten yards from the tracks and crawled into it.

It was damp and cold there, but he was glad he'd done as Spike had instructed because a minute later, two burly men with black clubs appeared at the rear of the train. They hurried to the rail car he'd just left and peered inside before continuing on, passing within a few feet of where he lay hidden. He stuck his head out and watched as they inspected two more cars. At the third car, both men yelled threats and climbed inside. There was a loud scream, and a body went flying out of the boxcar. Not content to throw the hobo off the train, the train bulls followed after the limping man, beating him to the ground with their clubs and kicking him, until he crawled into a chokecherry thicket.

Clint ducked back into the elderberry bushes and began to tremble. If he hadn't done exactly as Spike had instructed, that same fate would have befallen him. When the train bulls left, he hobbled along the tracks, curious to learn the fate of the beaten man. He crept into the chokecherry thicket and spotted the hobo. The man groaned and rolled over. His face was a mass of blood, but when he opened his eyes, Clint recognized the leering face from the boxcar last night. A knowing grin creased the man's split lips as he extended a pleading hand. Clint's eyes widened and he backed out of the thicket then hurried up the tracks.

He found a small stream a short distance from the tracks and drank deeply from it, then carefully washed the cuts on his hands and knees. His belly growled loudly, so he pulled out the paper bag that held the bread slices. They were mashed into a ball, but he gobbled them down and wished he'd brought more.

He skirted several wicked blackberry thickets and stopped in a grove of scrub oak about a hundred yards ahead of the engine. For a half-hour, workmen disconnected some cars and added new ones. Smoke belched from the locomotive's stack, and with a mighty lurch, it began creeping forward. The train bulls made another check of the cars, but were gone when the train passed by the oak thicket. He limped to the tracks and climbed into the first open car. He was asleep in minutes.

ooooo

Clint awoke when the train again slowed and left the car before it stopped. The water tower at the isolated station read: Milan, Ohio. The sun was now directly above, and his belly was growling again. Fifty yards away was a small corn field. He devoured several ears of half-ripe sweet corn and shoved two ears into his back pockets for later. That evening he picked strawberries and tomatoes from nearby fields when the train stopped, and he spent a relatively peaceful night in the bowels of a boxcar hurtling through the night.

Since the journey from home to the orphanage had taken two and half days, Clint figured the next morning would be the correct time to leave the train. Twice more he raided fields, munching on half-grown cabbage and lettuce. By dusk of that second day, his belly grumbled constantly, but there were no more crop fields nearby. He spent a restless night lying on the hard, dirty floor of a boxcar.

ooooo

Morning sunlight flashing through the billowing canopy of trees awakened him. His belly felt shriveled, and was now long past the grumbling stage. He even considered leaving the train to scrounge for food in the numerous crop fields that passed by, but the train was moving too fast. He pulled from a back pocket the empty paper bag that had held the bread slices and turn it inside out. Small pieces of bread and smears of butter stuck to the paper. He sucked at them, felt no sense of relief for his hunger then tore at the soiled sections of paper until most of the bag had been devoured. And still he was ravenous.

Excitement, mingled with relief, swept over Clint when he felt the train slowing. He poked his head out, and his heart began to thump loudly in his chest. Huge brick buildings and small factories paraded by. He was sure he recognized the Endicott-Johnson Shoe Factory, which was located on the outskirts of Binghamton. A wide grin spread across his face. He was only ten miles from home!

He bit his lip to keep from crying out when his blistered feet hit the ground. But, oh, how his spirit soared! By lunch, he'd be home! He climbed over the couplings of several idle trains pulling gondola cars of gleaming black coal. He'd seen coal cars before in Binghamton, but not this many.

Clint stood on the sidewalk, staring open-mouthed at the new sign on the front of the shoe factory. It read: Scranton Mercantile. He looked around, mouth agape as a wave of hysteria swept over him. The old brick structures had looked familiar, but this wasn't Binghamton.

Clint limped in a daze along a road that paralleled the tracks and stopped in front of a small building with a sign above the door that read: Scranton Anthracite Coal Company. The door flew open and four black men tromped outside. He'd seen a few Negroes in Binghamton, but these men were much blacker and stranger looking. For one thing, they had thin rings of white skin around their mouths and eyes, and white skin in their ears.

A sudden, gurgling cough erupted from the black man nearest him. He emitted a steady stream of hoarse bellows until he staggered and bent over, bracing his hands on his knees. The man made a loud hacking sound and spat a huge gob of dark fluid onto the dirty sidewalk. His buddies, who hadn't bothered to stop, laughed and yelled back taunts until he caught up to them on wobbly legs. Filled with morbid curiosity, Clint eased forward to inspect the dark deposit. It was a huge gob of spit, glistening black and shiny. It wasn't red like Momma's, but it still had the look of death.

He backed away from the slimy mess and yelled when he bumped into a hard body. A powerfully built black man stood with hands on hips, an amused smile on his black face. "Whatsa matter, kid?" he asked. "Ya never seen a coal miner's spit before?" He cleared his throat and spat his own death sentence onto the sidewalk.

Clint backed away from the sputum and stammered, "It's, it's black."

The man nodded and proudly announced, "It's coal dust, sonny. They call the plague the black death, but us coal miners call the coal dust our own black death. It'll kill us all someday, but there ain't no tougher men in the whole world than us."

"Is that what's on your face?"

The man's grin showed gleaming white teeth. He rubbed a thumb down his cheek, leaving behind a white streak. He laughed as he walked by, but turned back and yelled, "And you'd be smart ta stay the hell outta the coal mines, kid. Unless ya want an early grave!"

Clint now felt light-headed from hunger, so he limped across the street to the Scranton Anthracite Coal Company Store. He had eleven cents in his pocket—taken from a staff member's room when he'd planted Stallings' gift. He spent ten minutes trying to decide which items would furnish the most food for his money. The impatient clerk finally snapped, "If you're not gonna buy anything, kid, get out." Clint chose two of the largest apples, a candy bar, plus eight soda crackers. The clerk eyed him with annoyance and commented, "That's twelve cents worth, kid, but I'm feeling generous today. Now get out of here. You're filthy."

He walked into an alley beside the building and sat down with his back against a brick wall. He'd planned to ration the food, but his famished young body demanded every morsel. He ate the candy bar first, then the crackers. Momma had always peeled their apples, but now he chomped into the fruits, skins and all. He stared at the cores then devoured them down to the stems. He started to cast them aside, hesitated, then popped them into his mouth.

He was luxuriating in the feeling of a full belly, when a scuffing noise came from the street. He was startled to see three boys— one bigger and two smaller than himself—walking towards him. Both smaller boys hung back while the bigger boy swaggered forward until he stood over Clint with hands on hips. The big kid stuck out his chin and said, "What's the big idea? You're on our turf."

Clint struggled to his feet and stammered, "I'm, I'm lost. I got off the train at the wrong place. I'm supposed to be in Binghamton, New York."

The big kid scoffed, "This is Pennsylvania, stupid. You're really in trouble!" It wasn't the words, but his threatening tone that sent a jolt of adrenaline scorching through Clint's body. He began to tremble. "Give us your money!" The kid demanded, advancing menacingly as Clint stumbled backwards.

The fear, the hunger, the realization that he was still far from home welled up in him, and he began to cry. "Please leave me alone," he begged. "I'm lost. I don't have any money."

"You're lying, crybaby!" The big boy bunched his fists and a scowl creased his face. "Wanna fight, do ya? Let's see what ya got!"

Clint could barely curl his fingers into fists. In the few seconds it took the big kid to throw his first punch, Clint's mind ran through all the fighting techniques he'd learned. In his condition, only one would work. He ducked as the boy's looping right hand whistled over his head, then kicked him between the legs. The big kid screamed and grabbed his crotch before slowly crumpling to the ground.

Clint put on his meanest face and turned to the other boys, who were staring open-mouthed at their fallen hero. "Any of you guys want some of what he got?" They vehemently shook their heads and backed away as Clint mustered all his strength to walk past them without limping.

He hurried to the ticket office and approached the clerk, doing his best scared-little-boy imitation as he cried, "I'm lost, sir. I was supposed to take the train to Binghamton, New York, but I got off here by accident."

The clerk shook his head and replied condescendingly, "Son, you were supposed to get off here and then take the Black Diamond passenger train. It pulled out of here a half-hour ago. You'll have to wait for two hours for the next train. Have your ticket ready at boarding platform six."

Worried that the big kid might recover enough to seek revenge, he hid in an old shed next to the platform. When the huge black locomotive chugged up to the depot, Clint slipped down the tracks and climbed into an empty boxcar near the end of the train.

He had no idea how far Binghamton was from Scranton, Pennsylvania. With dread, he prepared for another day of boredom and gnawing hunger, but when the train slowed at the second stop, he was shocked to read on the water tower: Hancock, NY. He knew Hancock! He'd been here two years ago when his father had purchased a breeding mare. He looked ahead and spotted a familiar sight—the long steel bridge that spanned the Susquehanna River, whose waters separated the two states.

His heart began to pound in his chest. Home was just a few hours away! As soon as the train slowed, he jumped to the ground, winced, and hobbled toward the bridge. Even with his battered body, he felt a joy, bordering on giddiness, as he crossed the bridge into New York.

His excitement died, though, when he saw a road sign that read: Windsor 26 miles. But youthful glee soon returned as his eyes feasted upon the sign with his town's name on it. He looked around and then let out a loud, "Whoop!"

But after a half mile, it became obvious that he could walk no farther with his feet blistered and burning. He sat on the side of the road and stuck out his thumb. Several cars whizzed by, then a farmer in a hay truck stopped and took him six miles to a dusty crossroads in the middle of nowhere. A milk truck took him another ten miles. He rode in the back of a lurching, back-firing Model A pickup truck the last ten miles to his beloved Windsor. It was sundown when Clint, heart thumping wildly, limped onto the side road leading to his home less than a mile away.

Every muscle in his body ached as he stumbled along the lonely lane, while fighting an overpowering desire to lie down and close his eyes. He gritted his teeth, but finally his body screamed that it could go no farther. Then he remembered something Spike had told him—how he'd been able to put himself into a trance, blocking out pain and bad things from his mind when his drunken father was beating him. Clint focused on the road ahead, blocking out everything else—not by choice, but as a matter of survival.

Tears began to stream down his cheeks when the familiar alfalfa field appeared in the gathering dusk. And then there were lights ahead, and a white picket fence, and the front porch. He stood trembling outside the front door and took a few seconds to collect himself. Surely, Poppa would not want to find a crybaby son at his door. He spit on his hands and wiped the tears and grime from his face. He ran his fingers through his hair and hastily brushed off his clothes.

He was ready. With bated breath he rapped on the door, wincing as pain shot up his arm. Through the curtain over the glass, he saw a frowning Maura hurrying forward while glancing up at the wall clock. The door slowly opened. Maura stared at him—wide-eyed, mouth agape. "I'm home, Maura!" Clint blurted and fell sobbing against her breast.

Two hands reached up and grasped his shoulders, and he was violently pushed backwards. Maura's face was a mask of fury. "What are you doing here!" she screeched. She grabbed his collar and dragged him inside. "Albert!" she yelled. "Albert, get down here quick! We got trouble!"

Clint's mind struggled to understand Maura's actions and words. Maura didn't recognize him, that's what it was. When Poppa came, then it would all be made right. "What in tarnation are you yelling about, woman?" Albert Henley's voice boomed as his footfalls thumped loudly down the stairs. Upon entering the kitchen, he sucked in a loud breath and halted.

"Do something!" Maura yelled. "Don't let him get away!"

Clint rushed forward, fell to his knees, and hugged his father's legs. "Poppa, I'm back! I came all the way back by myself!"

Powerful hands gripped his shoulders and pried him away. Albert Henley's face was a mixture of shame and anger when he said, "What are you doing back here, Bartholomew? You are not supposed to be here!"

His lower lip began to tremble as the fragile glass of his mind began to crack, sending slivers of pain slicing through his consciousness. "But…but, Poppa. I'm your son. Oh, Poppa, I've grown so much. I won't be a problem for Maura. I just want to be home, Poppa. Please let me come back. I'll work hard. I can work now, Poppa. Like a man. I can…"

"Poppa?" a small voice floated down the stairs. "Is, is Bar down there? Bar…is that you?"

Bartholomew called, "It's me, Henrietta! I'm ho—"

Maura clamped a hand over his mouth and hissed, "Shut up!" She turned to Albert and barked, "Get him out of here before the girl finds out!" Albert Henley dragged the stunned boy out of the house and across the front yard. He unlatched the door to the vacant chicken coop and threw the boy down on the hardpacked dirt, then slammed the door and locked it.

ooooo

The large male wharf rat waited until the sounds had ceased before it ventured into the open. The rodent rose up on its haunches, tested the air, and eyed the inside of the chicken coop, seeking a female to breed, or another lesser male to kill and devour. The smell of fresh blood set its scaly tail to twitching, and it cautiously followed the scent trail.

The rat paused, staring at the inert form for any sign of danger. Emboldened by the lack of movement, it crept closer until it was mere inches away from the delicious blood. Its whiskers brushed the bloody hand. It leaned forward and licked the fresh blood.

Eyes blinked open, watching. The rat's pink paws padded onto the hand as its rodent teeth nibbled at the crusted ooze. Suddenly, the hand clamped around the rat, and the enraged animal sank its sharp chisel teeth into the soft flesh between thumb and forefin-

63

ger. The hand squeezed tighter, until the rat stopped biting and began squealing in terror and agony. Tiny rib bones snapped, and the rat's scream became a gurgle.

# CHAPTER 5

*A*t first light, the door to the chicken coop flew open and the hired hand threw a canvas bag at Clint. The man tied a rope around Clint's waist and jerked him to his feet with the warning, "Don't try ta run away from me, kid. I ain't as nice as old man Henley. Ya try anything with me, and I'll strip the hide off'n ya."

Clint trudged outside to an idling motor car. Dull eyes stared unseeing at familiar sights as dawn broke over the farm country of New York's Southern Tier. At the train depot in Binghamton, the hired hand pushed him at a porter and handed the man an envelope. The hired man clamped a hand on Clint's shoulder and squeezed hard enough, under normal circumstances, to make a grown man cry out. When he got no reaction, he leaned forward and whispered, "Stay where they're sendin ya, kid. Ya ain't wanted back here. Make yer own life somewhere else. I catch ya back at the place again, I'll make sure ya disappear fer good!"

ooooo

He was watched closely on the train by a succession of porters, but their vigilance was wasted. Clint rarely moved from his seat, listlessly staring out the window—seeing nothing, hearing nothing, thinking nothing. But even in his numbed state, his young body demanded to be fed. He ate the three sandwiches in the canvas bag and accepted food without a word when it was offered. This time, he didn't bother to ask the porter where he was going.

Two days later a porter grabbed Clint's arm and led him from the train to a familiar wooden siding. His heart began to beat wildly in his chest when he spotted the tall, slim man in rumpled brown suit waiting impatiently. Mr. Johnson cast a withering glare at him, read the note and nodded at the porter. He grabbed Clint's collar and dragged him away. Once out of sight, he whispered furiously into Clint's ear, "Cause me trouble, will you?" He reared back and brought his open hand forward with all his might.

Clint's head exploded in a shower of light, then darkness. He was dimly aware of Mr. Johnson jerking him to his feet and dragging him forward. By the time Johnson roughly pushed him into the motor car, Clint was mostly conscious, though the back of his head throbbed and he felt nauseous.

Two other boys, new to the orphanage and nervous, sat across from Clint. One boy fought back tears, while the other attempted some tough-guy talk, but Clint silenced him with a menacing glare before turning to stare out the window. The drive to the orphanage took twenty minutes, but for a boy in a stupor, it was a brief interval. At the sound of the wrought iron gates creaking open, his eyes blinked rapidly and a feeling of dread crept over him. The field crew glared at the new arrivals, and Clint recognized a few of them—Raker, Bo, Jonesy.

The other new boys were shocked and terrified, but Clint endured with detachment the humiliating delousing treatment. During supper he was made to sit at the same table with the new kids, but he received several welcome nods. He juggled his place in line so he'd be placed in Room Eight. When Clint shuffled in, Bo looked up and exclaimed, "Hey guys, Clint's back!" Several boys crowded around and peppered him with questions: How far did he get? How did he get caught? Do they really come after you with bloodhounds?

Clint sat on his cot and stared at the floor. "Whatsa matter, Clint?" Bo asked. "Did they beat ya?"

He shook his head and replied, "I made it all the way back home to New York." He gulped and fought back tears, then continued in a subdued voice, "Spike was right. They don't want us kids back. They just want rid of us. My own father sent me back here."

Someone muttered, "Geez!"

Clint noticed that the bunk above was empty. "Where's Mugsy?"

Bo avoided Clint's eyes and sucked in a deep breath. "I got some bad news. Mugsy fell out the fourth floor window up where they store the classroom books. Killed him dead."

Clint gasped and recoiled. "How? How did he fall? I've been up there. Those books aren't even in a room with windows."

Bo's words were slow and careful. "They say he mighta committed suicide."

Clint spread his arms, mouth open, and shook his head in bewilderment—unable to speak, unable to comprehend. "One more thing," Bo added and glanced at the other boys. "Stallings's back. They do keep him away from the other kids, though." Clint's eyes opened wide, and he gulped loudly.

Bo protested, "Clint, there was nothin' we could do ta protect Mugsy. Either Stallings threw him out that window, or he jumped ta get away from him."

Clint nodded, blinking back tears. Stallings knew who had left that "gift" on his bed, and who had run away that same night. He was as good as dead himself, if he didn't get out of there quickly.

A boy whom Clint didn't recognize walked through the door, spotted him, and swaggered over. The boy stood in front of Clint—legs spread, hands on hips—and said, "Outta my bunk, punk, or else."

Bo was rising to mollify the other boy when Clint rammed a fist into his challenger's belly. He flew at the fallen boy, pummeling him with fists and feet until two staff members rushed into the room and dragged him, kicking and screaming, into one of the detention cells. He spent the night lying on a cot and staring at the ceiling, thinking about life with dry eyes and dead heart while brushing bedbugs from his face.

For the first time in his life, he felt like a true orphan. He had no family to go home to. His best friend had run off to Chicago, a little boy he'd promised to protect was dead, and now a monster was lurking somewhere nearby—waiting. He began shivering, though the night was warm.

His mother had preached to him about a benevolent God who knew all, saw all. How could there be a God in a world like this? How could such a God let little kids be treated like this? How could grown-ups treat their own children this way? Spike had been right when he'd cautioned Clint, "Don't try ta understand it. It'll drive ya nuts. Just don't be a victim of it." Maybe when he was grown up he'd understand, but he doubted it.

He was still staring at the ceiling in the morning when a staff member he knew only as Mr. Jennings came for him. Mr. Johnson was chatting with a young couple when Jennings opened the door and nudged a reluctant boy with angry eyes into the dreaded office. Mr. Johnson cast a fake smile at Clint and said, "This is Bartholomew Henley, one of our newer boys. He came all the way from New York to join us."

The man, short and slim with thinning brown hair, stood and extended his hand. He said in a cheery voice, "Well, hello there, young man. I'm John Hoffman and this is my wife, Mabel. We're with the Chicago Orphan Society."

Clint stared straight ahead. John Hoffman self-consciously lowered his hand, but continued smiling. "We're here to give a few lucky boys in this institution a wonderful opportunity to be placed in adoptive homes. We've been taking entire trainloads of unfortunate children just like yourself out West to be adopted by pioneers, settlers, and ranchers who don't have children, or who have opened up their hearts and homes to accept another home-less child."

Mabel Hoffman, short and stout, sighed and added, "This train may be the last opportunity we have to place nice boys like yourself into loving families. Our government, in its well-meaning, but misguided way, may pass a law stopping this wonderful samaritan gesture."

She smiled warmly at Clint. "And Mr. Johnson tells us you're the kind of boy who might be interested in an adventurous new life out West."

Mr. Johnson cleared his throat and said, "Now, Bartholomew, we know you don't like it here, and you've proven that you know how to run away. These folks are part of a nationwide children's group who help wayward boys like yourself find a suitable match. They'll take…"

"I'll do it," Clint cut in.

Mabel and John Hoffman glanced approvingly at each other and then turned to Clint. "Wonderful!" John Hoffman exclaimed. "Our train of hope will be passing through Franklin the day after tomorrow, and we look forward to seeing you there and getting to know you a little better."

As Clint was being ushered out of the office, Mr. Johnson leaned close to Jennings and spoke in a low voice, "Keep this kid under your supervision at all times, and make sure Stallings doesn't get to him. We don't want another accident around here. These people donate a lot of money to this place, and I want to hand this boy over to them in one piece."

Clint was kept in a locked spare room next to Jennings at night and closely watched during classes and field work the next day. Jennings handed Clint a new pair of knickers for his trip, but he refused them and demanded grown-up long pants. And dressed that way, he stood on the boarding platform the next morning beside Mr. Jennings and eight other boys from the orphanage whom he knew only vaguely. Where this journey would take him, he didn't know, but as far as Clint was concerned, anywhere was better than this place.

A huge locomotive belching a black plume of smoke eased to a stop, and John Hoffman jumped onto the platform. He addressed the group in a loud voice brimming with excitement. "Well boys, this is going to be an adventure that you'll never forget. Are you ready to meet the challenge?"

The other boys cheered and surged toward the train, each carrying a single cardboard suitcase. Clint came aboard, to Hoffman's dismay, tight-lipped and surly.

ooooo

These steel-wheeled vehicles that lumbered across America's heartland to deposit children far from where they were becoming a problem were called Orphan Trains, but that term was a misnomer because usually just the last few cars carried the children. The remaining cars handled normal railroad commerce. On this train, the last four cars were reserved for the orphans. Three cars held upwards to forty children apiece, while the last car was used for eating and crude offices for John and Mabel Hoffman.

The Chicago Orphan Society had sent several orphan trains West, so the people in charge knew from experience that the cramped conditions on board often caused discipline problems among the children. Each rail car had two adult leaders who made sure older boys never sat together—each older boy instead being relegated to suffer the company of younger boys and girls.

Clint was led to a car stuffed with children of various ages and gender. He spotted an empty seat at the rear of the car and hurried for it, but Mr. Hoffman gently grasped his arm and said, "Bartholomew, you sit here."

He jerked his arm away and snapped, "My name is Clint Henley."

John Hoffman searched his eyes for a few seconds, then smiled and nodded. "Okay, Clint. This is your seat." Clint was dismayed to find a girl a bit younger than himself sitting there, staring out the window. He started to flop down on the seat across from her, but Hoffman said, "Sit next to, uh, Jenny."

Clint gave him a suffering glance and sat stiffly next to the girl. He glanced at her, taking a moment to appraise her profile. She had long dark hair and smooth white skin free of girlish blemishes. Already her body was beginning to bud into woman-hood. Clint thought the girl to be pretty.

But there also seemed to be a vacancy behind her slightly crossed eyes that unnerved him. The girl turned back to the window, nodding her head, and said, "My name is Jenny Briscoe, and I'm on this here train to find a new momma and poppa." Clint looked pleadingly at Mr. Hoffman, who smiled and shrugged before walking to the back of the car. "Are you looking to get a new momma and poppa?" the girl asked, still staring out the window. Clint sensed something not right in the girl and decided to ignore the question.

John Hoffman returned with two younger children. The little boy sat across from Jenny, and the girl sat opposite Clint. Hoffman pointed to each youngster as he spoke. "This is Jonathan Fortine. He's nine. And this is his sister, Hanna. She's eleven. And this is Jenny and this is Clint. Unless I change the seating arrangement, you are to sit in the same seat, understand?" All nodded, even Clint.

The little boy wore short pants and swung his skinny legs back and forth, a hopeful smile on his face. But Clint's attention was riveted to the girl. She smiled self-consciously at him, exposing two slightly buck teeth, then shyly looked away from the big boy who stared open-mouthed across from her. Clint's heart beat furiously, and his mind fought desperately to separate this lit-tle girl from the sister he'd left behind. Her long dark hair tied in pigtails, upturned nose, and large brown eyes made Hanna a near twin of Henrietta. "Hi, my name is Jenny," came the familiar words from the strange girl sitting next to Clint. "I'm on this here train to find a new momma and poppa. Are you lookin' to get a new momma and poppa?"

Eyes wide and face suddenly animated, Jonathan nodded vigorously and lisped, "Me and Hanna awe gonna get 'dopted togethow." Clint smiled at the youngster's speech, which became so muddled at times that his sister had to interpret for him.

Hanna glanced approvingly at her little brother. "We are a package deal," she announced, crossing her arms. "Momma said we go together, or not at all." She paused, then corrected herself. "That is, until she comes to take us home."

Clint leaned forward and extended his hand to Jonathan. "Hi, I'm Clint." Jonathan's tiny hand reached out and shook his. He then turned his attention to Hanna. Her slim white hand slowly reached out and gave itself to him. He held it gently and said, "Hanna, you look just like my little sister, Henrietta."

Hanna brightened the car with her smile. "Is your little sister and you a package deal, too?"

His expression clouded, and he released her hand. "No, she lives back in New York."

Jenny, staring out the window, said, "Well, just so's you all know. I'm on this here train to find a new momma and poppa."

Clint had scanned a map back at the orphanage and decided that it would take about a day and a half to get out West, but he had no way of knowing that the train would be stopping at a score of major cities throughout the upper Midwest to pick up a handful of children at each stop. By the time the train pulled away from Minneapolis, the orphan cars were packed with boisterous, hopeful, fearful children looking for country folks who would open their hearts and homes to them.

ooooo

The volunteers worked feverishly to compose a small folder for each child. On the second day, John Hoffman sat Clint down at a small table in the rear car and began asking him questions about his former life. But the more questions he asked, the darker Clint's mood grew, until he became largely unresponsive.

Hoffman finally put down his pencil and sighed. "Bar, uh, Clint," he began, "we can't place you with a nice new family if you won't cooperate. These families want to know something about the children they are adopting."

Clint studied the man for several seconds before his eyes lost some of their hardness. But his tone remained dubious. "Are there really that many families out there to take all of us?"

It was question John Hoffman had been asked hundreds of times before, and he was prepared for it. "We have placed many children in good homes. I assure you, there are families out West who are looking forward to this train stopping in their town."

It was an answer cloaked in nuances that easily went over the young man's head, but Clint had one more pointed question. "Will Jonathan and Hanna get adopted as a package?"

"That's the plan," Hoffman replied as he jotted notes on a yellow paper.

Clint was quiet now. He dropped his head and slowly wrung his hands. His voice was low, hesitant. "Would a family want to adopt someone like me?"

Hoffman raised his head, surprised by the boy's sudden change. He placed a hand on Clint's shoulder and said, "Trust me, Clint. There is a nice family out there waiting just for you."

Before he could stop it, a single tear cascaded down Clint's cheek. He turned away in embarrassment. Still unconvinced, he said in a hoarse whisper, "My own father got rid of me. Why would somebody want me, if my own father didn't want me?"

John Hoffman put his arm around Clint's shoulders and assured him, "There are people out there who would never think of giving up a nice young man like yourself. Honestly, Clint, we find homes for lots of older boys like yourself." For the first time since he'd been sent back to the orphanage, Clint felt a twinge of hope. During the walk back to his assigned booth, a quick succession of likely scenarios raced through his mind. He saw himself atop a black horse, herding cows; then driving one of those new motor cars delivering supplies for his new father; or working in a mercantile where there was lots of fruit and candy.

Back in the booth, he spent a thoroughly enjoyable day playing games with Jonathan and Hanna. Jenny continued staring out the window, but Clint noticed that a smile creased her face whenever Jonathan screeched with delight. After a playful roughing up from Clint, Jonathan sat back, eyes sparkling, and asked, "Cwint, would you be ow big bwuddow?"

"That all depends on Hanna," Clint teased. "After all, you're a package deal. Maybe she wouldn't want me for her big brother."

Hanna flushed and dropped her eyes, then shyly glanced up at Clint and nodded. "I would," she said as a radiant smile spread across her face. "Momma said we might join a family that's got other kids. Maybe we could all be adopted together. Do you think we could, Clint?"

Clint shrugged and said, "Maybe, Hanna. Especially after they see how nice you and Jonathan are."

Jonathan nodded his head and repeated, "We awe a package deal. Even Jenny." His little hand reached out and patted her knee. Jenny continued staring out the window, but the corners of her mouth curved up as she blinked back tears and nodded.

Once the initial seating arrangements had been made, the volunteers became too busy to discipline children who swapped seats. Four older boys gravitated to the large seat at the rear of the car and began acting up—pestering, teasing, and bullying nearby children. Several times, Clint heard kids crying behind him.

The older boys had noticed the swell of Jenny's bosom when she'd walked past on her way to the washroom. They began making whispered remarks that became louder and more lewd:

"Hey, little girl! Come on back, we have some candy for you."

"Hey girly, you got a cold? I see your chest is all swollen. Ha! Ha!" Clint ignored the remarks as long as his group was left alone.

The biggest boy, emboldened by Clint's inaction, swaggered by and stopped to leer at Jenny. He was joined by another boy who snapped a warning glare at Clint before turning to ogle Jenny.

The big kid leaned across the back of the seat, very near Jenny's head, and whispered, "Hey girly, wanna come back and visit? We got candy back there." Jenny stiffened and vigorously shook her head.

Clint slowly stood and faced the troublemaker. "Why don't you go back to your seat?"

The boy charged around and stood in front of Clint, legs spread, fists ready. He jutted out his chin and challenged, "You looking for trouble, punk?"

The boy misread the backward movement of Clint's head as a retreat and sneered. Clint's head shot forward, and a loud smack echoed through the room as the head-butted boy's eyes rolled upward, and he dropped.

The other boy stared at his fallen cohort and complained in a loud, frightened voice, "Hey that ain't fair!"

Clint grabbed a fistful of hair and pulled the wailing boy's face close to his. "You drag your buddy back to your hole. And if I hear another kid crying back there, I'll come back and finish what I started."

Jenny continued staring out the window. She reached back and patted Clint's arm, saying, "My big brother, too."

Later that evening, with Jenny and Hanna curled up asleep, and Jonathan stretched across his lap, Clint found himself wondering what kind of new family he'd have out West. He guessed he'd probably be the big brother to a passel of younger siblings, and he'd have to ride herd on all of them. Of course, he would be their protector. And the faceless mother and father would tell him over and over how happy they were to have him.

The next morning Clint stared out the window and guessed that they were close to the West because desolate, treeless prairie stretched as far as the eye could see, with only an occasional rundown farmhouse in the distance. Jenny mumbled, "No color."

The merciless late summer sun had baked the Nebraska ground to a hardpan and sizzled the moisture from the buffalo grass. It was in this land—where bitter cold and blizzards made life almost unbearable in winter, and the sun parched it in summer—that the orphan train made its first stop.

ooooo

One hundred and twenty children, ranging from toddlers in diapers to sixteen-year-olds, paraded awkwardly onto the railroad boarding platform in the town of Kearney. Jonathan and Hanna skipped onto the platform, and Clint had to grab their arms to keep them in line. But even he felt a giddy excitement as he stood in the long line of hopeful children waiting to be inspected by prospective families who had been notified in the local newspaper of the train's arrival.

There was a flurry of activity at the beginning of the line where the younger children were kept. A young couple had chosen a ruddy-cheeked little girl barely able to walk. Then a family who lived on an isolated ranch chose a ten-year-old girl to keep their daughter company.

Several grown-ups stopped to appraise Jonathan and Hanna, but when they were informed that it would be best if both children were adopted by the same family, the people continued on. No one made eye contact with Clint, who was beginning to feel very out of place in this lineup of mostly younger children. After a half hour of scrutiny, five children had been chosen, and the rest were herded back onto the train.

Jonathan swung his little legs, a perplexed look on his face, and asked, "Cwint, why wewen't we 'dopted?"

Clint smiled and tousled Jonathan's head until the boy giggled and returned his toothy grin. Hanna leaped forward and urgently shook his arm. "I know why, Clint!"

Clint put his arm around both children and squeezed until they screeched with glee. "Why, Hanna? Why weren't you and your brother taken?"

Hanna's soft brown eyes were wide with expression. "Because the perfect family wasn't there. They're maybe gonna be at the next stop."

But they weren't at the next stop, or the next one, either. And as the train stopped at smaller towns, less children were chosen, and some of the families didn't smile a lot. In a small Colorado town, a twelve-year-old girl named Cynthia, who was standing next to Hanna was poked and prodded by a short, stout, red-faced woman with huge forearms. "You're kinda scrawny," the woman griped. "You ever do any real work?"

Cynthia's face became florid. "Yes, ma'am!" she declared. "I done lots of washing and house work and cooking at the orphanage back in Ohio. I'm, I'm a hard worker."

The woman grunted. "You damn well better be, or you won't get none of my food." She turned toward the adoption desk at the end of the lineup and yelled, "I'll take this one!"

A dour-faced, middle aged couple slowly passed among the children, roughly poking and prodding them, mumbling to each other about this child being too skinny, and that one being too fat. They stopped in front of Jenny, and the woman said, "She looks like she could do some work."

The man sized her up, front and back, then grunted his approval. "Open yer mouth," he ordered and brought a grimy, tobacco-stained hand up to her face.

Jenny frowned and turned her head away from the filthy paw. The man grabbed her jaw and growled, "Open up! I wanna see yer teeth. I ain't takin' no kid with rotten teeth."

He tried to force his finger into her mouth, but Jenny clamped her teeth shut. The man swore and threatened to backhand her, but a volunteer hurried over and intervened. The disgruntled couple finally sulked away. Jenny stared straight ahead, smiling bravely while tears spattered in the dust at her feet.

ooooo

With most of the babies having been taken, the train headed into the heartland of Colorado, where the families were more rawboned and businesslike. Older children who could help with chores in the house and fields were now in demand. Several men approached Clint, but he purposely acted surly and insolent, and they passed him by.

The day finally came when the children were paraded onto a train platform in Aurora, but none were chosen. At the next stop, only one older girl was chosen. At the rough mining town of Leadville, only four couples and a few stragglers came to survey and prod the dispirited youngsters, taking two. The train then headed north into Idaho where the exhausted children were paraded at town halls and railroad sidings on the average of three times each day.

It was during this period that Clint and the other children in the booth began to formulate a plan. After a half-hour of rough-housing, Hanna sat back, her face flushed and glowing, and said what Clint had been thinking, "Maybe if none of us get picked, we could all just find a place and live together."

"Yeth!" Jonathan yelled with glee, raising his scrawny arms. Even Jenny giggled and clapped her hands in approval.

"I could keep house," Hanna volunteered.

"I could thweep the flow," chirped Jonathan.

Jenny gave an exaggerated nod and announced, "I c'n sew real good."

The words tumbled out of Clint's mouth, "I'm old enough to work. I could get a job, and we could maybe live in an old house near a small town."

They were all talking at once, even Jenny, about their dream home together when the train whistle blew. A volunteer entered the car and announced, "Children, get ready. We're stopping in Dillon, Montana, in fifteen minutes."

Hanna's eyes widened and she said, "What if one of us gets taken?"

Clint rubbed his chin for a few seconds, then replied, "I'll come and check on anyone who gets taken. If you're happy, you can stay there. If not, you can come and live with the rest of us." Everyone nodded enthusiastically.

ooooo

John Hoffman came out of the telegraph office and glumly read the telegram. He walked over to his wife and said, "Congress is going to vote on the bill outlawing the interstate transportation of homeless children within the week."

Mabel Hoffman brought a hand to her breast and said, "What will we do with all these children? We're not even halfway through our tour."

Hoffman sighed heavily and said, "We have no choice. Once they pass that law, we have to stop." He was lost in thought for a few seconds, idly rubbing his jaw. "We've got to place as many of these kids as we can in the next week."

ooooo

Only five people climbed the platform to inspect the children in Dillon. Two couples had come to adopt infants, but when they learned there were none, they left. A tall, skinny man in dirty clothes remained. He scowled as he passed by the boys, but a gleam came to his eye when he studied the girls.

Clint's palms began to sweat. He'd seen that look before. The man spotted Hanna and his eyes widened. "What's yer name, pretty little lady?" the man asked and grinned, showing broken, tobacco-stained teeth. "Hanna," came her hesitant reply.

The man reached out and caressed Hanna's shoulder. He licked his lips and his voice became husky. "Would you like to go home with me, Hanna, and be my little girl?"

Clint jerked Hanna from the man's grasp and pointed at Jonathan. "They're brother and sister. They go as a package deal, or not at all."

The man's face hardened and he growled, "Keep yer mouth shut, boy. Ain't nobody talkin' ta ya."

Mabel Hoffman hurried over and asked, "Can I help you, sir?"

Clint stepped forward and protested, "This man's trying to take just Hanna!"

"Well," Mabel Hoffman said, then hesitated. "We were trying to adopt Hanna and her brother, Jonathan, as a package."

The man glanced at a smiling, hopeful, Jonathan and adamantly shook his head. "Ain't got no need fer a runt kid. The wife's home sick and wishin' fer a little girl just like this one here, and I intend ta get 'er what she wants."

Clint was relieved when Mabel walked over to confer with John Hoffman, who frowned and looked at Hanna and Jonathan. Mabel glanced nervously at Clint, then addressed the man, "Come up to the desk, please, and we'll do the paperwork."

"No!" Clint yelled and pulled Hanna back. "Leave her alone, you scumbag!" The old man brought back his hand, but John Hoffman grabbed Clint and led him away.

Clint tore free and ran back to the train. He fell into the booth and burst into tears. "Lies!" he raged. "They were all lies!" A half-hour later John Hoffman found Clint curled up on the seat and gently patted the boy's shoulder. Clint looked up, and violently pushed Hoffman away.

"Easy now!" Hoffman cautioned. "I know you're upset, Clint, but we had to break those children up. It's just too difficult to get people to adopt two orphans. I wouldn't be a bit surprised if Jonathan—"

"You're a stupid liar!" Clint yelled, chest heaving, face livid. "What do you think that old geezer wanted Hanna for?"

"Oh, now wait a minute, Clint." Hoffman protested, his voice rising as he fought to retrace in his mind the events of a half-hour ago. "That man has a sick wife at home. He—"

"Shut up! You're...you're so stupid!" Clint screamed. He squeezed his eyes shut and brought his knuckles to his temples. He spoke in a trembling voice barely above a whisper. "I saw that same look in a man's eyes at the orphanage I came from, and now a little boy is dead." John Hoffman raised both hands to reply, but a rush of guilt froze the words in his throat. Clint turned to stare out the window.

Ten minutes later the children tramped quietly back to the car. Clint continued staring out at nothing, but felt a small body press against his side. "Cwint, whewe's Hanna?" Clint forced himself to look at Jonathan. The little boy's eyes showed hope, but his angelic smile had disappeared, and his skinny legs no longer swung back and forth. Clint swallowed hard and croaked, "A nice family adopted her, Jonathan."

Jonathan's eyes studied the floor for a few seconds, then he looked back at Clint and asked, "And when wiww they come fow me?"

"Soon," Clint whispered, and stifled a sob. It was all he could think to say. He could not bear to look at Jonathan for another second, and turned his head to look out the window, but found Jenny studying him with sad eyes. Simple-minded Jenny—dumb in the ways of the world, but not in heartbreak. Her head shook ever so slightly, telling him what he already knew.

For the rest of the evening, Clint had Jonathan sit next to him, and he put his arm around the frail body. "Dear God," Clint prayed, "if you're out there, please help Jonathan and Hanna get back together someday." As an afterthought, he added, "And please help me and Henrietta to find each other someday, too. Amen."

The next morning, the train slowed as it entered a narrow canyon with stark sagebrush hills along both sides of the tracks, but the mountains above were covered with huge evergreen trees. A volunteer poked his head into the car and announced, "Get ready, children. We're about to stop at a small depot near Anaconda, Montana.

Clint held Jonathan's hand as they walked onto the platform to be inspected by the serious and the curious from nearby Anaconda. Several couples slowly walked by, and three children, a boy of twelve, and two older girls, were taken.

An enormous, rotund man dressed in a dark suit flounced onto the platform and started down the line. He was followed by a slim, timid-looking blond-haired woman and two blond children—a boy and girl about Clint's age. The man prodded and poked the older boys, sizing them up as if they were livestock, but disdainfully shook his head at each one, as he worked his way down the line. He strode past Jonathan and stopped in front of Clint.

The man's huge jowled face had a small upturned mouth surrounded by a large drooping mustache which made him appear jolly, until you looked at his eyes. Clint insolently returned the man's cold stare. Gustav Schmidt glanced at his wife and said, "Dis von. I don't like the vay he looks, but he is strong." Schmidt extended a meaty hand, and Clint squeezed it with all his might, but could not budge it. "Ha!" the big man laughed. "You are pipsqueak! You vill never have the power of Gustav Schmidt. But you are strong for your size." Schmidt spun around and waved his cane high in the air. "Ve take dis von!"

John Hoffman hurried forward, carefully avoiding Clint's smoldering eyes. "This way, sir," Hoffman said. "A few papers to sign, and you can be on your way."

As Clint was led away, a small voice called out, "Bye, Cwint!" He waved without turning back, but a sob erupted from his throat.

"Ach!" Gustav Schmidt grunted and jabbed Clint hard in the back with his cane. "No cvybabies!"

While he waited to sign the adoption papers, Schmidt bragged to the attendant, "I have big sawmill up Timber Gulch, just like Black Forest in Germany vere ve come from. I make good beams, planks, boards. I need another strong hand. This von is a cvybaby, but I vill make him strong. He vill get food and a bed, but he vill vork for it every day."

Clint stared straight ahead with dead eyes as John Hoffman nervously approached him. "Clint, uh, uh," Hoffman stammered, "this situation can work for you. Give it a try." When he got no response, he mumbled defensively, "Well, it's better than an orphanage." Without acknowledging the man, Clint walked away.

# CHAPTER 6

Clint followed behind the huge man and his family in a daze. Frightened and bewildered, he fought the impulse to run away. Yet amid his turgid emotions, a spark of hope surfaced. This was his new family—a mother and father, even a brother and sister. Gustav Schmidt herded the children and Clint onto the flatbed of a large lumber truck, then squeezed his enormous bulk into the cab beside his wife. The girl, almost as tall as her brother, sneaked a peek at the new boy. She whispered something to her brother, but he frowned and shook his head.

She cast an annoyed glance at her brother, then shyly turned to Clint. "Mein, uh, my name is Greta. My brother's name is Wilhelm."

Clint stammered, "I'm, uh…my name is Clint." Wilhelm turned away, but Greta extended a slim hand. Suddenly aware that he'd been holding her hand and gazing into her deep blue eyes, Clint pulled his hand back and looked out at the steep, towering mountains.

The truck bounced up a rough, winding road, then dropped into a narrow, timbered basin. At the far end was a large sawmill surrounded by decks of logs and a huge pile of sawdust. The truck jolted to a halt in front of a quaint Bavarian cottage with a steep roof of hand hewn wood shakes that extended to the ground. Schmidt threw open the door and bellowed, "Out! Evybody out!"

Wilhelm and Greta hurriedly jumped down and stood shoulder to shoulder, while Clint slowly climbed down and stood uncertainly. Schmidt barked orders in German at his children and they scurried away. He put his hands on his ample hips and appraised Clint, who fidgeted nervously under the enormous man's glare. Finally, Schmidt snorted and said, "Come vit me, cvybaby. I show you vere you vork."

Clint followed two massive, undulating buttocks up a winding path. Schmidt stopped at a mountain of wood blocks fifty yards below the mill. He swung a massive arm through the air and announced, "Dis is ver you vork. You chop vood for fio. Fio make steam. Steam make mill vork. You skinny as chicken, but Gustav Schmidt make you stvong. You are cvybaby now, but I make you tough, body and mind."

"Yes, sir," Clint quickly replied. "I'll work real hard, Mr. Schmidt. I've, I've never spilt wood before, but I'll sure try."

Schmidt grunted and grabbed a heavy double-edged axe. He thrust it into Clint's hands and placed a two-foot thick block of wood on a massive chopping block. Schmidt gestured toward the block and ordered, "You chop vood now."

Clint struggled to bring the heavy axe above his head then brought it down as hard as he could. The sharp blade sliced into the wood and stuck there. Clint pulled frantically on the handle but could not free the head. "Ha!" Schmidt bellowed. "You are pipsqueak, but Gustav Schmidt make you a man." He clamped one paw around the handle and jerked the axe free. Schmidt then swung the axe in a long overhead arc and neatly split the block of wood.

Clint's eyes widened at this awesome display of power. Schmidt eyed him triumphantly and boasted, "You nevow be able to do vat Gustav Schmidt do." He picked up three steel wedges and a sledge hammer that were lying on the ground and threw them at Clint's feet. "You use these to pound into vood until it splits."

Clint began pounding a wedge into the center of another block of wood, but Schmidt stomped his foot on the ground and yelled, "Nein! You are stupid! Bang it in side." Clint hurriedly pounded another wedge off to the side, and after several blows a crack appeared at the outer rim and ran toward the center.

Schmidt barked, "Now hit other side vit axe." Clint struck the opposite side with the axe, and though it was not a hard blow, the block cracked. Schmidt grunted. "Each block, you make six pieces. You load on conveyow belt. Two times each day you come up to front room and stack in neat pile. Then you come back, split more. You vant to sleep in my house, eat my food, I make you vork for it."

Clint nodded submissively. "Yes, sir."

Schmidt pointed at the wood pile and ordered, "You vork now. You vork hard, you get food. No vork, no food."

Clint nodded and tried to split a half block, but the axe became embedded again. "Use wedge, pipsqueak!" Schmidt bellowed. While Clint nervously pounded on a wedge, Schmidt shook his head and grumbled in German as he stomped up the path to the sawmill.

A minute later, the large round saw blade began to spin, then screamed as it sliced through a log. Slab after slab fell away from the log until only a neat pile of boards remained. Schmidt noticed Clint watching and angrily gestured for him to get back to work.

With every swing of the axe, his sense of foreboding about his new home and the giant man with smiling face and hard eyes increased. So did his fatigue. Instead of improving at the chore of splitting wood, he became more inept as the heavy axe and blocks of wood sapped his strength. The soft skin on his hands blistered, then broke, sending a slick, bloody ooze onto the axe handle. But Clint dared not stop.

Three hours later, the sun dropped below the timbered ridge to the west, and the temperature dropped with it. The pristine forest now became a brooding beast, casting ominous shadows where minutes before there was sunshine. Sweat soaked his clothing and rose from his fevered body in the form of steam into the chilled evening air.

Lights glowed in the cottage below. His belly grumbled continuously, and he feared he'd been forgotten. Then he spotted Wilhelm's blond head bouncing up the path through the dusk. Clint stopped chopping and grinned at the boy. "I thought you might have forgotten about me."

Wilhelm's eyes widened. He took a step back and averted Clint's eyes. "Du kommst..." He stopped then spoke in the American language, as he'd been ordered, "You come for supper now." At the door Wilhelm stopped, looked past him, and said, "You take off shoes now."

Shoes in hand, Clint stepped inside. He was met by a blast of warm air permeated with the pungent aroma of fresh-baked bread and spices. A mixture of excitement and anticipation flooded his senses, and he allowed himself the giddy thought, *So this is my new home.*

He stared in wonder at the ornately scrolled woodwork and shelves filled with figurines and clay dolls. A large grandfather clock began to chime, and Clint stared open-mouthed as a tiny yellow bird shot out of a small door and chirped, "Cuckoo!"

The blond woman emerged from the kitchen, smiled nervously at the wide-eyed boy and said, "I am Katarina." She pointed to a small door. "You vash hands and face. Then come vait for supper."

A few minutes later, Clint entered the kitchen and noticed Greta and Wilhelm seated along the wall facing the table. The front door flew open and the floor shook as Gustav Schmidt stomped into the kitchen and dropped heavily into one of the two chairs at the table. "Where, uh, where should I sit?" Clint asked.

Schmidt jumped to his feet, grabbed Clint's arm and dragged him to a chair beside Wilhelm. Schmidt declared, "Ha! You not only cvybaby pipsqueak, you have no manners. You sit and vait for grown-ups! Then you eat. This is old country vay. German vay. You vespect elders at all times."

"Yessir," Clint mumbled, the hunger in his belly replaced now by tension.

Katarina Schmidt carried a huge ring of steaming hot sausage to the table, followed by red sauerkraut, boiled potatoes, and thick slices of dark bread. The pungent, spicy aromas made Clint's mouth water, and his hunger returned.

Schmidt surveyed the table with satisfaction then Katarina heaped his plate with half the sausage, kraut, and potatoes. She waited by his side while Schmidt sliced a two-inch chunk of sausage and jammed it into his mouth. "Mmph!" he grunted and nodded as bits of chewed meat and juice dribbled onto the oil cloth. Katarina smiled and patted his shoulder. She sat in the chair next to him and placed dainty portions on her plate.

While Schmidt chewed, he glanced at Clint and spoke in German, "Der Junge ist ein schwachling, aber ich will eine mann aus ihm machen, oder sonst." (The boy is a weakling, but I will make a man out of him, or else.)

Katarina cast a furtive glance at her husband then replied, "Er scheinst ein netter Junge zu sein, Gustav. Er kennt die alten landarten nicht. Er wird lernen." (He seems like a nice boy, Gustav. He just doesn't know about the old country ways. He will learn.)

Schmidt stuffed another huge chunk of sausage into his mouth and sniffed. "Ja, Ich werde ihn klein kriegen und dann wieder aufbauen." (Yes, I will break him down and then build him up.)

She reached over and patted his huge forearm. "It takes a real man to teach such things."

Schmidt grunted with pleasure and turned his gaze to Clint. "Vat you last name, pipsqueak?"

"Henley, sir."

Gustav Schmidt froze in the midst of slicing his sausage. He slammed his knife and fork on the table. Wilhelm and Greta jumped, but a gloating smile raised Schmidt's jowls, and his rotund body shook like a gigantic bowl of flesh-covered jelly. Schmidt joyously roared, "You Johnny-bull!"

Clint frowned and leaned forward. "Sir? Uh, what's a, a…"

Schmidt still smiled, but there was a hard edge to his voice. "Johnny-bull! English! Ha! Now, I know vhy you are such a cvybaby pipsqueak!"

Gustav Schmidt's face hardened as he wiped juice from his mustache. "Ve destroyed de Englishmen in de gveat var." The smile, now dark and sinister, returned. "I kill many of you Johnny-bulls. Too many to count."

Clint gulped. His father had told him of an Uncle Charles who went off to a place called Verdun in France and never came back. He also remembered his history lessons of the English Empire. His mother's proud English blood welled up in him. Two short words barely above a whisper tumbled out: "We won."

But they'd been heard. Katarina sucked in a loud breath and brought a hand to her breast. Greta and Wilhelm slouched low in their chairs.

Gustav Schmidt hunched forward like a huge, flesh-covered buddha, a large piece of sausage poised to enter his cavernous maw. He showed no emotion—except for a crimson hue creeping into his jowls. Katarina's hand hesitantly touched her husband's shoulder and continued upward to caress his thick neck. "Nein, Gustav. Er ist nur ein Junge. Ein dummer Junger der nichts von krieg weiss. Nur was er von den Englandern gelernt hat." (No, Gustav. He is just a boy. A stupid boy who knows nothing about the war. Just what he has been taught by the English.)

Gustav Schmidt spoke in a low, menacing voice, "Vat did you say, English pissant?"

The color drained from Clint's face as he stared into the huge mask of hate. He probably could have ridden out the storm, if that English bull-headedness had not resurfaced. "I…I said, uh, my mother told me the English won World War One."

"Nein!" Schmidt exploded and smashed his fist onto the table. Wilhelm and Greta jumped. "Ve slaughtered you English! You fought as fools, fodder for our guns. If these stupid Americans had not interfered, Deutschland vould be across the English Channel today. Next time, Ve vill be better prepared, and ve vill take America vit de storm tide."

Gustav Schmidt's hands clenched and unclenched, and his chest heaved as his beady eyes bored into the trembling boy. His voice was low, furious, "Ich werde dich umbringen, fur das was du gerade gesagt hast, du samen von einer Englischen hure." (I will kill you for what you just said, you sperm of an English whore.)

Katarina lunged forward, hugging her husband's neck and kissing his jowls. She petted his balding head and urgently whispered, "Nein, Gustav! Nein! Der Junge wird dein sklave sein, und er will das holz haven, so dass du geld machen kannst fur unsere ruckkehr zum Vaterland. Was fur eine bessere art ihm zu zeigen dass du uber ihn bist. (No, Gustav! No! Just think of it. The English boy is your servant and cuts the wood for you like a slave. What better way to show him you are supreme over him.)

Gustav Schmidt blinked as his wife's words sank in, then growled, "Raus mit ihn von here. Er wird in meinem haus weder essen noch schlafen. Bring ihn in die Scheune mit dem rest von raubwild." (Get him out of here. He will not eat in my house or sleep under my roof. Put him in the barn with the rest of the vermin.)

Katarina Schmidt jumped up and rushed to fill a plate. When she sliced into the sausage, Schmidt ordered without taking his eyes off Clint, "Nein. Kein fleisch fur ihn." (No. No meat for him.)

Katarina shoved the plate into Clint's hands and snapped, "You come vit me now."

Clint numbly trailed behind her to the barn. Katarina gestured to the hay pile and said, "You must sleep in de hay. It vill get colder. I vill get you some blankets. And some boots and a coat. And maybe gloves."

Clint fought back tears and spread his arms wide. "Mrs. Schmidt, what did I do that was so wrong? The war was over before I was even born."

She vigorously shook her head. "Nein. Not for Gustav. He had to flee to America to escape de communists who took over because the English and French allowed them to. You must not speak of this again. And you must not do anything that would anger Herr Schmidt. Do you understand?"

Clint lowered his head, fighting back tears, and nodded. Katarina placed a consoling hand on his shoulder and said, "It is not your fault. You could not know. I vill try to put a little piece of meat in your soup to keep you strong, but you must promise that you vill never provoke my Gustav again. He is a proud man." She paused then added, "America does not understand the pride of the Fatherland."

Clint nodded again, tears cascading down his cheeks, and whimpered, "I promise. I'll, I'll do whatever he says." Katarina hurried away, leaving Clint to collapse onto the hay and wonder how his life could get any worse. But it did get worse—quickly. Though it was still a week shy of September, the cold increased during the night to near-freezing and quickly seeped through his thin shirt. He spent a miserable night burrowed deep in the hay, in a vain attempt to escape the bone-chilling cold.

In the morning, Clint poked his head out of the hay burrow when the hinges creaked on the barn door. Greta came forward self-consciously with a bowl of porridge and thick slice of bread. Clint took the food and mumbled, "Thanks."

The girl lingered while he hungrily spooned the steaming, nutritious grain cereal into his mouth. She turned to leave, but stopped and turned back. "Father is not so bad as you think. In time, maybe he will like you, like he does Wilhelm."

"And what about you?" Clint asked, but regretted his words when he saw the hurt in her eyes.

She stared at the floor and spoke in a voice barely above a whisper, "Poppa wanted all boys—to be soldiers when the Fatherland is restored."

Gustav Schmidt's voice boomed outside, "Come on, cvybaby Johnny-bull! You vork now for your food!"

Clint gulped down the last of the porridge and stuffed the bread into his mouth before scurrying outside. "Good morning, sir," Clint said in a meek voice.

Schmidt scowled, pointed toward the woodpile and gruffly ordered, "Go!"

The axe handle was coated with frost, which burned his hands until his body heat melted it. Within minutes he was warm again, and a half-hour later he was sweating. The blisters from yesterday reopened and new ones sprouted. At noon, Katarina hiked up the path lugging a burlap sack and a food tray. She placed a bowl of dark beef soup and slice of bread on a stump. "Show me your hands," she ordered. "Ach!" she exclaimed when she saw the mass of bloody, blistered skin, then pulled a small tin of ointment from a pocket in her long dress. "Put this on at night. It vill make de pain go avay and heal de skin." She then pulled a tattered old coat from the sack, along with a cap, boots and gloves. "Take care of these. There vill be no more for you, and it vill get much more cold."

"Thank you, Mrs. Schmidt," Clint said, searching her eyes for some sign of motherly affection. Katarina Schmidt hesitated for a moment and threw a furtive glance towards the sawmill before hurrying down the path to the house.

ooooo

The next three days of Clint's life were a blur of fatigue-numbed muscles that cramped at night, and blood-crusted hands that festered and oozed a slimy yellowish-red liquid. But on the morning of the fourth day, his hands had stopped bleeding, and a hard covering of calloused skin began to form over the sores.

One evening while Clint rummaged through the barn for a file to sharpen the blade of the heavy axe, he came across a smaller double-bladed axe. Its weight was half that of the cumbersome axe he'd been using, and its thin head took a sharp edge quickly. But he was disappointed with its performance because the light axe lacked the heft needed to drive the head deep enough into the wood to split it. A hard overnight frost had turned the ground icy, and as the thin axe bit into a large block of wood, his foot slipped, putting sideways pressure on the head. To his astonishment, the block split in two. After some experimenting he discovered that if he twisted his wrists as the thin axe head bit into the wood, even the biggest blocks split in two.

After a few more weeks of hard work, his calloused hands could grip the axe handle tightly all day, and his hardened muscles sent the thin axe head slicing through block after block of wood from dawn until dusk. Now, instead of cramping, his muscles yearned for the first vigorous swings of the axe in the morning. His lunches became more hearty because Katarina sneaked extra pieces of meat into his bowl. Another nice thing about his lunches was that Greta brought them. Clint felt a glow of satisfaction as he sat on a stump slurping his soup, knowing that this striking girl's hungry eyes followed his every move.

One day Wilhelm brought Clint's lunch. The boy carelessly dropped the soup and bread onto the stump. Grinning, Clint wiped sweat from his face and said, "Thanks, Wilhelm. I'm starved."

But when Clint started toward the stump, Wilhelm stepped in front of him and stood with legs spread, chest out, arms folded. Gone was his shy demeanor, replaced now by a haughty glare. "I think you are wrong!" he blurted. "My father told me we won the war."

Clint took a step back, remembering his promise to Katarina, and replied in a cordial voice, "That was a long time ago between other people, Wilhelm. Let's just let it go as a piece of history and be friends."

Wilhelm vehemently shook his head and spat, "We could never be friends!"

"Why?"

"You are English. You killed my father's father and his brother. Soon, we will leave America to go back to the Fatherland and prepare to reclaim it for Deutschland."

Clint shook his head and sighed. "Come on, Wilhelm. You and me don't even know what those old people were fighting about. It was some dumb war between two countries that happened before we were born."

Wilhelm's jaw jutted out as he declared, "We are the superior race. One day we will rule the world."

Clint felt the flush of heat in his cheeks, but quickly checked it. He sucked in a deep breath and spoke carefully, "Read any history book, Wilhelm."

The boy retorted, "My father says the English and French put lies in the books about us. And I believe what he says about the English pigs."

A fleeting picture of his mother passed through his mind, and Clint battled the impulse to strike back. He reluctantly returned to the woodpile and picked up his axe. "Go away, Wilhelm. Just leave me alone."

Wilhelm turned to leave, but stopped at the stump where the soup lay steaming, its tantalizing aroma beckoning Clint's grumbling stomach. He put a finger against the bowl, cast a smirking glance at Clint, then slowly pushed the bowl off the stump.

Clint watched in horror as the soup spilled onto the ground, but dared not give the gloating boy the satisfaction of knowing how much his actions had hurt. Clint turned away, threw a large block of wood onto the block and swung the axe downward with all his strength. Up at the mill a beaming Gustav Schmidt watched from the window.

ooooo

Clint's life became a routine of long, brutal hours of labor followed by cold nights shivering in the barn's hay loft. Eventually, Katarina furnished him with two old wool blankets. However, there was one surprising benefit of his plight. Hard muscles had begun to appear where a few months before there was flaccid flesh and bones. When he passed by a window, Clint was startled to see in the reflection a young man with broadening back and thickening chest. His fair hair had also begun to turn brown, and his high cheekbones had become more prominent, making him look even more English.

But it was the isolation that gnawed at him most—alone chopping wood all day, and alone all night in the barn. The highlights of his day were the two times he went up to the mill to stack the split wood. Gustav greeted visitors with a hearty handshake and booming, "Hello!" His affable, even jolly, outward demeanor made his mill a favorite gathering place for lumber buyers—store owners, farmers, miners—who sat around the big potbellied stove in the front room and sipped free coffee. But privately, Gustav Schmidt voiced disdain for these men who filled his cash box with dollars.

One morning while Clint stacked wood at the sawmill, a hardware store owner from Anaconda arrived. "Good morning, Gustav Schmidt, my friend!" the short, balding man called, as he climbed from the cab of his flatbed truck.

Schmidt's eyes took on a hard look, and his tone lacked its usual robust cordial air when he said, "You vant something, Mr. Horowitz?" He failed to offer the man a seat near the warm stove or cup of coffee.

After the truck loaded down with lumber had roared off, Clint listened intently to hear what derisive comment Schmidt would make. The big man stood silently, scowling at the handful of greenbacks in his hand. He dropped them carelessly into the cash box before muttering, "Kike." Then he stomped over to the wash basin and scrubbed his hands. Clint frowned and made a mental note to ask Greta what *kike* meant.

ooooo

On a cold, snowy morning in October, Clint stamped into the front room of the mill with an armload of wood for the stove and was surprised to find it filled with milling men talking excitedly. He stacked the wood and kept his head down but his ears open.

A short, stout man with a ruddy face pulled at his suspenders and said, "I heard there was guys in New York City jumping out of hotel windows yesterday after the stock market crashed. They lost everything overnight. I mean, millions of dollars in stock ain't worth a penny this morning."

A tall man with a big nose said, "I got a brother, works in a carpet mill in Vermont. He called this morning asking if there was any work out here. Said the big boss come through yesterday at quitting time and shut the whole plant down."

Another man added, "Geez, sounds like the whole country back there is going down. I'm glad I live out here."

"Hey, it's happening here, too," an Irishman with stooped shoulders cut in. "I get these beams from Gustav for the mines in Butte. The foreman called this morning and cut me off. Said he's cutting back on all the subcontractors, and big layoffs in the mines are coming soon."

Gustav Schmidt had listened quietly to the good news of the American economic collapse, until he could no longer contain his glee. "Ha!" his voice boomed. "De news in Germany is all good. Ve haf our own industrial revolution in the Fatherland as I speak.

Dere is a good job and good vage for every man. And a new man is leading the National Socialist Party to veclaim the Fatherland from de Communists."

Someone in the crowd joked, "Hey, Gustav, teach me German and I'll go back to the Fatherland with you." The other men laughed, but Gustav Schmidt's eyes danced.

ooooo

Katarina found out that Wilhelm had purposely spilled Clint's soup. Much to Greta's delight, she was permanently assigned that duty. Wilhelm usually trailed behind a short distance, sulking and casting insolent glances at Clint. As snowflakes floated to the ground on a gray November day, Greta arrived with lunch, and as usual, cast a shy smile his way. "There is much meat in the soup today," she announced proudly. "Because, because I made it myself." She blushed when Clint tasted it and proclaimed it the best he'd ever eaten.

"Greta," Clint asked as he swirled the bread along the rim of the empty bowl, "your dad called Mr. Horowitz a *kike*. What does that mean?"

Greta cast a furtive glance at Wilhelm. "Not now, Clint. You shouldn't ask such..."

"He's a Jew!" Wilhelm spat. "Father says the Jews are even worse than the English. They are the true enemies of the Fatherland. Soon we will go back there and rid the land of them."

The words tumbled from Clint's mouth. "Your father was wrong about the English losing the war, so I would imagine he's wrong about the Jews, too." Clint inwardly cringed and wished he'd remained silent when he saw the outrage in Wilhelm's face. "How dare you talk about my father like that!" Wilhelm stomped forward and pushed Clint backwards. "Stop it, Wilhelm!" Greta screamed. "Leave him alone!"

Clint struggled to control his rage, fighting the impulse to beat his adversary into the ground.

Wilhelm turned on his sister. "And you! I see the way you look at him! If father knew what you were thinking, he'd cut this English pig's throat!" Greta burst into tears and ran down the trail.

Before he could check himself, Clint latched onto the collar of Wilhelm's coat with one hand and his belt with the other. He ran the struggling boy headfirst down the path for twenty feet then gave him a hard shove.

Wilhelm stumbled, then pitched headfirst and tumbled several times. He slowly rose to a kneeling position. His eyes grew wide and his face paled when he saw the blood on his hands. He emitted a loud wail and hurried down the path toward the house.

Clint walked slowly back to the woodpile. His hands trembled as he reached for the axe. What had he done? Would Wilhelm squeal on him? Had Gustav Schmidt been watching? After a few minutes of splitting wood, he glanced up at the sawmill, relieved to see nothing unusual. But as he swung the axe down on a block of wood, a dark shadow moved from the window.

# CHAPTER 7

Falling snow sifted through the trees most of the afternoon, then the sun broke through the clouds and turned the snow covered forest a brilliant white. At sundown an opaque full moon rose above a timbered ridge to the east, and the temperature plunged to six degrees below zero. The frigid air froze the damp hair on the top of Clint's head and burned his lungs before it was exhaled as a billowing plume of frosty breath.

Five hours had passed since the incident with Wilhelm. His sense of relief bordered on euphoria. A loudly grumbling belly reminded him that it was almost supper time, and he hoped for another bowl of Greta's soup with its generous portions of meat. He placed one last block of wood on the chopping block and raised the axe.

As if the cold had suddenly penetrated his body, he froze, arms and axe reaching to the sky. Slowly, the arms came down, and the axe fell from his hands. It felt like a giant hand was squeezing the blood from his heart. His knees buckled. He staggered backwards—mouth agape, eyes wide at the sight...of Gustav Schmidt striding down the path from the mill with Wilhelm hurrying a few steps behind.

As Schmidt drew closer, he saw the man's face—a mottled mask of anger and hate—and he began to tremble. His breath came in short, ragged gasps. "Momma," he whimpered, "please help me. I'm so scared!"

Gustav Schmidt stomped up to Clint, and his huge belly bumped the terrified boy backwards. Schmidt put his hands on his hips and barked, "My Vilhelm says you attack him from behind!" Clint opened his mouth to protest, but Schmidt wagged his head up and down. "You are dirty fighter, like all English."

Schmidt turned and stomped away, and for a fleeting moment Clint thought it might be over. But Schmidt turned back and stood with legs spread and arms folded. "Now you fight fair because I am here." Schmidt turned to his son and nodded.

There was fear in Wilhelm's eyes as he took two hesitant steps toward Clint. He threw a worried glance at his father, then stuck his chin out and croaked, "Now, you fight fair."

Clint folded his arms and slowly shook his head. His trembling voice was barely above a whisper. "I will not fight you, Wilhelm."

Wilhelm's eyes showed surprise then a gloating smile spread across his face. Without taking his eyes off Clint, he turned toward his father and called, "He is afraid of me now, Poppa, like you said. He does not want to fight me fair."

Schmidt smashed a fist into his palm and roared, "Schlag ihn!" (Hit him!)

Bolstered by Clint's reluctance, a sense of bravado swept over Wilhelm. He rose to his full height, chest pushed out, fists raised. "Fight now!" He ordered. Clint gulped, closed his eyes and shook his head.

Unsure how to proceed, Wilhelm drew back his right fist and held it there. Schmidt shook both fists at the boy and bellowed, "Dann schlage ihn zu boden!" (Then beat him down!)

Wilhelm landed a feeble blow that barely staggered Clint. He opened his eyes and the two frightened boys stared at each other for several seconds, then Wilhelm began swinging wildly. The blows at first were ineffective, but eventually Clint staggered backward and fell. He curled into a fetal position as Wilhelm punched and kicked his body.

Wilhelm, his face flush with victory, jumped up and down with fists raised skyward. "I won, father!" he exulted. "I beat the Englishman!"

Schmidt clapped his hands and exclaimed, "Guter Junge, Wilhelm!" (Good boy, Wilhelm!). He strode forward and draped a heavy arm around his son as they walked victoriously back up the path to the sawmill.

Down at the house, Greta turned from the window and burst into tears. Her mother dropped heavily into a stuffed chair and covered her face with her hands. "Vat haf ve become?" she moaned over and over. "Vat haf ve become?"

Clint lay on the ground for several minutes. As the effects of the beating wore off, he brought his hands to his face and began to weep—not from the beating, but from the shame of his fear.

ooooo

It was dark now. Snowflakes alighted and melted on the prostrate, convulsing body at the woodpile. He slowly sat up and numbly wiped blood and tears from his face. The physical damage was superficial, the other severe.

Black clouds parted and a full moon bathed the land with an eerie glow. Trees cracked and popped from the intense cold. It was a time when families were comfortably snuggled close to their stoves, luxuriating in the powerful heat provided by the burning wood. But at the wood pile below the Schmidt sawmill, a different fire had ignited.

Gustav Schmidt and his son were exuberant during supper, in contrast to a reserved Katarina and a despondent Greta. During a dessert of apple strudel and cream, the Schmidt family was startled by a primal sound that seeped through the walls—low at first, then increasing in volume and fury. They listened in tense silence until Wilhelm, face still aglow, asked, "Maybe a wolf, father?" Gustav Schmidt ignored his son's question. He knew.

At the woodpile, the madman stood in the moonlight and again bellowed his rage. He grabbed the axe and viciously murdered a cowering block of wood. Again the axe came down, and again and again and again. And then was thrown to the ground. He tore off his coat, faced skyward with arms raised and chest heaving, and raged, "Momma, you lied to me!" His hands became hard fists, which he shook at heaven. "All your nice-nice was a lie! It was all just lies! There ain't no good in this world!"

Words were not enough to express his torment and outrage. He gritted his teeth, grabbed a chunk of wood and threw it at the moon. Still incensed, he hopped onto the splitting block to get a few feet closer to heaven. He again shook both fists and railed at heaven, "Where were you, Momma? Where were you when I needed you? Momma, you lied to me!"

His rage increased. He threw two more blocks of wood at the heavens and hopped back atop the block. His chest convulsed and he sucked in several breaths before screaming, "A father? You call that a father, Momma? What kind of a father would throw away his own son?"

A tortured moan escaped from his lips. He fell to the ground and wept bitterly. But after a few minutes, he carelessly wiped the tears away and stood up. He wasn't finished having his say. Not by a long shot. He hopped back onto the block and yelled, "No more, Momma! I will not be a victim no more! No one will do this to me again!" As if to increase his chances of being heard by the heavens, he cupped his hands to his mouth and screamed, "I...WILL...NOT...BE...A...VICTIM...AGAIN!"

Down at the cottage, Greta could stand the pitiful wailing no longer and started for the door. "Nein!" Gustav Schmidt bellowed and threatened the girl with a backhand. Greta covered her ears and ran to her room. Katarina gathered up the leftovers, including a piece of meat for the soup and started for the door. Schmidt growled, "Lass ihn hungrig gehen." (Let him go hungry.)

Katarina stopped and stared at the door, carefully assembling her words. "He is English, my Gustav, but ve need him to be strong to chop de vood for us." Schmidt grunted loudly, but said nothing as Katarina slowly turned the door handle and stepped outside.

Clint was still raging between vicious swings of the axe when Katarina stepped into view. He looked away, embarrassed, but continued battering the blocks of wood. Katarina spoke in a soothing voice, "You must stop for de night and rest, young Clint. Here is some nice hot food. I even put a big piece of meat in it for you."

She smiled and showed him the soup. Clint stopped and glared at it then snatched the piece of meat out of the soup and slammed it to the ground. Katarina gulped and laid the tray down on a stump. Her hand reached out to touch him, but it stopped an inch from his fevered body. Slowly, she withdrew it and turned away. Within minutes the rantings began again. Throughout the bitter cold night, the Schmidts' ears were assaulted by the raging diatribe of a tortured soul, each outburst punctuated by the metallic clang of the axe on frozen wood.

ooooo

The Schmidt family sat glumly at the breakfast table in the morning. Sent to retrieve the dinner tray, Greta hesitantly approached the young madman dripping with sweat, still pounding at the chopping block. A light snow had fallen overnight and covered the frozen, untouched soup. With trembling hands, Greta picked up the tray and whispered, "I am sorry." A ragged sob escaped from her throat, as she turned and ran.

For the next week, a howling blizzard blasted western Montana, with blinding snow and below zero temperatures that idled the sawmill. But not the lone figure wearing only a shirt and viciously swinging the axe. With the darkness, the figure faded from sight, but the maddening clang of the axe continued through the night, its ringing indictment seeping through the heavy feather pillows pulled tight over the heads in the house below.

Though Katarina sneaked meat into his soup, Clint left it in his bowl. He methodically split the wood, trance-like, for up to eighteen hours, and then collapsed into his hay burrow.

The nutrition deprivation, physical and mental exhaustion, and inner rage brought on hallucinations. He sometimes saw Henrietta watching him split wood. Then his mother would sit on a stump and watch. And Albert Henley would sit on a stump with Maura on his lap, smirking, and he would throw the axe at them. And he saw Hanna sitting on the old geezer's lap. Pink spots danced in his eyes until he shook his head violently enough to make them disappear, and sometimes he would swing the axe at blocks of wood that weren't there, then slump to the ground in a stupor until the cold revived him.

Hours ran together. Days had no beginning or end, running into weeks, then a month, then more. He welcomed the exhaustion, looked forward to the hallucinations. For even though it was madness, at least the undulating apparitions were often someone he knew, and it brought a sense of mournful longing deep within his soul as he raged at each demon or angel who pranced through the icy fog of his tortured breaths.

And visitors to the sawmill began to notice, not only the madness, but also the brutal explosions of power of the crazy, shirtless boy assaulting the woodpile below. Men began to comment, much to Gustav Schmidt's ire, of his strength and stamina.

One a snowy Monday morning, several customers huddled around the potbellied stove. Some of the men complained about the sudden drop in business since the Great Depression had begun and voiced hope that the worse of it would be over with spring coming soon. But most of the men watched the crazy kid below split block after block of wood. A man named George

Canfield remarked, "Hey, Gustav, I bet that kid could outchop even you."

"Ha!" Gustav snorted. "That pipsqueak can do only vat I show him. No vone beats Gustav Schmidt at de vood block."

George Canfield pulled a dollar bill from his pocket, winked at his grinning cohorts, and challenged, "A buck says the kid can outsplit you." Other men at the stove fumbled in their pockets and drew out wrinkled bills to add to the bet.

Gustav Schmidt bellowed with laughter. "Dis is no bet. Dis is like taking candy from a baby!"

ooooo

The contest, set for Saturday, was simple. Whoever split a full cord of wood first, won. Of course, no one had approached the other contestant yet. On Wednesday, George Canfield wandered down the path and stood safely back, watching Clint split huge blocks of gnarly wood with single, deadly swings of his slim axe. Canfield finally spoke, "We're gonna pit you against Schmidt in a wood splitting contest. Gustav says you don't have a chance, but I've been watching you, boy. I think you can beat him."

George Canfield grunted loudly as he picked up a two-foot block of pitchy wood and staggered to the chopping block. He stepped back and wheezed, "All that pitch, you better use a couple of wedges to pry it apart."

Clint had ignored the man up to that point, but now he stopped and glared at George Canfield. Without taking his eyes off the man, Clint whipped the axe in a looping overhead circle. As the axe bit into the wood, he snapped his wrist, and the big block popped apart. "Whew!" Canfield whistled and shook his head. Then his eyes narrowed and he studied Clint. "I been watching you around, Gustav. You really hate him, don't you, boy?"

For the next two days, Clint ate all his food, worked less hours, and hit the hay sooner. However, as the meager heat of the Friday afternoon sun waned, so did his resolve. He raised the axe, hesitated, and the blade clattered to the frozen earth. Slowly, he sunk to his knees and began to weep. Unable to face a mother he had so recently cursed, he allowed himself only to sob and mouth her name over and over again.

Saturday morning dawned cloudy, with a light, sugary snow falling. Though the temperature had risen to a balmy fifteen degrees, the crowd of about a hundred men, women, and children shivered as they circled two huge piles of wood blocks cut from a gnarly old red fir tree.

Gustav Schmidt arrived, stuffed into heavy wool pants and shirt under a bulky mackinaw coat. He shook his twenty-pound axe at the crowd and announced, "Now ve see vat this cvybaby can do ven he comes against a man." He walked to within inches of Clint, but this time the young man stood his ground and glared back at his adversary.

Slowly, Clint removed his coat, then his shirt. Without taking his eyes from Schmidt, he slowly removed his long undershirt. The crowd gasped, and someone murmured: "God, the kid'll freeze! He musta snapped or something!"

"Contestants, get ready!" George Canfield called out. Schmidt spit on his hands and rubbed them together before grabbing his mighty axe. At three hundred pounds, he had bulk and power as his method, and arrogance as his motivation. As Clint grasped the thin, double-edged axe, his eyes bored into Gustav Schmidt's. At half his opponent's size, he lacked the brute strength, but his entire body, mind, and soul were infused with the narcotics of revenge and hate. "Begin!"

The crowd roared when Schmidt's axe delivered a tremendous blow, sending the halves spinning. He quickly stood up each half block and split them also. He grabbed another block as easily as if it was a toy and placed it on the chopping block.

Over and over again, Schmidt popped the blocks. In fifteen minutes he was already halfway through his pile. He put his hands on his hips and snorted contemptuously at his opponent, who was barely a third through his pile. Schmidt took a long pull from a bottle of Schnapps and, amid raucous cheers, raised his arms in a preliminary victory celebration.

Steam rose from Clint's bare chest, and ice formed on his damp hair. He worked methodically, efficiently, oblivious to the din of the pressing crowd and his opponent's bravado. Only a few spectators cheered him on. Most of the crowd clustered around Gustav Schmidt, roaring their approval every time he brought down the mighty axe and raised the bottle of Schnapps. Someone in the crowd, worried about his bet, yelled, "Hey Gustav! Better get going. The kid's almost pulled even with you." Schmidt scoffed as he leisurely grabbed his axe and split another block.

The blocks at the top of each pile had come from the ends of the old fir trees where very little pitch had concentrated, making the splitting process much easier. But at the bottom of the pile the blocks not only became larger and heavier, but huge seams of frozen pitch made splitting them much more difficult. Now, Gustav Schmidt was not splitting the blocks with one mighty whack. He often had to pound them two or three times before they fell apart. His supporters noticed with alarm that his opponent was having no such problems.

With each snap of Clint's wrist, the thin axe's murderous downward inertia was transferred outward, ripping through the pitch seams and neatly popping the blocks. Twenty-five minutes into the contest, someone excitedly yelled, "They're dead even!" The crowd cheered wildly.

Schmidt's arrogant demeanor had dissolved into rivers of sweat pouring down his face. His chest heaved as he stumbled backwards. Someone in the crowd yelled, "They each got six blocks left!" Schmidt bellowed in outrage and delivered a tremendous blow to a large block, popping it in two, but he staggered as he bent over to stand the split halves upright.

The last three blocks showed thick seams of amber-colored pitch. Schmidt delivered an off-balance blow to a block, but the axe sank into the wood without splitting it. The pitch held the steel blade tightly, and the exhausted man was unable to pry it loose. "Ach!" Schmidt exclaimed, gasping for breath. "Too much pitch. You give him de easy blocks."

At those words Clint walked over to his opponent's pile. He whipped his axe in a wide arc and neatly split Schmidt's block, freeing the big axe. The crowd roared while Gustav Schmidt—enraged, but gasping for breath—angrily snatched up his axe. He took a long pull of schnapps and threw the bottle into the snow. His face was beet-red as he raised the axe and brought it down, but it again became hopelessly embedded in the pitch.

Clint quickly split his remaining three blocks, as a humiliated Gustav Schmidt looked on, his hands opening and closing in helpless rage. George Canfield hurried forward and held up Clint's hand, declaring, "The winner!" Amid applause, Canfield asked, "Well, boy, what do you have to say for yourself?"

Clint declined, but the crowd clamored for a word from the strange boy who stood before them with steam rising from his naked, heaving chest. At almost six-feet tall and wide shouldered with sinewy muscles rippling under taut skin, he was no longer the skinny little English boy who had arrived in this frozen corner of hell six months earlier. But the crowd had no idea that the changes were far more than physical. The prolonged yoke of sadistic cruelty, instead of breaking him, had metamorphosed into a virulent strain of hate that now nurtured his psyche with a purpose for living.

He turned his full attention to Gustav Schmidt and spoke in a low voice that belied the fury within, "The Englishman beats the German, again."

Gustav Schmidt's nostril's flared, and his sweat-soaked face turned a bright crimson. He grabbed his axe and broke the handle over his knee before pushing through the crowd. He stomped back to the sawmill where he locked the doors and put a "closed" sign out front.

ooooo

The crowd had long departed. Clint was still splitting wood as the sun dipped low in the sky. He glanced up and saw Gustav Schmidt, bottle in hand, staggering down the path. He gripped the axe tightly. This time would be different. Fortunately for Schmidt, he stumbled and plopped down on a block of wood twenty feet short of his death and stared bleary-eyed at Clint. Between swings, Clint met the drunken man's stare with steely eyes.

Schmidt took a long pull from the bottle and growled, "The English swine, son of a whore, cheats Gustav Schmidt. But I tell you, Johnny-bull scum, nobody cheats Gustav Schmidt. Nobody shames the fatherland and lives to joke about it. I vill kill you slowly, with my bare hands. You filthy little—"

"Gustav! Gustav!" Katarina Schmidt called as she hurried to her husband's side and threw her arms around his neck. She stroked and kissed his face, and snuggled her cheek against his sagging jowls. "Gustav," she purred, "I have your favorite food vaiting for you, my big strong man. Don't let the cheating little English pipsqueak ruin your meal." She continued kissing and caressing him. Schmidt's drooping eyelids fluttered as he basked in the pleasure of his wife's caresses.

Schmidt spat on the ground and muttered, "Englisches schwein." (English pig.)

Katarina kissed his face and whispered, "Kamme jetzt mir mir merab, mein wundervoller starter mann." (Come down with me now, my wonderful strong man.) Then she turned to Clint and spat at him. "Da! Lasse den Englander das zum abendessen!" (There! Let the Englishman eat that for his supper!)

Gustav Schmidt's eyes danced, and he bellowed his approval. He also spat at Clint. "Da! Englisches schwein. Esse auch das

zum abendessen! (There! English pig. Eat that also for your supper!) Pleased with himself, Schmidt struggled to his feet and
staggered down the path to the house, with his wife struggling
mightily to keep the huge body upright.

That evening Greta brought Clint's meal of black bread and
soup loaded with meat and vegetables. She stood uncertainly and
whispered, "I'm glad you won."

Clint allowed himself a faint smile and said, "Thanks."

Katarina's distant voice called from the house, "Greta, come
help me with your poppa." Reluctantly, she left, and Clint wolfed
down his supper.

Early the next morning, the big truck drove away with a load
of lumber. Clint had just begun splitting wood when Katarina
Schmidt strode up the path and ordered, "You come vit me."

He followed her to the house. On the front porch, she grabbed
a canvas bundle and thrust it into his arms. "Take dis and go.
My husband is gone to deliver lumber. I vill take you down to
de valley."

Katarina pushed her open hands up and outward, as if the
hurry him along. "You must go quickly. When my husband comes
back, he vill kill you. My Gustav is a good man, but your English
insolence has damaged him. You American young people don't
have the vespect like ve have in the old country."

Clint nodded curtly and said, "I was getting ready to leave on
my own, anyway." He paused for a moment and glanced past her.
"I have just one more thing to do before I leave."

Katarina Schmidt read his eyes. She folded her arms and
stamped her foot. "Nein! I have hidden the boy until you leave."

Clint nodded, satisfied with Wilhelm's cowardice, and turned
to Greta, teary-eyed and wringing her hands. He brushed a tear
away and said, "Goodbye, Greta. You are a nice person in a family
of monsters." Greta sobbed and fell against his chest.

Katarina Schmidt's face paled and she snapped, "Ve go now!"

ooooo

A half-hour later Clint stood at a deserted railroad siding and watched the Schmidt's motor car roar away. A rusty water tank hovered close to the tracks. Water dribbled down from a hastily plugged bullet hole midway up the tank, and a jackrabbit furtively eased into the open, studied Clint for a few seconds, then hopped back into the sagebrush. Across the tracks was a weathered corral with a rickety loading chute leading towards the tracks.

He walked to the water tower and sat down, feeling strangely at a loss for something to do. Then a smile slowly spread across his face. He didn't have to work every daylight hour anymore, and he didn't have to submit to that enormous "thing" up at the sawmill. He was free. He plucked a few green shoots of grass, lifting them to his nose to smell their freshness, then carefully placed them in a small pile for the jackrabbit. He stretched out on a board and luxuriated in the warmth of the early spring sun. He smiled and closed his eyes, then blinked them open and wondered, "When was the last time I smiled?"

Clint dozed, and awoke with the memory of his sister on his mind. What grade would Hen be in now? Probably sixth, maybe seventh. Did she ever think about him anymore? No telling what Poppa, no, that man, and Maura might have told her. Probably told her he was dead, or didn't want to come back home. He dozed again and dreamed he was back in the barn with a malevolent presence nearby. He jerked upright, gasping for air, but slowly settled back and closed his eyes. He had no idea where these tracks would take him, but whatever lay ahead had to be better than where he'd been.

An hour later, a freight train pulled in to take on water. Clint eased out of the sagebrush and climbed aboard an open boxcar as the train slowly pulled away. Two stops later, the train pulled into a station near the small town of Deer Lodge. Clint jumped from the train and hid in a brushy stream bed two-hundred yards away. Hunger gnawed at his belly, so he unwrapped the bundle and selected a long sausage and chunk of thick dark bread. He fought back the impulse to devour the other sausage and bread.

The blast of the train's whistle jarred him, and he hastily tied the bundle. The train was already moving when he got to the tracks. He spotted two open boxcars coming up and easily hopped aboard the first car. With his belly full, he was overcome by a euphoric sense of freedom as he sat watching the sagebrush hills go by.

Clint tensed and snapped his head to his right. He peered into the back of the boxcar. From behind the gloomy depths came a scraping sound. He scrambled to his feet as a tall, gaunt man emerged from the gloom, wearing a gray sweat-stained hat with two snake rattles pinned to the band. The man grinned, showing rotten, tobacco-stained teeth and said, "Well, hello there, sonny boy."

He sensed someone behind him an instant before his head exploded in a shower of stars. He was dimly aware of men cackling above him and hands fumbling with his belt. Then darkness enveloped him.

# CHAPTER 8

*H*owling wind and wet snow pounded horse and rider like a swarm of angry hornets and quickly soaked man and animal to the skin. The big roan's ears sagged under the weight of the heavy snow as its muddy hooves clomped over the mushy white landscape, leaving behind a trail of mud-spattered divots. The horse swung its head back and gave its master a suffering look. Henry Crenshaw snapped at the reins and groused, "Don't look at me that way, Dancer. We're not heading back to the barn until I get every calf out of this godforsaken weather.

He pulled the cowboy hat low over his curly red hair and leaned into the wind, but the snow still stung his face. "Yep," he muttered, "it's falling faster than cattle prices." He snorted at his black humor. Everybody was blaming this Depression thing for the low prices, but Henry Crenshaw was convinced it was all a ruse by the cattle buyers to keep the profits for themselves.

A frantically bellowing heifer, broad back covered with snow, materialized out of the white void. He reined the horse and hopped off in front of a shivering newborn calf. "This is all I need," Crenshaw grumbled as he shook out a tattered wool blanket. "Calves born in a spring blizzard. Bluebird weather for a week until my cows start dropping calves, then this." He threw the blanket over the prostrate calf then hoisted the half-dead animal across the front of his saddle. He mounted and spurred the horse toward the barn a half-mile away.

Bent low to keep his weathered face from freezing, he glanced down toward the railroad tracks a hundred yards away and spotted another calf in a gully. "How in hell did that calf get through the fence?" he fumed. The mother was nowhere in sight, and that fact alarmed him, what with the railroad tracks being so close.

He hesitated, torn between getting the shivering calf he was holding back to the barn, and inspecting the motherless calf in the gully, finally deciding to make the short detour. Maybe the damn thing was already dead, and it would be one less problem he'd have to deal with. He rode to his fence, quickly opened the barbed wire gate and trotted Dancer toward the gully.

He reined the horse at the edge of the gully, but a fierce gust of wind forced his head down low to the horse's neck. When the squall eased, he jerked upright and grunted in surprise at the sight of a man lying at the bottom of the gully. He eased the calf onto the ground and hurriedly slid down the muddy slope.

Henry Crenshaw forgot about the wet snow and wicked wind, and the water trickling down his ribcage. He kneeled in the white mush and studied the body for any broken bones, like an arm or leg bent the wrong way. Nothing. He'd already surmised that the faceless, nameless human was just some old bum from the train, but when he gingerly pulled back the coat collar, he grunted in surprise at the young white skin. He laid the back of his hand on the skin. It was warm to the touch. He carefully turned the body over, revealing the blood-covered face of a young man. At first he thought the youth was dead, but then a tiny groan escaped from the boy's mouth. Henry Crenshaw scooped up the body and scrambled, slipping and sliding out of the gully.

ooooo

Floating colors of gray and blue slowly seeped into the black void. Dim awareness came, then faded, then came again—a ceiling, a light, a voice then oblivion. Finally, Clint opened his eyes and stared into a woman's smiling face. "Momma?" he mumbled.

The woman smiled and said, "I'm Julia Crenshaw."

But Clint groggily persisted, "Am, am I in heaven, Momma?"

"No," Julia answered softly. "You're not in heaven. You're alive, thank God. You've been hurt. We found you along the railroad tracks yesterday."

Clint blinked several times at the dark haired, freckle-faced woman. A look of bitter disappointment spread across his face, and he turned away from her. She was not his mother. And he was still alive.

An hour later, Doc Hastings shuffled out of the room and addressed the Crenshaws. "From the wallop on the back of his head, I'da sworn he'd have brain damage, but the kid seems lucid. Most of his memory's back, and I'm happy to change my prognosis from guarded to good. I think the kid's gonna be just fine, but he's got a severe concussion. He'll have to be careful to avoid bumping that head for a while."

"Oh, good!" Julia Crenshaw exclaimed and clapped her hands.

Henry Crenshaw's reaction was more to the point. "Now we gotta find out who he is, where he came from, and what he was doing laying down there by the tracks."

Doc Hastings scratched his head and replied, "Well, he says he got waylaid by a couple of bums on the train."

Henry Crenshaw was not appeased and countered, "Then what's a young kid like him doing riding the rails when he should be in school?"

Doc Hastings shrugged and changed the subject. "Did you get a look at his hands? They've got the hardest callouses I've ever seen." He rubbed his left wrist and added, "And that grip! He grabbed my wrist when he was delirious, and I couldn't hardly

115

pull away. Wherever that damn kid came from, he sure as hell worked hard."

The salty, underpaid, overworked country doctor winced under Julia Crenshaw's withering glare and hoped to avoid her patented sermon about his cussing. Instead, Julia Crenshaw protested, "Let's give the young man a chance to heal. Just because he looks like he's been working hard doesn't mean he's fresh off a chain gang."

Henry Crenshaw said, "At least he's not from here."

Julia Crenshaw's jaw dropped and she turned to her husband with hands on hips.

Henry Crenshaw threw up his hands and defended his actions. "Honey, we can't allow any old stranger in our house, what with the state prison a couple miles away. I went ahead and checked to see if anybody'd escaped. And by the way, nobody's escaped in six months."

"Just the same," Doc Hastings mentioned as he pulled on his coat and headed for the door, "you should find out who this kid is before you give him the keys to the house."

The front door flew open, and a freckle-faced teenage girl in bib overalls and tattered Carrhart canvas coat charged inside, almost knocking Doc Hastings over. "Oh!" Ann Crenshaw declared. "Sorry, Doctor Hastings."

She pulled off her wool cap, freeing two brown pigtails. Her voice rose with excitement, "Guess what, Pop? I found that calf alive and standing when I went down to get the wool blanket. I brought it back to the barn."

Henry Crenshaw looked down at his teenage daughter, and a big grin spread across his face. Fourteen years old and already his little Ann acted and looked like a grown woman. Then his eyes narrowed. He damn well intended to find out who this strange kid was and where he came from.

Henry Crenshaw's assessment of his daughter was more accurate than he dared to admit. Ann Crenshaw was turning from a tree-climbing tomboy into a woman in both body and mind. And at the moment, she was excited about a lot more than a calf. When she'd come home from school yesterday, she'd caught just a glimpse of the strange boy lying in her bed, but the sight of his pale, gentle face caused a stir that disturbed, yet tantalized, her. For one thing, it sure perked up their mundane existence out here on the ranch. She turned to Doc Hastings and asked, "Is he okay? Is he gonna live?"

Doc Hastings smiled and yanked at a braid of hair. "Oh, in another couple days he'll be pulling your pigtails." Ann blushed and smiled. And Henry Crenshaw frowned.

ooooo

Clint lay in bed wondering where he was. It wasn't a hospital. Two clay dolls adorned the dresser, along with bobby pins and a hair brush. Though he was covered with a blanket, he felt uncomfortable lying in a girl's bed. He spotted his clothes neatly folded on a chair and struggled to sit up, but gasped at the sharp pain that in the back of his head. He lay back for a minute until the pain subsided, then drew back the blanket and slowly rolled out of bed. He shuffled across the room while steadying himself against the wall.

It took five minutes of effort and pain to struggle into his pants and shoes. He was about to pull on his shirt, but stopped, momentarily struck by its clean look. He pressed it against his face and luxuriated in its fresh smell. Other than a few quick wipes with a damp rag soaked with icy snow-melt, he hadn't been clean in months. His eyes widened. Who had bathed him?

It was then that he glanced into the mirror—and was stunned. There were several cuts and large bruises on his face, but it was the rest of his body that shocked him. The face that stared back at him was much older looking, with darker brown hair. And those muscles. Where had they come from? His shoulders and chest were as broad as a man's, with sinewy arm muscles running into massive forearms that resembled cord wood.

But then dark thoughts seeped back into his consciousness of a sawmill and a huge, ugly man—no, a monster. The face in the mirror hardened as he buttoned the shirt. He wasn't about to go through the same thing again. A scraping noise outside the room brought him back to the present. He slowly opened the door and saw a woman, back turned and working at the sink. When she turned her head sideways, he saw that she was younger, maybe his age. He stood uncertainly, watching her wash dishes and hum.

The woman turned, spotted Clint and gasped. A large bowl fell from her hands and crashed onto the floor. Henry Crenshaw burst through the door and said in a loud, harsh voice, "What's going on in here?"

Clint stared speechless at the angry man's face, but the girl hurried forward and said, "Daddy. It's okay. I, I just turned around, not expecting anyone, and this, uh, this person was standing there."

Henry Crenshaw studied Clint with suspicion for several seconds before relaxing a bit and asked, "How are you feeling? Doc Hastings didn't expect you up for another day or so. Maybe you ought to get back in bed."

Clint placed his hand on a kitchen chair to steady himself. No way was he going back into a girl's bed. "I'm, I'm feeling all right. I just have a little headache."

Henry Crenshaw stepped forward and took the reeling boy's arm. "Here," he said, "sit down before you keel over." He looked down at the broken bowl and sighed. "Ann, you better get that bowl picked up while I get your mother."

Ann Crenshaw kneeled and began gathering the broken shards of pottery. She glanced into the eyes of the strange boy—and could have died. Here was this handsome guy staring at her dressed in dirty bib overalls. And pigtails of all things! She blushed under his scrutiny. "Ow!" she cried and looked down at a small cut on her palm oozing a trickle of blood.

He was beside her now, carefully cradling her hand. "It's not too bad," he said and gently ran a finger over the cut. "I don't think there's any glass in it." The cut forgotten, she gazed into his deep green eyes. "Here," he said, "let me help you." Both of them nervously picked up the larger pieces, and Ann quickly swept up the rest with a broom.

Julia and Henry Crenshaw came through the door, and Ann stammered an apology for breaking the bowl. "Accidents happen," Julia said while staring wistfully at the remains of her last good mixing bowl.

Feeling totally out of place in a house full of strangers, Clint stammered, "Well, I, uh, I appreciate your helping me. I guess, I'll be on my way now."

Julia Crenshaw put her hands on her hips and pursed her lips. "You'll do no such thing, young man! Doc Hastings says you won't be ready to travel for another week." And much to Henry Crenshaw's dismay, his wife added, "Until then, you'll be our guest."

"In the meantime," Henry Crenshaw's tone was impatient, "I've got some questions I'd like answered."

Julia snapped an annoyed glance his way. "There'll be time to talk later. Now you two men get out of the house while Ann and I start supper. Clint slowly walked outside, but stumbled as he stepped off the porch. Henry Crenshaw grabbed his arm and said, "Easy, boy, let's sit you here on the bench."

Clint felt intermittently nauseous and normal while he watched Henry Crenshaw hustle around the barnyard, first feeding a half-dozen squealing pigs a mixture of water and vegetables and fruit too spoiled to sell at the Deer Lodge Mercantile. In exchange, he furnished one pig annually to old man Prescott, the store owner. Next came the force-feeding of six calves too weak yet to nurse from their mothers. Clint yearned to help, but knew in his condition he'd better stay put.

His mind drifted back to the train, and he bitterly derided himself, "I thought you weren't going to let yourself be a victim anymore?" He closed his eyes and slowly shook his head.

His eyes roamed over the place. The old white farmhouse badly needed a new coat of paint. The big barn listed to one side, and some of the lower boards had rotted away. Baling wire and twine kept the drooping corral from collapsing. If he had to stay here for a whole week, he would begin helping with chores in the morning.

After a half-hour of sitting, Clint slowly rose and grabbed an old hoe to steady himself. He shuffled across the yard to a grove of cottonwood trees along a small creek and looked out at the bleak landscape. Unlike the heavy forest surrounding the Schmidt sawmill, this land was almost devoid of trees. Cattle could be seen grazing on rolling hills covered with sagebrush and grass that stretched for miles, with steep green mountains in the distance.

It had been more than a day since Clint had eaten, and by supper time he was almost beside himself with hunger. Julia seated him in a chair between Ann and Henry, and they both extended a hand to him. Not knowing why, he took the offered hands. The Crenshaw family then squeezed their eyes shut and prayed fervently to God for Clint's health and the bounty of the food they were about to eat. The meal consisted of a chicken, mashed potatoes, and home-canned green beans. Never had such simple fare tasted so good to him. He could have eaten the whole chicken, and probably another one. Instead, he took a leg and thigh, eating them slowly and sucking every morsel of meat from the bones.

Henry Crenshaw fidgeted while the women cleared the table. His life had certainly changed for the better since his wife had found religion and brought it home. He'd resisted her attempts to drag him into church with a bunch of do-gooders. But after a few visits to the Deer Lodge Methodist church, Henry began to look forward to attending—at first to visit with other ranchers, then to listen to the pastor's sermons about this gentle son of God named Jesus. Long before the world would use it as a catch phrase, Henry Crenshaw became a born-again man and put aside his drinking and carousing.

It was the evilness of that other life that he remembered all too well as he scrutinized the young man across the table. A total stranger, yet they had him sleeping in his daughter's bed! Who was he? Where did he come from? Was he dangerous? Well, one thing he didn't have to worry about was the kid stealing any money from them. There was none. With the table cleared, Julia cast a condescending look at her husband, allowing the inquisition to begin. Henry cleared his throat and said, "Now, young man, we'd like to know…"

"Hold on!" Julia cried and jumped up. "I forgot about dessert. Let me get some canned peaches and cream."

Henry gave his wife an exasperated look and sighed deeply before slumping into his chair. As soon as the last bowl hit the table, he loudly cleared his throat and began, "Young man, we know your name is Clint, but we don't know anything else about you. If you're going to live in my house, I'd like to know who you are and where you came from."

Clint had no intention of recounting his humiliating ordeal with the Schmidt family. He looked out the window and said, "My name is Clint Henley. I'm an orphan."

Henry Crenshaw leaned back in his chair and folded his arms. There was a twinge of impatience in his voice when he said, "So, you're an orphan. You still had to come from somewhere. You're how old?"

Clint turned to his inquisitor, thought for a moment, and said, "Fifteen, I think." Ann's eyes widened. She thought he was much older.

Henry rubbed his chin and said, "Okay, so you 'think' you're fifteen. What's a fifteen-year-old boy doing riding a freight train in the middle of the school week? And how'd you end up almost dead in that gully?"

Julia Crenshaw smiled and patted her husband's hand. "Now, now, Henry. Not all at once."

Henry Crenshaw ignored his wife's plea and drummed his fingers on the table.

A slow feeling of dread crept over Clint as that first supper at the Schmidt house fluttered through his mind. He sat up straight and turned defiant eyes on Henry Crenshaw. He began in a low voice, "Like I told you, I'm an orphan." His mouth became a thin line, and his voice rose. "I got sent by the orphanage to a family who worked me like a dog and treated me like one. And then they asked me to leave. The train was the only way to get away from them. Two hobo's jumped me, robbed me, and…"

Clint looked away. His eyelids blinked, and a slight tremble came to his lips. He said in a low, vague voice, "And then they hit me over the head."

Henry was still not satisfied, but before he could continue his interrogation, Julia reached over and patted Clint's arm. "Oh, you poor dear! Were you part of those Orphan Trains they sent out here?"

Clint slowly nodded. "We heard about them," Ann volunteered. "They helped orphans find homes."

Clint folded his arms and snapped a hard look her way. "All I saw that they did was make slaves out of little kids." Ann flushed at the rebuke.

Henry got to the point, "Where are you headed?" Clint shrugged and shook his head.

Julia put her hands to her face and said, "Oh! We can't send you away like this, with nowhere to go. Surely, there must be somewhere you could stay."

Ann blurted, "He could stay here with us!"

A scandalized look came to Henry Crenshaw's face, but Julia nodded and said, "We have a storage room in back. "We could put a cot in, and you could go to school with Ann."

Henry cleared his throat again and said, "We, uh, we may be getting a little ahead of ourselves here."

Julia gave her husband an impatient look and quoted scripture, "Suffer the little children, and send them not away. That's what Jesus said."

Henry Crenshaw sighed heavily. He knew his wife too well to argue, especially when it came to children. Even before she'd become religious, Julia Crenshaw had been caring for the needy children in the Deer Lodge area—be it a coat for a girl in winter, or a sandwich for a hungry boy at school.

Ann volunteered to clean out the back room. Clint felt well enough by then to help move some of the boxes to a far corner. His eyes kept straying to the young woman sweeping the floor, and she stole an occasional glance at him. Reluctantly, she finished and started for the door, but stopped and turned back. She cast a shy glance at him and stammered, "I, I'm glad you're staying." Then she fled.

On her way to school the next morning, Ann stopped by her best friend's house. Karen Jenkins asked, "How's the man doing that your Dad found by the tracks?"

Ann leaned forward and spoke in a low voice, "He's not a grown-up. He's our age."

"Really?"

"Yes, and he's real cute, too."

Karen Jenkins rolled her eyes and her tone was dubious. "How cute?"

A smug smile spread across Ann's face. "You can see for yourself in a couple of days. He's coming to our school."

At that moment three teenage boys jumped out from an abandoned building next to the schoolhouse. The biggest boy yelled out, "Hey girls, want some company?"

Ann's voice was cold. "Leave us alone, George Brumley." She self-consciously folded her hands over her chest, and Karen pressed close to her. "What ya hiding there, Annie?" Tommy Brookings asked as snickers erupted from two other boys.

Karen warned, "Leave us alone, or we'll tell Mr. Thompson."

George Brumley snarled, "You're safe enough, Jenkins. Ain't nobody interested in you, with your flat chest."

On the way home from school that day, Karen asked Ann, "Is this Clint boy like George Brumley and the others? Always bullying little kids and trying to touch the girls?"

Ann vigorously shook her head. "No, he's a real gentleman. He'd never act fresh."

Karen sighed and said, "What'll happen is George Brumley and his bunch will take him into their gang, and he'll act just like them to fit in."

"I don't think so," Ann said. She frowned and added, "If he does, he won't be living in our house."

Before she entered the clearing where the Crenshaw house stood, Ann hastily combed her hair. She felt absolutely immoral as she watched Clint, shirtless and muscles rippling, turning the soil in the vegetable garden. "Hi!" she finally called and waved.

Clint stopped digging, and his eyes feasted on the vibrant young woman smiling at him. "Oh, hello," he said. "I thought I'd turn the garden now that the frost is out of it. When you're ready to plant, I'll turn it again." He quickly put his shirt on and apologized, "Sorry, I'm used to working with my shirt off."

Ann flushed and stammered, "Oh, uh, that's okay. My dad does it in the summer all the time." Then she mentioned, "You must be feeling lots better."

Clint smiled and nodded. "I am. My head doesn't hurt anymore when I bend over. I guess I'm just about over it."

A small frown creased Ann's face, and she pursed her lips before saying, "Uh, about school. There's some guys that are real jerks. The best thing to do is just ignore them. Their fathers are guards at the state prison across town, and they think they're something special."

Clint rammed the pitch fork into the ground and jerked up a large clod of soggy soil. He turned to her and spoke pointedly, "I'm not looking for trouble, but if I have to, I can take care of myself."

ooooo

The next morning, Clint and Ann began the one mile trek to school. There was some small talk, separated by long stretches of strained silence—he, feeling awkward to suddenly find himself going to school again; she, feeling an excitement to have this strange boy walking beside her, but with a foreboding of the day ahead. Ann was relieved when they arrived at the Jenkins house. Karen bounded off the porch, then slowed when she saw the new boy. Ann said, "Karen. This is Clint, the boy I told you about." Clint smiled self-consciously and said hello, while Karen blushed and mumbled a greeting.

The same four boys were in the old building, smoking cigarettes, but hesitated when they saw someone with the girls. George Brumley, the leader of the gang, was a sixteen-year-old freak of nature who stood six feet-two inches tall and already weighed 215 pounds. Added to that combination was a mean father and alcoholic mother to create a classic bully. Brumley flicked a cigarette butt onto the ground and asked, "Who's the sissy punk?"

Tommy Brookings, always anxious to stay in Brumley's good graces, said, "I never seen him before. Maybe he's a new kid."

Brumley spat on the ground and sniffed. "He looks like a girl. Acts like one, too."

Tommy Brookings chuckled, then volunteered, "I'll find out if he's one of us or not."

The school bell rang, and the students assembled at the front door in a single line. Clint was sandwiched between Ann in front and Karen behind. Tommy Brookings jumped in front of Ann, and she immediately folded her arms over her chest. As the line began moving forward, Tommy Brookings stopped, then leaned backwards. "Stop it, Tommy!" Ann hissed and warded him off with her elbows.

Tommy Brookings smirked. "I ain't doing nothing." He leaned back again, but bumped against hard muscle. A hard shove sent him sprawling to the ground. He jumped up with fists ready, but stopped when he saw the new boy standing with feet spread and hands on hips. Tommy gulped. The new kid was taller by two inches, and muscles bulged under his flannel shirt. "Hey, what's the big idea?" Tommy Brookings complained.

Clint stood with arms folded and said gruffly, "You need to learn some manners."

Principal Thompson yelled from the doorway, "You two boys! Get back in line."

Tommy Brookings' bravado returned, and he muttered, "This ain't over."

Clint was assigned to Ann's ninth grade class, where the teacher discovered that Clint was intelligent, but behind in his studies. At lunchtime, Ann led Clint to a small table where Karen and two other girls sat. Clint felt uncomfortable sitting with a bunch of girls, but Ann had the sandwiches.

Karen glanced up, and a look of terror spread across her face. George Brumley swaggered to the table and stood, chest out and arms folded. He glared at Clint, while Tommy Brookings and the two other boys stood nearby with sullen faces. Brumley nudged Clint hard with his knee and challenged, "Heard you been pushing my friend around?"

Clint jumped to his feet. Though now almost six feet tall and 175 pounds, he was dwarfed by Brumley, but not intimidated. He jabbed a thumb at Tommy Brookings and said, "You mean the punk who doesn't have any manners?"

Brumley's face clouded over, and he shoved Clint hard. Ann jumped up and angrily pushed at George Brumley's chest. "You stay away from him, George Brumley!" she screeched. "He has a head injury."

Principal Thompson charged between the two boys and scolded them, but as Brumley strutted away, he looked back and said in a loud voice, "The sissy has to hide behind a girl. I'll be waiting after school."

Ann and Karen pestered Clint about taking the long way home to avoid a beating, until he erupted, "Enough already! I'll meet him after school."

Ann protested, "But your head!"

A hard look came to Clint's face when he replied, "I don't intend to let him hit me."

But Ann persisted. "Nobody can beat George Brumley. He's too big and strong."

Clint placed a hand on Ann's shoulder and looked into her brown, fearful eyes. His voice was low, confident. "I can."

As Clint walked away, Karen sidled up to Ann and murmured, "I saw that l-o-o-k." Ann blushed and jostled her friend, but her heart was thumping in her chest.

Ann was ashen-faced and trembling as she followed Clint's purposeful gait down the path to the old building, where a crowd had gathered, watching George Brumley flex his muscles and shadow box. When Brumley saw Clint, he strode forward and stood in his path with hands at his side, balled into tight fists. The crowd circled the two boys. "So you're looking to get your face smashed in, are ya?" Brumley growled.

Clint retorted, "Not from a punk like you."

The new boy's audacity sent a shocked murmur through the crowd. Brumley's eyes bulged out at the insult, and he threw a powerful roundhouse right. Clint ducked, and before Brumley could regain his balance, Clint put his shoulder behind a straight right hand that smacked against Brumley's cheek with a loud thud.

Brumley staggered backward, his eyes glazed over, and he dropped hard into a sitting position. A loud gasp rippled through the crowd. Clint moved in to finish it, but Brookings jumped on his back, and then he felt other hands pulling him down. George

Brumley shook his head and scrambled to his feet. He leaped forward and landed a glancing punch to Clint's forehead before two teachers, warned about a fight, charged into the fracas, and pulled the boys apart.

Brumley, Brookings, and the other two cohorts strutted away. Brumley, having regained his composure, yelled back, "Monday, we'll finish it!"

Ann hurried forward and slipped her arm through Clint's, while Karen slipped her arm through the other, and both girls looked up adoringly at him. Other youths who'd been victimized by the Brumley gang descended upon Clint and hailed him as their hero.

After Karen and the other kids had wandered off to their homes, Ann maintained her hold on Clint's arm. He didn't resist. "Oh, Clint," she murmured, "I'm so worried. Those guys won't quit until they beat you up, and Doc Hastings said you need a month for your head to heal."

Clint scoffed, but he was worried. Brumley's glancing blow had brought back the headaches. "Where does George Brumley live, anyway?" Clint casually asked. "In an old brown house down by the creek behind the Deer Lodge Mercantile. Why?"

"Oh, just wondering."

That evening Henry Crenshaw pulled his daughter aside. "What's this I hear about our new boarder getting in trouble at school already?"

An offended look spread across Ann's face. "Trouble? George Brumley and his gang are the trouble! Clint just stood up to Brumley after Tommy Brookings started…"

"Started what?"

Ann tried to avoid the answer. "Well, they've just all been fresh lately."

Henry Crenshaw's eyes narrowed and he leaned his head forward. "What do you mean, 'fresh'?"

Ann flushed and stammered, "Uh, well, you know."

"No, I don't," Henry snapped. "Why don't you quit beating around the bush and answer my question, young lady?"

Ann dropped her eyes and spoke in an embarrassed voice, "They make dirty remarks at the girls and try to touch us."

"And Clint stepped in to stop this?"

Ann looked up, and nodded. Henry Crenshaw's demeanor changed. He grunted and walked away.

On Saturday morning, Clint announced that he was going in to Deer Lodge to look for some part-time work. Ann volunteered to go along, and Clint was relieved when Mrs. Crenshaw reminded her that there were three loads of wash to do. That evening Clint returned home after dark and announced that he'd found a job splitting wood behind the Deer Lodge Mercantile.

The Crenshaw family took Clint along to the Deer Lodge Methodist Church on Sunday. The pastor's wife, Mary Talbot, taught youth Sunday school, which was comprised of Ann, Karen and four other teens, plus Clint. Unfamiliar with the Bible, Clint fumbled hopelessly through the pages, searching for answers to scripture questions.

Mary Talbot said, "Okay, class. Now we're going to look at what Jesus had to say about children." She wrote two scripture verses on the blackboard, and the students rifled through the pages of their bibles.

Clint jerked open his Bible and was startled when his eyes fell upon the first verse. There was a quickening in his spirit as he scanned the words. He read aloud, "Suffer the little children to come to me, and forbid them not, for of such is made the kingdom of heaven."

"Very good!" Mrs. Talbot praised, and both Ann and Karen patted his shoulders.

Amazingly, Clint's Bible fell open to the next verse, and he eagerly began reading, "If anyone should harm one hair on the heads of these children, it would be better for him that a millstone was tied around his neck and he was thrown into the sea, than to face the day of judgment." His mind flashed back to little Mugsy, and he stopped reading.

All eyes were on him as Mrs. Talbot said, "Read the next verse also, Clint." He shook his head as he fought furiously to hold back the tears. Two large drops spattered on the pages of his Bible.

Ann fought the urge to throw her arms around him. She did the next best thing by volunteering, "I'll read it." For the rest of the class, Clint stared at the floor.

When class was dismissed, Clint rushed for the door, but Mrs. Talbot called him back and said, "You seemed upset by those scriptures about God's love for children, Clint. Is there anything you want to discuss about them?"

Clint's frowned for a few seconds then asked, "Does God really care about what happens to the children in the world?"

"Oh, yes! God especially cares about what happens to the children."

Clint's frown turned into a scowl as he shot back a reply, "Well, I don't think he cares. If he did, he wouldn't let all this bad stuff happen to kids." He folded his arms and awaited an answer. Mrs. Talbot's jaw dropped. Sensing the boy's turgid emotions, she was about to respond when the church bell clanged.

ooooo

Julia Crenshaw had just placed a huge pot of chicken dumpling soup on the table for Sunday dinner when the phone rang. Henry picked up the receiver and spoke while the rest of the family took turns ladling out their soup. Julia watched her husband's expression change from surprise to concern. As soon as Henry replaced the receiver, Julia asked, "What's wrong, dear?"

Henry Crenshaw walked to the table shaking his head. "You won't believe this," he said as he sat down and grabbed the ladle. "Pastor Talbot just told me that George Brumley got bit by a black widow spider last night in bed."

Ann gasped. Her spoon clattered onto the table. She slowly turned wide-eyed and open-mouthed to Clint, who blew on his soup and said, "Pass the biscuits, please."

# CHAPTER 9

*H*e idly balanced the pitchfork in his right hand. His head slowly swiveled back and forth as he took in the atmosphere of the barn. The sweet smell of hay tantalized his nostrils, and freely mingled with the healthy sour odor of leather. From a rusty nail hung four small steel traps, a necessity to eliminate the rats and skunks that constantly invaded the place.

He wanted to feel fear, even outrage, for this barn was not much different from the barn of Gustav Schmidt. Instead, he felt a warm sense of well-being. For, unlike that monster's ugly prison of weathered boards, death and hate, this barn furnished life and peace.

Unfortunately, not all the life in the barn was at peace. A tremendous bellow that rattled the dirty windows startled him from his reverie. "Oh, shut up, Flossie!" Clint bellowed back at the milk cow and threw a pitchfork full of loose hay in her face. Clint laughed as the beleaguered cow, with calf sucking loudly at her swollen udder, shook the hay off her face and greedily munched dinner.

The door to the barn squeaked open. He tensed for an instant then relaxed. Without looking, he knew who it was. Ann stood beside him, studying his face for any sign of—what? He knew she was there, but continued humming as he spread bedding straw in the pen. Her words came in breathless flurry. "What do you think about George Brumley getting bit by a black widow spider?"

Clint shrugged and rammed the fork into the hay pile. "It's spring. Spiders come out."

That wasn't the answer Ann was seeking, so she pressed on. "Gee, Clint, he was gonna fight you tomorrow. Now, Dad says they have to cut a big chunk out of his right shoulder because it got gangrene in it."

"Humph!" Clint grunted. "I guess he won't be fighting anybody for a while."

Ann's heart raced as she worked up the courage to ask him another question. But in the end, she silently walked out of the barn.

Supper at the Crenshaws that evening was chicken soup, but this time without the chicken. On the way to school the next morning, Clint mentioned, "Your folks are having a tough time, aren't they?"

Ann was silent for a moment, then nodded. "Dad bought this ranch two years ago. The land payments take up just about all the money Dad makes on the ranch. Sometimes we don't even have a chicken to put in the pot. We just have broth and dumplings."

Clint nodded with a frown. "I can help with that. Besides the money I'll make chopping wood, I think I can find some more work after school."

Ann gave Clint a long, radiant look, then slipped her arm through his and laid her head on his shoulder. "You're so nice, Clint."

The fragrance of her freshly washed hair and the heat of her body electrified him. There had been moments of sexual awakening in the past, but nothing like the way he was feeling at the moment. Every nerve in his body tingled, and a delicious trembling overtook him. But when he glanced down and saw the bulge, he faked a sneeze to put some distance between them.

At Karen's house, the door flew open and she hurried out, a look of intrigue on her face. "Did you hear the news? George Brumley got bit by a black widow!"

Tommy Brookings had also heard about George Brumley. He tried skipping school, but his mother chased him out the front door. At least there was still Joe and Jake to hang around with until George got back. He hurried to the old building next to the school to plan a strategy with his cohorts. The other guys weren't there yet, so he lit a cigarette and waited. At the sound of oncoming footsteps, he turned. The cigarette fell from his open mouth. Standing in the doorway was Clint.

With the memory of George Brumley staggering backwards still fresh in his mind, Tommy Brookings began to tremble. Clint held up his hands and said, "I'm not here to beat you up, unless you're a bad listener. We've got some stuff to talk about. I'm going to do the talking, and you're going to do the listening."

Tommy Brookings turned out to be an excellent listener. Without their leader to hide behind, the Brumley gang's reign of terror evaporated. At lunch hour, small children got to eat their lunches without fear of having them pilfered, and young girls skipped across the school grounds unmolested.

After Karen was dropped off, Ann slipped her arm through Clint's and they walked home that way. Clint liked having Ann close, but he was also unnerved by her attention. While he liked the feeling of her body brushing against him, he also felt an urgency to get away from her—to flee from those adoring eyes because he wasn't the hero she thought he was.

On the other hand, Ann felt no such uneasiness about being close to him. He was the most courageous, beautiful boy she had ever seen, and she often daydreamed about the two of them, married and…She would blush at the thought, but those fluttery feelings were like a narcotic to her, and she often sought them as her rapidly developing womanhood sent confusing, delicious signals soaring through her body.

The next day after school, Clint stopped by Doc Hastings' office for a scheduled checkup. While Doc Hastings studied Clint's pupils, he mentioned, "I heard you thumped that big Brumley kid the other day."

"Where'd you hear that?"

Doc Hastings sniffed and replied, "This is a small town. Word gets around, especially when a bully like George Brumley gets a taste of what he's been dishing out for so long."

Doc Hastings wheeled his chair away and Clint stood up. While he buttoned his shirt, the doctor said, "Your concussion is healing fast." He paused, then spoke in a low voice, "The first time I checked you at the Crenshaw house, I found blood on your legs. How are you doing down there?"

Clint stiffened then looked away. "All right," he mumbled.

"Good. Enough said about that."

ooooo

Spring planting season had begun, and Clint was able to pick up hourly work selling vegetable seeds and starter plants at the Deer Lodge Mercantile after school during the week. On Friday, Julia Crenshaw was dumbfounded when Clint handed her a five dollar bill—enough to feed them for two weeks, the way she stretched things. She protested weakly, but Clint was adamant about paying his way.

While the money ingratiated Clint to Julia, it had the opposite effect on Henry Crenshaw. Years of living off the land had created in him a stubborn self-sufficiency that was now threatened by some strange kid who could go into town and make more money than Henry could earn on the ranch right now. And it caused a rare argument in their bedroom that night when he folded his arms and ordered his wife to give the money back.

Julia quit stroking her hair and slapped the brush onto the scarred old dresser. Her eyes flashed with anger, and her voice echoed her frustration over their financial situation, "There's no money in this house! You said yourself the boy would have to carry his own weight. Five dollars a week will feed this family and pay the light bill until you can sell the calves to the prison ranch."

A flush came to his face. The ranch foreman had offered him only two cents a pound for the calves. Henry tapped his finger on the dresser. "And just where did the kid get all that money? That's what I'd like to know. Old man Prescott at the Mercantile is as tight as an old whore. No way he's gonna pay that kid five bucks a week for part time work."

Julia put her hands on her hips, a look of outrage spreading across her face. "Henry Crenshaw, besides talking filth, you're also accusing that boy of stealing!"

Her rebuke infuriated him, and he shook his finger in her face. "We still don't know a damn thing about that kid. These people that ride the rails have ways of getting money that ain't legal."

Julia flung her arms out and whispered in a furious voice, "I hate it when you act like this! Not only is your mouth in the gutter, so is your mind. You can't even bring yourself to trust a boy who is trying to help us."

Husband and wife stood glowering at each other. Henry turned away and flounced into bed, turning his back to his wife. "I smell a rat," he grumbled, "and I intend to find it."

The next morning he ate his pancakes in silence, while Julia stood at the sink washing dishes. Finally, he cleared his throat and said, "I'll be taking four calves into town to sell this morning." Julia nodded, but didn't turn around as he walked out the door. He hated to part with the young animals before they had a chance to put some weight on, but the monthly mortgage payment was due in three days, and he was still two dollars short. On his way out of town, he stopped by the Deer Lodge Mercantile to pick up a few items with the dollar left over after he'd paid the bank.

John Prescott was a short, balding man with wire-rimmed glasses that hung on the bridge of his nose. He didn't bother to look up from his ledger. "Morning, Henry."

"Morning, John," Henry said, then busied himself weighing out a pound of ten penny nails and five pounds of flour. When he handed over a wrinkled dollar bill at the counter, Prescott shook his head and said, "No need for that. You've a dollar and a half credit on your account."

"What?" Henry sputtered.

Prescott nodded. "That boy you've got staying with you wouldn't take any money for his after school work. Said to put his earnings on your account, since he's eating you out of house and home."

Henry leaned forward, an incredulous look on his face. "You mean to say, you never gave him any money?"

Prescott shook his head. "I gotta admit. That's one hard working kid." Henry grunted and stomped out the door.

Julia Crenshaw sat quietly at the kitchen table, morosely shaking her head as her husband related his conversation with Prescott. She sighed and said, "I guess I was wrong. He just seemed like such a nice boy. Mrs. Talbot said he's even taken an interest in the Bible."

Henry gave his wife a condescending smile and patted her shoulder. "It's not your fault, dear. It's just your nature to think the best of everyone."

Julia sighed heavily and said, "Ann will be crushed. She's taken a real liking to that boy."

"So I've noticed," Henry commented dryly.

At the supper table that evening, Ann detected a tension between her parents, but she attributed it to the money problems they were having. With the meal finished, Henry cleared his throat and said, "Ann, why don't you clean off the table."

Clint stood and volunteered, "I'll do the dishes."

Henry motioned him down and said, "Ann can do the dishes. We want to talk to you about something."

Ann stood uncertainly beside the table and asked, "What's the matter? What's wrong?"

Henry pointed at the sink and ordered, "You get over there, young lady, and do as you're told."

Ann flushed and hastily gathered up an armload of dirty dishes before retreating to the sink. Clint slowly sat down, wondering how they'd found out about George Brumley.

Henry Crenshaw got right to the point. "I talked to Mr. Prescott today. He tells me you don't take money for your work."

Clint's mind feverishly searched for some understanding of where the conversation was headed. He nodded slowly and said, "That's right. I thought if I lived here, I should pay my way."

"And you put all your wages to credit?" There was an edge to Henry's words that startled Clint, but he nodded warily.

Henry glanced at his wife then fished the five-dollar bill from his pocket. He held up the wrinkled paper for a second, then threw the damning evidence onto the table and demanded, "Then where'd you get this five dollar?"

Now, Clint understood. He glanced at Ann, who stood frozen at the sink, confusion and fear on her face. He slowly picked up the bill and studied Henry Crenshaw. "So you think I stole this."

Julia leaned forward and placed a hand on his forearm. "Clint, that's a lot of money for a young man in school to come up with. We just want to know where you got it."

Ann rushed to the table and blurted, "Clint wouldn't steal money! He's, he's honest and, and nice."

Henry folded his arms and leaned back in his chair, waiting. Clint met his steely-eyed glare without wavering and shot back, "You think I stole it, don't you?"

Henry lurched forward and jabbed a finger at the five dollar bill. "I want to know where you got this money."

Clint gave Ann a long, sad look, which hardened when he turned back to Henry Crenshaw. "You're right," he began, "Mr. Prescott didn't give me a cent. I put all my earnings from the Mercantile toward credit." Henry cast a knowing glance at his wife. Julia lowered her head and stared at the table.

Clint continued, "But Mr. Prescott doesn't own that big pile of logs behind the store. He just sells the cord wood for a Mr. Jasper who logs up Gold Creek. For every cord of wood I cut, split, and stack, he pays me a half dollar. I did ten cords, that's five dollars." Clint picked up the bill, examined it again then flicked it onto the table. "That's where it came from." He rose and walked outside.

Ann ran after him, but stopped at the door and turned on her parents. "You two are so, so..." She spun away and hurried after Clint.

ooooo

There was another meeting at the Crenshaw home later that evening, with Henry Crenshaw awkwardly explaining that they were simply asking where he'd gotten the money, not accusing him of stealing. Clint sat quietly, but he knew better. If it hadn't been for Ann, he would have left immediately.

The misunderstanding served to forge a closer bond between Ann and Clint, and they often sought each other's company doing farm chores and at school. And much to Henry Crenshaw's chagrin, Ann and Clint began sitting together in church.

On Sunday afternoon, Ann and Clint decided to plant the vegetable garden while Ann's parents were away visiting. Clint turned over the black soil again and smoothed it, then made shallow planting furrows with the handle of the pitchfork. Ann watched his deft movements and commented, "Boy, you sure know a lot about gardening."

An image of his mother carefully examining every plant in her garden flashed through his mind. He smiled and said, "My mother always…"

He froze as the words hit his ears. Ann gave him a startled look and asked, "What?"

"Nothing," Clint muttered. They planted the garden in silence for the next hour. Ann finally stood and brushed the dirt from her overalls. She avoided his eyes and spoke in a vague voice, "I have to go and prepare dinner."

Clint placed a hand on her shoulder. "Wait. Could we talk for a minute?" Hurt eyes stared back at him, but she nodded. They sat on a mound of hay in the cool air of the barn. Clint gathered his thoughts and said, "I'm not an orphan." And then he began—telling her about his early life, the loss of his mother, the orphanage and a sister left behind when he'd been sent away."

Ann finally asked, "Will you go back and find your sister? You, you could bring her back here."

Clint shook his head, and his voice betrayed the bitterness he felt when he replied, "They don't want me back there."

Ann touched his arm and whispered, "Oh Clint, I'm so sorry. How could people treat children that way?"

Clint sighed and said, "There's more." And then he told her about the children on the Orphan Train. And about little Mugsy, until a sob choked his words. He made a futile gesture with his hands and spoke falteringly, "I should have brought him with me when I left. I could have taken care of him. He'd be alive now, if I'd…"

Ann put her fingers to his lips and whispered, "Don't. You were just a little boy yourself. You did all you could." He turned and looked into her eyes. And then they kissed, softly at first, then passionately. Bodies strained against each other, then Clint suddenly pulled away and croaked, "We, we shouldn't be doing this. Someone might come by."

Ann's breath came in loud, ragged gasps, "You're…right. We, we shouldn't." A few seconds later, the drone of the Crenshaw's old truck rose above their labored breathing. Julia Crenshaw thought her daughter's flushed face was the result of the hard work in the garden, while Henry Crenshaw frowned when he noticed she wasn't wearing her bra.

ooooo

For the next month, life at the Crenshaw ranch continued to improve. The credit from Clint's part time job carried the family until Henry finalized a deal to sell twenty calves to the prison for five cents a pound. And the garden was now furnishing early season produce such as sweet peas, carrots, and radishes.

Henry Crenshaw should have been at ease, but suspicion about the young stranger living in his house still gnawed at him. For one thing, he didn't like the way his daughter looked at the boy. They were always together, whether it was work or school. No, he didn't like it one bit, and he became grimly determined to get that boy out of his house before "something" happened. He visited Pastor Talbot, explained his dilemma, and inquired about a state orphanage that could take the boy off his hands— the sooner the better. His wife would throw a fit if she knew what he'd done, but he was sure she'd eventually see that it was best for everyone.

Clint made sure that the "something" Henry Crenshaw worried about didn't happen. Behind the barn, when Ann's body pressed desperately against him, it was he who pulled away. Ann loved him all the more because she thought he loved her too much to go all the way before they were married. But for Clint, his desire for her was tempered by the fear of a commitment. She was already hinting about their lives together as husband and wife, while he still wrestled nightly with the ghosts of his past. And if he couldn't keep the commitments he'd made to his mother and the children on the Orphan Train, how could he make a lifetime commitment?

And this thing called love that Ann talked about. What was it, anyway? Could young people have it, as Ann claimed she had for him? Could he ever love her like she said she loved him? But another question haunted him even more: After what he'd been through, was he even capable of love?

ooooo

It was a brilliant Sunday morning in late July when the Crenshaws arrived at church. The Sunday school lesson was in the book of Matthew, Chapter 5, verses 1-11. These verses were called *The Beatitudes*—Jesus's famous sermon on the Mount of Olives. Clint devoured the scriptures, awed by their poignant beauty and power. As if he had discovered a treasure, he scribbled them down on a yellow sheet of tablet paper:

> Blessed are those who mourn, for they will be comforted.
> Blessed are those who hunger and thirst for righteousness, for they will be filled.
> Blessed are the merciful, for they will be shown mercy.
> Blessed are those who are persecuted because of right-eousness, for theirs is the kingdom of heaven.
> Blessed are the peacemakers, for they will be called sons of God.

At the end of class, Clint carefully folded the paper and put it in his pocket. He smiled at Ann's beaming face and felt a warm glow unlike any emotion he'd ever felt. Was this love, this wonderful feeling that made him want to gaze into her beautiful face forever?

ooooo

Pastor Talbot had invited the Crenshaw family to his house for Sunday dinner after church. He'd previously informed Henry Crenshaw that the state orphanage in Helena was willing to take the boy, and he'd made arrangements for Clint to be sent there on Monday. Henry Crenshaw thought it would work best if Pastor Talbot broke the news to Julia and the boy, explaining that state law required his placement there. That way, Henry wouldn't end up looking like the heavy. Besides, the kid was probably getting bored with ranch life and would welcome a change.

The Talbot's house was only three blocks from the church, so the pastor and his wife usually walked during nice weather. With an eye on saving a penny's worth of gas, Henry Crenshaw opted to have the family walk with the Talbots to their house. Ann and Clint reluctantly followed a short distance behind the grown-ups.

At the corner of Main and Fifth Streets, two bums sat on the steps of the bank. One of the men spotted the pastor's clerical collar, removed his hat and called, "Morning, folks. God bless ya. Would ya happen ta have a dime fer two hungry souls?"

Henry Crenshaw ignored the man, but Pastor Talbot fished a dime from his pocket, showed it to the bum and began preaching about the evils of idleness and hard drink.

Clint was explaining to Ann how to protect tomato plants from early frost when he glanced over and spotted the bums thirty-feet away. His words died in mid-sentence. He took two quick steps and squinted at them. A fury rose within him as he scrutinized the hatless man nodding submissively at Pastor Talbot's finger-wagging speech.

Ann saw the hard look in his eyes and asked, "Do you know those men, Clint?"

With the impromptu sermon finally over, the bum nodded and thanked Pastor Talbot for the dime. He smiled, showing tobacco stained teeth before placing the hat back on his head. A flush came to Clint's face. He breathed loudly though his nose.

Ann grasped his arm, her voice rising. "Clint, what's wrong?"

Clint's eyes were riveted to the hat—gray, floppy and sweat-stained. And two snake rattles dangled from the front of the band. He shouldered past Pastor Talbot and stood spread-legged in front of the bum, hands clenched into tight fists at his side. "Remember me?" he asked in a hoarse voice.

The bum pushed his hat high on his forehead and grinned up at Clint, but his eyes showed no sign of recognition. "Hi, sonny boy. Ya wouldn't happen ta have a…" Clint kicked the man hard in the groin.

The bum screamed and pitched forward. Clint kicked him twice more in the back then began furiously punching the man's head. Strong hands gripped his shoulders. He spun around and swung blindly. The blow landed low, but still carried devastating power. Henry Crenshaw staggered backwards, grabbed at his lower midsection, and dropped.

ooooo

He'd been sitting on the rickety kitchen chair for the past hour, staring straight ahead. Julia Crenshaw silently padded around the kitchen in front of him, casting an occasional troubled glance his way, which he ignored. Muffled sobs emanated from Ann's bedroom.

A car pulled up in front of the house. The front door banged opened and Henry Crenshaw gingerly walked in, followed closely by a stern-faced Pastor Talbot. Julia hurried to her husband's side and asked, "Is there still blood in your urine?"

"Doc says I'll be fine," Henry grunted, then cast a withering glare at Clint.

Arms crossed, Clint returned the man's glare with unrepentant eyes. Crenshaw shuffled towards Clint. "You!" The word came as a furious whisper as he snapped an accusing finger at Clint. "Just what in the hell was all that about? Why did you attack that man?"

Clint turned and stared out the window.

Julia wrung her hands and asked, "Is that poor man going to be all right?"

Pastor Talbot volunteered, "Doctor Hastings says he might lose his, uh, testicles."

"Good," Clint muttered.

Henry Crenshaw's face turned beet red, and he lunged at Clint, but Pastor Talbot and Julia stepped in front of him. "You almost killed that poor man!" Crenshaw raged. "Maimed him for life, and then you say *good*?" Clint remained silent, but defiantly met the man's angry glare.

Crenshaw's eyes narrowed to slits. He spoke in a low, furious voice, "I always knew you were no good. I never wanted you in my house. I knew you were trouble. You're just a bad seed—mean through and through.

Julia Crenshaw cautiously touched her husband's arm and said, "Henry, maybe there's a reason why the boy…"

Henry silenced her with a vicious wave of his arm. "I know all about you and your bullying at school. And that spider. How'd that black widow get in George Brumley's bed the day before you two were gonna fight? His mother said she found a drop of pitch mixed in with the squashed spider. How'd that get there, huh?"

Clint's silence infuriated Henry Crenshaw even more. He pointed a finger at the boy and growled, "You're just no good. We don't want you around here no more. I want you out of my house right now."

Pastor Talbot stepped forward and solemnly announced, "I've found an orphanage in Helena that will take the boy. Tomorrow, he'll be sent…"

"I won't go." Clint's voice was low, but firm. "I won't go back to an orphanage."

Pastor Talbot cleared his throat and said, "Young man, you have no choice. This is for the best. You need special help with your temper."

From the depths of his mind came one of the Beatitudes he'd learned that morning: "Blessed are the merciful, for they will find mercy." He scanned the room, desperately seeking mercy in their eyes, but found none.

Clint gulped and stood. He announced in a tight voice, "I'll leave the way I came, on a train. I'll get my stuff and be gone."

"No!" Ann screamed from her room. The door flew open and she ran toward Clint. Henry Crenshaw grabbed her arm and roughly pushed his daughter back into her room. "You stay in there, young lady," he bellowed, "or I'll put the strap to you!"

Clint started for the door, his body tense, but Henry Crenshaw made no move to stop him. Julia scurried about the kitchen and called to him, "Wait, I'll send something along for you to eat." Clint slammed the door behind him.

While he gathered his few belongings in the barn, Ann climbed out the back window and ran to him. She collapsed into his arms and wept bitterly. "Don't go, Clint!" she wailed. "Just tell me why you did it, and I'll talk to my parents. I'll beg for another chance."

Clint held her at arms length and smiled sadly at her tear-stained face. "There's nothing to be done. They want me gone, so I'll leave."

"Then take me with you," she begged. "We can run away and get married. We can…"

Clint shook his head. "No, Ann. It's not right. We're too young."

"But, but," Ann blubbered, "I love you, Clint!" She searched his eyes, then whispered, "You love me, too, don't you?"

Clint scowled and looked away. "I don't know what I feel anymore."

Ann closed her eyes. Her lower lip trembled, but she bravely announced, "I love you more than anything in the whole world."

She opened her eyes, stifled a sob, and said, "Someday, when we're grown up, we'll meet again."

Clint smiled and touched her face, then walked away. Ann followed, sobbing, to the edge of the barnyard and called after him. "I love you, Clint!" She cupped her hands around her mouth and called, "Please come back for me!"

Clint slowed his pace, looked back, and nodded briefly. He walked swiftly out of sight, then stopped and pulled the yellow paper from his pocket. He studied his scribblings, the beatitudes, then let the wind carry it away.

ooooo

A dark figure ran alongside the slow-moving midnight freight train. Clint swung aboard an open boxcar and sat catching his breath. Suddenly, he stiffened and whirled around. "It's okay!" a voice called from the dark. "I ain't gonna hurt ya."

A short, squat man dressed in rumbled coat and battered hat stepped into the moonlight with his hands extended to show he had no weapon. The stubble-faced stranger said, "Ya wouldn't have any food by any chance, would ya? I ain't ate all day."

As powerful hands clamped onto the man's shoulders, the frightened hobo cried out, "What the…" A second later he was flying through the dark void beyond the boxcar. As the screams faded, Clint sucked in a ragged breath and roared into the night, "I will not be a victim!"

ooooo

Henry and Julia Crenshaw were sitting at the table early Monday morning sharing their first cup of coffee when a motorcar lurched to a halt outside. Henry Crenshaw looked out the window and said, "It's Doc Hastings. Wonder what he wants."

Julia said as she padded to the door, "He probably wants to check on your bladder."

Doc Hastings barged inside and said, "Where's the boy? Is he still here?"

Henry Crenshaw folded his arms and remarked in a cold voice, "He's gone, and good riddance."

Doc Hastings shoulders sagged. He shook his head and moaned, "We made a big mistake with that boy."

"What do you mean?" Julia asked, her voice rising.

Doc Hastings poured himself a cup of coffee and sat at the table. "Well," he began, "I didn't think it was anybody's business at the time, but that boy got more than his head worked over when he was jumped on that train."

Now it was Henry Crenshaw's turn to ask, "What do you mean?"

"I mean when I checked him out that first time in this house, I found blood coming out of his behind. He'd been raped."

"Oh dear God," Julia gasped and brought a hand to her breast.

Doc Hastings continued, "I got to wondering why that boy would attack a stranger for no reason. So I started asking that bum some questions, plied him with a little booze I keep for medicinal purposes. He admitted everything."

"Oh dear Lord," Henry Crenshaw groaned as Ann's bedroom door flew open.

# CHAPTER 10

*R*olling thunder and heavy rain buffeted the Henley farmhouse in the early hours of August 2, 1930. Albert Henley had been awake all night, sipping whiskey and staring out the kitchen window into the black void. It was an hour past dawn, but the black clouds hanging low over the land pushed back the light.

He'd hoped for a bright, sunny day—one last chance to feel warmth. Instead, the air was as cold as his heart. One last cup of coffee would be nice, but that bitch Maura had stolen most of the cooking pots, including the coffee pot, when she'd run off last month after the money had run out.

Albert Henley fought back tears and dropped his head into his hands, moaning, "How did it all go so wrong?"

But he knew the answer. He'd always been a weak man. The chance for easy money, and the allure of the flesh had been entice-ments he could not resist. He'd married a good woman—stern, but rock solid and upright in character. But that wasn't enough for him. He'd chased after an ambitious hussy who'd deserted him when he needed her the most—something Elizabeth would never have done.

And the money. That miserable stock market had seduced him into borrowing against the farmland his father, and his father's father had wrestled from the wilderness. Paper riches was all it had amounted to. Lots of money on a white sheet, leading him down a path to financial ruin. In just a few hours Constable Jacobs would arrive with the bank's eviction notice.

But it was a much more horrendous crime against nature that haunted his mind during the day and robbed him of sleep at night, and brought him to this precipice of his life. He squeezed his eyes shut, hoping for one last respite from the torture, but he was defenseless against the image that screamed forward into his consciousness: terrified eyes and a small voice pleading for mercy. Even now he could feel the pressure on his leg where the son he'd betrayed had clung desperately to the father he loved.

Father, the boy had called him. He was no father! No husband, either. Not even a man when the money had run out. He'd cast aside everything good in his life for his own selfish desires.

And now it was time to pay the piper. A ragged sob escaped from his throat. He sat up straight, peered out the window at the first rays of sunshine streaking through breaks in the dark clouds, felt the cold steel against his temple. Hoping they'd all hear his last words, he whispered hoarsely, "I'm sorry."

ooooo

The Great Depression settled upon America like a shroud and instantly suffocated a national economy built on paper riches. Now, the plush Pullman railroad cars begged for a few of those high rolling entrepreneurs, but overnight the new rich had become the new poor. And those who had not jumped out windows on Wall Street or jammed a gun into their mouths were now selling apples on Times Square in New York City.

One thing can be said for the Depression. It chose no favorites. Every man, woman, and child—young or old, rich or poor, new money or old–had been affected by a national malady that no one seemed capable of correcting. Unable to change its course, a bewildered nation was forced to hunker down and weather a crisis unlike anything that war or weather had ever wrought upon America.

The West was one of the least affected areas of the country during the Great Depression. Isolated ranchers, farmers, and homesteaders were mostly self-sufficient, growing their own crops and livestock, making their own clothes, soaps, saddles—even grinding their own wheat by hand with crude stone mortar and pestle as the Indians had done for centuries.

Some of the large ranches in the West had enough orders for beef from the military to continue operating with a reduced herd and a skeleton crew of men who were willing to work for room and board, but no wage. Clint Henley fit into this niche. Though just fifteen years old, his physique and surly demeanor fooled most folks into guessing his age at about twenty.

After leaving the Crenshaw ranch, he'd worked odd jobs along the southern rail route through Colorado, until he found himself at an isolated railroad depot just north of Denver. There, he stumbled upon the huge Bar S Ranch stock holding pens, and was hired for the simple reason that he didn't request a salary, just room and board.

During the lonely days tending cattle on the desolate prairie, Clint wrestled with the painful memories of the past. As he lay in his bed roll at night, the feel of his lips upon Mugsy's cheek tortured him. The winsomeness of Hanna and the innocence of Jonathan sliced through his soul, exposing over and over his failure to protect them. And what of Jenny? Slow, simple Jenny. If the world could ravage him, what hope did she have?

An occasional memory of Henrietta would surface, but he'd drive it from his mind. The thought of his little sister being preyed upon by some oafish monster such as Gustav Schmidt was more than he could bear. Besides, that life was behind him now. Those people didn't want him, and he'd be damned if he'd ever open himself up like that again.

Bill Westen, the Bar S foreman, liked Clint's hard work ethic, and he became a favorite among the other men when he stood his ground against twenty-four-year-old Jimmy Walker, a wannabe tough guy and bully. After a night of drinking, Walker had urinated in his own bed. The next evening, he ordered the youngster to switch beds with him. Clint scoffed and replied, "Sleep in your own mess."

Walker grabbed Clint by the hair and jerked him to his feet. Bringing back an open hand, he growled, "You snot-nosed, punk. I oughta—" Clint rammed a knee into his groin. Walker staggered backwards, groaning, then a look of pure hate flooded his face as he stalked forward with a long-bladed knife in his outstretched hand. Westen stepped forward and cracked Walker's head with a club he kept handy to settle bunkhouse fights. They dragged the semi-conscious man to the rail yards and threw him into an open boxcar on a southbound freight train.

The next Friday, Westen handed Clint a silver dollar, but reminded him that only the hard workers could expect a dollar at the end of each week. Clint had not seen many silver dollars because the eastern half of the nation had gone almost entirely to paper money, while the West still used silver dollars extensively. He stared at the large shiny coin in his hand and remarked, "It's almost too pretty to spend."

Westen clinked several of the heavy coins in his hand and said with a smug grin, "The ladies sure like the sound of 'em too. Ya ever wanna impress some dame, grab a couple a those rusty old washers along the railroad tracks and put 'em in your pocket with the silver dollar. She'll hear 'em clunkin' in your pocket, and ya can show her the one ya got."

Clint accompanied Westen and several other cowboys into Denver on Saturday night, and the bartender asked no questions when he self-consciously bellied up to the bar. His first taste of whisky quickly made him drunk, sending him whooping and hollering through the bars, until he fell to his knees, retching, and heaving. The Bar S men watched with amusement then dragged the delirious lad back to his bunk. But anyone who thought the new kid had learned his lesson was mistaken.

Clint Henley had discovered the one remedy to ease his pain and make his ghosts go away, if only for a night. The alcohol that gushed through his bloodstream and turned his mind numb became a necessity whenever he received his dollar's pay at the end of the week. By guzzling down a pint of cheap fifty-cent red-eye whiskey beforehand, he was able to quickly attain the numbness of the drunkard before he entered the saloons, where he scraped by for the rest of the night with a few drinks over the bar.

The hangovers from the rotgut booze were wicked, but even this throbbing pain in his head was a relief from the more agonizing pain of memories that continued to torture him—the face of a scared little boy here, a helpless little girl there, and a mother shaking her head at a drunken son.

While booze was an elixir, prostitution became a salve for Clint. His first and only lady of the night was named Diamond Lil. Thirty-year-old Lillian Prentice had the wholesome, muscular build of a homesteader's wife, with stretch marks and hips a bit wide from bearing two children, but her fair English features of fine cheekbones, tawny hair, and pale skin made her a favorite at Denver's Velvet Parlor.

Most of the other working girls lured in their "Johns" with coarse talk and lewd conduct. One disgruntled cowboy complained, "It would sure be nice if at least one of 'em was a lady."

Then along came Lilly. She offered a sensual feminine alternative to the gyrating hips of the other girls. But the one thing Lilly had in common with the other girls was an untold story—a tale that the men were not interested in hearing, so these intimate stories of tragedy and despair were kept safely tucked away in feminine hearts long ago calloused over.

None of the women at the Velvet Parlor had planned a life of squalor and deprivation—having random relations with a dozen different men nightly and the dripping, pussy venereal diseases that came with it. When they had finished for the night—after gasping for breath under the weight of a dozen drunken, sweating men with putrid breath—they would retreat to their lairs and drink away the memories of the night and the nightmares of the past.

For Lilly, it was suicidal to ponder the past. Lacking food and basic medical care that first winter of the Depression, she'd stood by in anguish as her two children slowly died of pneumonia in a damp sod hut on the bleak Wyoming prairie. At the burial of her second child, she'd watched in numbed detachment as her husband hastily threw dirt over the small bundle she'd tenderly placed in the bottom of the hole.

Her husband, desperate to ease his wife's pain, said, "Aw, don't worry, Lilly. You're young. There'll be more babies in the years to come."

She remained silent, near mad with grief. But of one thing she was certain. There would be no more babies in her life. Never again would she expose herself to a heartache so severe that it tore away part of her heart. That night, Lilly Prentice tiptoed past her snoring husband and out the door.

She walked and hitched rides to Denver, but quickly discovered that even in the big city there were no jobs. On her third day without food, she allowed a man to buy her dinner and drinks. The next morning when she groggily awoke, the man was gone, but a shiny silver dollar lay on the pillow.

Lilly had been selling herself for almost a year when Clint nervously walked through the door of the Velvet Parlor, flanked by two Bar S cowboys. Bill Westen and Joe Harley had scraped together a dollar when they guessed that Clint was still a virgin. "Here's some new blood, Lil," Joe Harley announced with a grin. "Break him in right, will ya?"

Lil smiled and nodded demurely. She stepped forward and admired the boy's jade green eyes, then ran a slender hand along his cheek. "English," she said in a soft voice. "You must be English with that face." She took his hand and led him upstairs.

Most of the men she took upstairs were drunk and such episodes ended, mercifully, after a few minutes. Lilly wanted it that way. She had no desire to know them intimately or otherwise, and it freed her to get back downstairs to work. On a good weekend night, she could take care of a dozen men. At a dollar a poke, with four bits going to the parlor madam, that left her with six dollars to stash away.

Clint became a regular with Lil. There were lots of other prostitutes around the seedy bars in the red-light district near the stockyards, but Lil's English features and soft warmth were a salve to him. However, Lil presented him with a financial dilemma. His pay of a dollar a week took care of his whiskey needs, but the extra dollar for Lil was hard to come by. Clint solved the problem by contracting with several businesses to deliver firewood. His income skyrocketed to four dollars per week, allowing him to be drunk three days each week, while still visiting Lil.

ooooo

It was a Saturday night in early May 1931, and the Stockmans Bar was filling fast when Clint sauntered in, feeling the satisfying bulge of three dollars clinking in his pocket. He spotted Joe Harley and Bill Westen at the far end of the bar and pulled up a stool beside them.

Joe Harley slapped Clint on the back and chuckled. "Well, if it ain't Diamond Lil's favorite treat. The hormones must be ragin' tonight."

Clint blushed, but smiled and called to the bartender, "Three whiskeys for me and my two friends." He'd already slugged down a pint of redeye behind the saloon, and the alcohol had brought a numbing glow to his brain. He raised the whiskey glass and studied it. "I think today is my birthday."

"Oh yeah?" Bill Westen asked with a grin. "How old are ya? Thirty? Maybe thirty-one?"

Both men guffawed and rose their whiskey-filled shot glasses to him before throwing back their heads and draining their drinks. Bill Westen shook his head and said, "I gotta hand it to ya, kid. You're about the only one around here who's got money. I don't know how ya kin split all that wood after working the Bar S all day."

Joe Harley wiped his mouth and said, "I hope ya ain't lookin' fer Lil tonight."

Clint grinned and replied, "Well, I thought I might go see her in a while."

Bill Westen sadly shook his head and mentioned, "Bad thing, it was. In my opinion, she was the best whore in the whole place."

Clint's voice rose. "What happened?"

Joe Harley sucked on a tooth and said. "The way I heard it, Jim Freeman got mean drunk and beat her up last night. Broke all her front teeth out, blackened both eyes, broke her nose. She won't be much good for nothin' now."

Clint's jaw dropped. He studied Harley's face to see if the man was teasing him again. When Harley remained somber, Clint said, "You're...you're joking, aren't you?"

Harley belched and said, "'Fraid not."

Clint stumbled off the bar stool and said, "Where is she?"

Bill Westen placed a consoling hand on Clint's shoulder and admonished him, "Look, kid. She's just a whore. Don't go gettin' attached to any of these girls. They'd all roll ya as soon as look at ya. Besides, this kinda thing happens to all of 'em sooner or later. They know what they're gettin' into."

Clint lurched away from the bar and staggered out the door. He burst through the front door of the Velvet Parlor and was met by a tall girl named Jill. "Where's Lil?" he blurted.

Jill thrust her hips at him and taunted, "Lil ain't much good no more, but I can take care of anything ya want done to ya."

Clint grabbed the girl's wrist and squeezed. Jill gasped, "You're hurting me. Let go!"

"Where's Lil?" he demanded.

The frightened girl fell to her knees and wailed, "She's upstairs packing!"

Clint bounded up the stairs and rapped on Lil's door. A faint voice came back, "Who is it?"

"It's me, Clint."

"Go away."

Clint turned the knob. As the door opened, he caught a glimpse of Lil's disfigured face before she spun away. "Go away. I don't want you to see me like this," Lil mumbled through puffy lips and returned to packing her suitcase.

"Where...where are you going?"

A tear left a glistening trail down her swollen jaw. "There ain't much demand for a toothless whore around here."

"You don't have to go," Clint said, stepping closer. "I'll take care of you, Lil. I'll rent a room and—"

Lil threw a bag of hair curlers into the suitcase and spoke in a low, furious voice, "Stay away from me! I don't want nothing to do with men."

Clint stepped back and gulped, then asked, "Where will you go?"

Lil replied glumly, "I got a sister in Oregon. Maybe she'll have pity on me."

Clint took a step toward her and croaked, "I'll take care of you. I'll love you and—"

"Stop it!" she hissed and slammed the top down on the suitcase.

She turned and Clint winced at her misshapen face. Lillian Prentice put her hands on her hips and blinked back tears. She spoke in a low, trembling voice. "You don't know nothing about love. You don't find love in a whorehouse." Her breath came in short, ragged gasps as she pointed at the bed. "That wasn't love.

I did it for money. And after you left, I did it with another man and another one after that."

Clint stood open-mouthed, unable to respond. Finally, Lil turned away and said in a dead voice, "Now get out and leave me alone."

ooooo

Back at the Stockmans Bar, the warm glow of the whiskey had been replaced by a darkness that left Clint seething on the barstool next to Bill Westen. "Who's this Jim Freeman?" He asked through clenched teeth.

"Whoa there, partner!" Westen raised his hands and cautioned, "You don't want to go messin' around with a guy like Freeman. He's big and mean, and he wouldn't hesitate for a second to work over a kid like you."

Clint stared at his image in the mirror behind the bar. The whiskey had blurred his vision, revealing only the grotesque image of a pale young man wearing a floppy, sweat-stained gray cowboy hat. His eyes were mere slits, and his mouth had become a thin line. "Where's he at?" Clint asked in a low voice that hinted of the fury within.

Westen grabbed Clint's arm and whispered furiously, "Look, kid, let this thing be! Freeman'll kill ya. He's that kinda guy."

Harley chuckled and added, "Besides, if you're dead, who'll buy us poor beggars drinks." Both men laughed and slapped his shoulders, eliciting a wane smile from Clint.

Westen was right about one thing. He couldn't do anything at the moment. The whiskey had dulled his reflexes. He clunked a dollar on the bar and said, "Drinks are on me, boys. I ain't feeling so hot. If Lil's not available, I'm gonna head back to the Bar S."

Clint staggered out the door and held onto a post while he sucked in the cool night air. Heavy footfalls pounded on the boardwalk as two men emerged from the darkness. Clint pulled his hat low on his forehead and asked, "You guys seen Jim Freeman tonight?"

"Yeah," a voice replied as the men entered the Stockmans. "I seen him over at Red's Corner Bar."

ooooo

Calloused hands roughly shook Clint awake. Bill Westen and Joe Harley jerked him to his feet. Westen growled, "You're in big trouble now, kid."

Clint groggily shook his head and mumbled, "I've been asleep. What's going on?"

Joe Harley spat on the floor and countered, "Don't give us that bullshit, kid. Somebody hit Jim Freeman over the head with a bottle of gin last night."

Westen put his face an inch from Clint's and said, "Problem is, the bottle didn't break, but Freeman's head did."

Harley added, "Kid, they don't know if Freeman's gonna pull through."

"And we know you did it!" Westen said, poking an accusing finger into Clint's chest.

Clint stepped back. His eyes took on a hard look. "I've been sleeping. They can't prove anything."

Westen scoffed. "It don't matter what the law can prove. Freeman's got some friends that're already asking around about anybody who mighta had a grudge against him. Seems two guys gave some kid his whereabouts outside the Stockmans last night."

Joe Harley vigorously shook his head and said, "You're as good as dead around here, kid. And we don't wanna die tryin' ta protect some dumb kid who wouldn't listen ta reason."

Westen made a sweeping motion with his arm and demanded, "You get your stuff rounded up quick and get outta here. And don't come back. Freeman's got family in these parts. They won't forget."

Harley blew out a loud breath and said, "Listen ta me, kid. Things in the country is a mess. Ain't nobody gonna be lookin' fer some kid, what with everything else that's goin' on. Go up north somewhere. Lay low and keep yer nose clean. Ain't hardly nobody knows ya around here, so ya should be okay."

Bill Westen shot a disgusted look at Clint and slowly shook his head. "And kid, you better check that temper of yours, or it's gonna get you killed."

# CHAPTER 11

The next few days for Clint were an alcohol-induced blur of filthy boxcars and hobo camps. Food, he stole—hoarding his last few dollars to buy the cheapest rotgut whiskey in small towns along a route aimlessly chosen by taking the first train with open cars.

He awoke from his latest drunken state in Cheyenne, Wyoming. His head throbbed and he vomited, but his stomach was empty, so only a clear fluid slithered onto the ground. Again and again, his stomach convulsed with the dry heaves until he fell to his knees.

He knew what he needed—the hair of the dog that bit him. Near the rail yard he saw a man walking away from a small crowd with a bottle of whiskey in his hand. The man hid the bottle when he saw Clint approaching. He considered head-butting the guy and taking the bottle, but there were too many people milling around. "Where'd you get the whiskey?" Clint asked impatiently.

The man eyed him with suspicion, but nodded toward the crowd and said, "Over there. A Gypsy's selling it for only sixty cents a fifth. Can't beat that." The man then pulled out his bottle and grinned, adding, "Does the trick, too. I already got a buzz from one swig."

Clint hurried over and shoved sixty cents into the hands of a swarthy-complexioned man with a bandanna covering his hair and a large gold earring in his left ear. "You wanna the whisky?"

the gypsy announced. "I got good whiskey. Make you drunk quick. You come back, buy more."

As Clint walked away, he heard a voice rise in anger, "You no good Gypsy! All I got's thirty cents. Sell me half a bottle, or I'll just take it." Clint glanced back and saw the Gypsy shrug, then pour half a bottle of the reddish-amber liquid into a mason jar and hand it to the glowering man.

The evening was chilly, so after a quick pull at the bottle, Clint hid it under his shirt and walked toward a blazing fire at a hobo camp across the tracks from the train depot where a dozen men sat forlornly staring at the dancing flames. Two men sat off by themselves near a large bush and sipped from a bottle.

Clint dropped his canvas bag and sat heavily on the end of a long log near the fire that held four other men. The gypsy had been right. The whiskey tasted terrible, but it was potent. Already, his head was buzzing.

The man sitting next to him got up and threw another piece of wood on the fire. He was tall, with broad shoulders and huge hands. His hawkish nose and chiseled face made him appear fierce, but his brown eyes were soft. He studied Clint for a few seconds before asking, "What's your name, kid?"

Clint stared at the fire and replied numbly, "Don't call me a kid. I haven't been a kid for a long time."

The man snorted and an amused smile creased his weathered face. "Well, my name's Ben." He sat next to Clint and poked at the fire with a long stick. "If ya got any extra grub, there's a couple guys around the fire here haven't ate today."

Clint's eyes swept across the usual bunch of hobos who hung around the rail yards. Even if he had it, he wouldn't waste food on this bunch of bums. He pulled out his bottle and took another swig. Too late, he realized his mistake. All eyes were on him. A short, powerfully-built man wearing a faded black derby called from across the fire, "You oughta share what you have there, young feller."

He reluctantly passed the bottle to his right, but Ben jerked his head back and said, "Get that stuff away from me. It creates way more problems than it solves."

"Well, I'll have a pull," said a gaunt man with graying hair on the other side of Ben as he snatched the bottle away. He hastily pulled out the cork, tipped the bottle up and gulped twice. "Whew!" He coughed and wheezed. "Ugly stuff, but it's strong."

Clint watched helplessly as six of the eight men took long pulls. When he finally got the bottle back it was only a quarter full. He frowned and jammed it into his bag for later use.

One of the men back by the bush retched and groaned. The derby man glared in that direction and muttered, "Good, puke your guts out. That's what you get for not sharing."

Ben looked at the derby man and said, "Where ya headed?"

The derby man replied eagerly, "Seattle. My brother's got a line on a couple jobs for us. He went ahead to line things out then he'll send word for me to come."

Ben shook his head and countered, "Don't count on it. I just come from Seattle. Ain't no work there. Believe me, I looked."

The derby man spat into the fire. His face flushed with anger. "That's the problem with this rotten Depression. You always hear about work in some far off place, but it's never there when you get there. Ghost work, that's all it is."

Another man said, "I don't know how this country can go on like this much longer. It's been almost two years now. I got a wife and three kids back in Michigan. It's gotta end soon, or...or I don't know what'll happen."

The man next to him volunteered, "I heard it's supposed to break by next spring."

"Geez!" someone grumbled. "That's six months away. Everybody'll be starved to death by then."

A loud groan came from the bush where the two men were sitting, followed by a cry of pain. "Help!" came a tortured plea. "Help us! Me and my buddy is sick."

The men scrambled from the campfire and crowded around the two men writhing on the ground. One of the men was already incoherent. The other vomited a vile-looking, reddish fluid and groaned, "Oh God, my guts is on fire!"

The derby man kicked dirt at him and snarled, "That's what you get for not sharing!"

The men jumped back when the incoherent man screamed and began thrashing around on the ground and vomiting. Ben gingerly picked up the almost-empty whiskey bottle and read the label, "Old Montana Pure Whiskey." He brought the bottle to his nose and sniffed twice, then jerked his head back. "Lord a mercy!" he exclaimed. "This smells like it's got anti-freeze in it."

"You sure?" the derby man asked, concern evident in his voice.

Ben nodded and said, "I worked in a garage. Anti-freeze has wood alcohol in it, not grain alcohol like in whiskey." He grimly studied the men on the ground. "This stuff is deadly poison."

All eyes turned to Clint. The derby man stepped forward and demanded, "Where's that bottle of yours?" One of the men trotted back to the fire and returned with the bottle and handed it to Ben. "Same label," he muttered as he examined the bottle.

The derby man cursed and advanced menacingly toward Clint. His voice was accusing, threatening, "You gave us bad booze? Why, I oughta…"

Ben stepped forward and his long arm held off the derby man. "Just hold on there," he cautioned. "We don't know if this booze is bad."

The men stood there, silently watching each other—hoping. But Clint already knew. He was secretly fighting a losing battle to keep from vomiting. Then a searing pain ripped through his guts, and he fell to his knees and vomited.

Someone gasped, "Oh Lord, help us. We're poisoned."

There was another groan, followed by the splash of vomit onto the ground.

ooooo

Clint dimly remembered the wail of a siren then being carried across the railroad tracks. He awoke on a cot in the hallway of a hospital. As he struggled to rise, a middle-aged nurse with red hair hurried over and gently pushed him back down. She felt his forehead and said soothingly, "You're going to be all right. You're out of the woods. Stay still while I get Doctor Fullmer."

She hurried away and was followed back in a few seconds by a gray-haired man with intense eyes. Doctor Fullmer felt Clint's forehead, then studied his pupils. "Looks like you'll make it, young fella," he said. "You're one of the lucky ones."

The red-haired nurse called from down the hallway, "Doctor Fullmer, another one is coming around!"

A young nurse came by and made Clint sit up and drink water and eat some bread soaked in milk, which he promptly vomited back up. "That's good," the nurse assured him. "That will bring the poison up."

After several attempts, Clint was able to keep the bread down. The next morning, he was fed toast and oatmeal. When the young nurse came for the tray, he raised up on one elbow and asked, "How many died?"

She avoided his eyes and said in a low voice, "Seven, altogether. Three from your group."

Clint flopped back onto the cot and stared up at the glowing ceiling light. What had he done? Seven men were dead—three from the booze he'd given them. Ben back at the hobo camp had been right. Whiskey doesn't solve problems, it creates them. Tears of frustration brimmed in his eyes as he croaked, "And sometimes it kills."

He lay there, trying to make some sense of this latest disaster in his life. Where had he gone wrong? He thought when he'd walked away from Gustav Schmidt's sawmill that he was taking control of his life. Now, it seemed like a swirling madness had taken control of him, making him a victim over and over again. And it was getting worse. Not only was he still a victim, but now he was turning into a victimizer—throwing people off trains, kicking them in the balls, bludgeoning them with a bottle. And now, poisoning them.

Clint closed his eyes and rubbed his temples with his knuckles. Where had he gone wrong? He flashed back through the last year of his life—of bars and booze and whores and hobo camps. The muscles along his jaw twitched as the answer seeped into his consciousness: He was making a victim of himself. And it all revolved around booze. Now, just the thought of whiskey sickened him, and he swallowed hard several times until the nausea subsided. "No more," he whispered. "No more booze."

He brought his hands to his face and groaned, "Oh, what a mess I've made of my life." His mother would turn over in her grave if she could see him now. What happened to the promise he'd made her to take care of Henrietta? And what about his promises to Jonathan, Hanna, and Jenny on the Orphan Train? And what about Ann?

Those promises were the only honorable things he'd done in his life. The only things that had virtue in his miserable existence. A tightening came to his mouth, and his eyes narrowed. He would honor those promises. Or die trying. And at that moment, he really didn't care which came first.

Lunch was a toasted cheese sandwich and glass of milk. Clint waited until the attending nurse was gone, then hurriedly dressed, grabbed four extra sandwiches, and slipped out the door.

ooooo

Ben was sitting on a log at the hobo camp and poking a stick at the fire when Clint meekly stepped forward and picked up his bag. Ben's face turned grim as he stood with hands on hips, assessing the piqued young man standing glumly before him. "So, ya lived through it, did ya? You're lucky. Joe, Caleb, and Lawrence the banker weren't so lucky."

Ben's eyes suddenly flashed with anger, and he opened his mouth to speak, but he paused to suck in several ragged breaths. "They were good men," he began—his voice low, furious—not aimed at Clint, but at the senselessness of it all. "They were just down on their luck like the rest of us. Family men, trying to find a way to make money to send back home. And now they're dead because a gypsy talked some stupid kid into buying cheap whiskey with poison in it."

Tears streamed down Clint's cheeks. Ben's face softened somewhat when he saw the effect his words had had on the lad. "I hear that damn gypsy poisoned three other hobo camps here in Cheyenne."

Ben placed a consoling hand on Clint's shoulder. "It wasn't your fault, son," he said in a soft voice.

Clint shook his head, refusing the reprieve, and said in a quavering voice, "I've been my own worst enemy."

Ben's face now showed a fatherly concern. "Son, what're you doing out here on the road? Don't you have somewhere to go?"

Clint wiped tears from his face and shook his head. Then he paused, frowning, and a determined look came to his eyes. "Yes," he said with conviction. "I do have a place to go."

"Where's that?"

Clint picked up his bag and started walking toward the tracks. "I'm going to a town called Dillon, in Montana."

"You got family there?"

Clint turned back and stood for several seconds in deep thought. "Yeah," came his deliberate reply. "I hope so."

# CHAPTER 12

The Union Pacific freight train rumbled through the desolate sagebrush covered hills of southern Wyoming, often traveling for hours between stops. In this desolate land, where the modern conveniences of electricity and roads had not yet penetrated, the train chugged past an occasional small ranch. The inhabitants would hurry outside and watch as the train rumbled by, occasionally giving a forlorn wave.

Reminders of the old West were still in evidence in this lonely prairie country. Wagon ruts sliced through the thick buffalo grass, sometimes meandering past the remains of a covered wagon, its bleached wood appearing like the skeleton of a corpse. Old Indian encampments, with tepee lodge poles, which still held a few tattered pieces of buffalo hide flapping in the breeze, were seen whenever the train coursed through a draw or along a riverbank. Bison bones, bleached white, lay scattered throughout the land.

Wagon trains and Indians and buffalo—just as he'd read about in history class back in Windsor. The little boy surfaced in Clint, and he would have liked to roam through these haunted places, but the train rumbled through without stopping.

One pleasant surprise, Clint noted, was the absence of railroad bulls at the small town depots where the train stopped. Clint still hopped off to relieve the boredom, and to search for food. The cheese sandwiches were gone, so he spent a dime on four apples and a piece of pie at a small store in Rock Springs.

As the train pulled out, Clint sat chomping on an apple in an open boxcar just behind the engine. Suddenly, two heads bobbed in the open doorway, followed by two bodies rolling into the boxcar. He jumped to his feet, club raised and ready. A slim, hatless man in a dusty canvas jacket stood uncertainly at the opening, eyeing Clint with a mixture of fear and desperation. A small boy cowered behind him.

The man carefully raised his open palms and said in a low, careful voice, "Mister, we don't aim to cause you no harm. Me and my boy here are heading out to Washington to pick apples." Clint slowly lowered the club and nodded toward the back of the boxcar. "Much obliged," the man said, tipping his hat as he slipped past. The boy, small and skinny, stared at the apples at Clint's feet.

Listening to Clint chomp the big McIntosh apple was maddening for the father and son. Neither had eaten in more than a day. The father, fighting back tears, did the only thing he could think of to console his whimpering son. He put his arms around the boy and rocked him.

The man's head jerked up as a rolling sound echoed through the cavernous boxcar, then an apple bounced off his boot. A second later, another apple rolled against his son's shoe. "Thanky kindly," came the father's voice. "We ain't ate in a long time." Clint sighed and looked down at his last apple lying on the filthy wood plank in front of him. He eyed it wistfully for a few seconds then sent it on its way. At the next stop, he got off and made sure he was alone in the car when the train left the depot.

Clint lay back, placed his hands under his head, and went over his plan. He remembered Dillon to be a fairly small town. It should be no problem tracking down the old geezer who'd taken Hanna. Then he would rescue her. A glint came to his eyes as he idly rubbed the large folding knife in his pocket, a souvenir of his fight with Jimmy Walker back at the Bar S bunkhouse. If Hanna was harmed, that old geezer would never hurt another child.

He'd start asking at the local mercantile. Everybody went to those places. Surely, they'd know uh, uh…Clint bolted upright and gasped, "Oh, no!"

He couldn't remember the old geezer's name! He closed his eyes and could still see that dreadful scene: The old geezer leering at Hanna, his ugly paw on her little shoulder. He even remembered the man speaking his name to John Hoffman, but it now escaped him. And without that name, it would be impossible to find Hanna.

He began pacing. Hours went by while Clint spoke every name he could think of. "Damn that booze!" he raged as he pressed his hands against his temples. "Dirty rotten geezer," he mumbled over and over while walking swiftly in a tight circle. "Dirty rotten geezer! Dirty rotten geezer! Dirty rotten geezer Higgins!" He stood open-mouthed. Somewhere in the deep recesses of his mind, the name had popped out: Higgins, John Higgins.

ooooo

The sun was peeking over the horizon when the train pulled into the depot at Dillon, Montana. Even in July the morning air in this high-country town was chilly and hinted of frost. By the time Clint hopped from the train he was shivering, and he hurried into the empty depot, where a huge chrome-plated, pot-bellied stove in the middle of the room quickly warmed him. As he stood with his rear to the stove, his eyes roamed over a dozen mounted elk, mule deer, and antelope heads that adorned the polished oak plank walls. The stuffed heads, with their beady eyes staring lifelessly ahead, gave the deserted depot an eerie, foreboding air.

A sleepy-eyed clerk came from a back room to the ticket counter and informed him that it would be another hour before the stores in the business district opened, so Clint peered out the window to pass the time. Dillon was literally in the middle of nowhere, the nearest town being Butte eighty miles away. Sagebrush-dotted grassland stretched as far as the eye could see. This was cowboy country, and the sole purpose of Dillon was to support the large cattle railhead where thousands of cows from several huge ranches located in the fertile Big Hole Valley to the west were shipped to the meat packing houses back in Chicago.

Large corrals bordered the train yards, and that morning they held more than two-hundred milling, bellowing cows. A few cowboys sat on the top rails, while others impatiently herded stock into slatted cattle cars. Clint felt a tug of longing to be back at the Bar S. It had been one of the few times in his life when he'd felt accepted, even valued. He shook those memories from his head. It was time.

The clerk at the Dillon Mercantile looked up, startled, when the young man entered the store two minutes after he'd unlocked the front door. He stopped counting money into the till and slammed the cash register shut, then glanced below the counter to make sure the short-barreled Colt service pistol was there. He busied himself at the counter, but kept a wary eye on the young man browsing his way forward.

Clint noticed the clerk's nervous actions, so he pulled out the contents of his pocket into plain view. In his hand were two stick matches, three pennies, two quarters and a nickel. He chose three of the largest McIntosh apples from an oak barrel. The man's disposition improved when he saw the nickel. "Sir," Clint said in a cordial voice, "I was wondering if you could help me. I'm looking for my uncle."

The man dropped the nickel into the cash register and said, "If he lives in these parts, I'll probably know him."

"His name is John Higgins."

The man peered over his reading glasses, an incredulous look on his face, and remarked, "John Higgins is your uncle?" Clint nodded. The edges of the clerk's mouth curved up, and a chuckle escaped from his throat. "Have you ever met your Uncle Higgins?"

Clint shook his head. "No, but with things bad in Denver, my mother thought it would be good to come up here, stay with Uncle John and maybe find work."

"And you expect your Uncle John to help you find work?"

"Yes, sir," Clint replied.

The man's eyebrows arched. He shook his head and smirked as he pointed at the front door. "He lives up Sage Creek. Take Main Street outside the store to the right and follow it to the edge of town until you hit a dirt road. Take another right on that road and go about a half mile until you come to a creek. There's a trail takes off up the creek. Higgins's shack is about a mile up the trail."

∞∞∞

The sun quickly warmed the chilly morning air, and Clint was sweating by the time he arrived at a small bridge over Sage Creek. He stashed his canvas bag under the bridge and found the trail upstream. The earth was churned up from horse tracks, and many footprints were pressed into the sandy soil, but none were the small prints of a girl. Still, a sense of euphoria swept over him as he hurried up the path. All along, it would have been this easy to find and rescue Hanna. Maybe within the hour he'd be coming back down the trail with her. That thought sent his body tingling with excitement.

But when he caught a whiff of horse manure and wood smoke, his euphoria was replaced by a sense of foreboding. Just ahead lived someone who might be very dangerous. He remembered how Higgins had roughly shoved him back when he'd tried to rescue Hanna at the depot. The guy might even be packing a gun.

That thought stopped Clint in his tracks. He couldn't just barge up to Higgins's place and pound on the door. He found a

172

stout red fir tree limb lying on the ground and broke off a four-foot chunk, then whacked the ground several times to make sure it would not break.

A rusted tin roof came into view, followed by a dilapidated clapboard shack. A rickety corral next to the shack held an emaciated, sway-backed old horse who'd slipped its head between two rails and strained to reach a few morsels of grass. Clint slipped through the underbrush and waited at the edge of the clearing for a half-hour, but detected no signs of life inside the cabin. Finally, he slipped around back and eased up to a small window, pressing his nose to the filthy glass and shielding his eyes until they became accustomed to the gloom within.

The inside of the cabin was one large room. Below the window was an old table with a frying pan that held a fly-covered, putrefying mess. Opened can of beans and corned beef hash lay next to the frying pan. A rusted wood stove sat in a near corner. Clint pressed hard against the window glass and scoured the room for some sign of Hanna.

He squinted into a far corner and deciphered the outline of an old bed. A hand suddenly dropped from the bed onto the floor next to an empty whiskey bottle. It was a gnarled old hand, not the hand of a girl. Then came soft snoring, and the dim outline of a fully clothed man lying on the bed. He was relieved that Hanna was not on that bed. But if she wasn't in the cabin, then where was she?

A loud pounding on the door roused John Higgins from his drunken stupor. He rolled over and spat onto the floor. Two more impatient raps came to the door. Groaning loudly, he rolled out of bed and rasped, "Stop the goldarn pounding, Curly. I told you I won't have another batch a shine ready fer a week."

He jerked open the door and staggered outside, throwing up a hand to shade his eyes from the brilliant sunlight. "Curly, where..." There was movement to his right, followed by a hard blow that sent him sprawling and bellowing in pain. An instant later his mind exploded in a shower of light, then darkness.

ooooo

A splash of cold water brought Higgins back to consciousness. He found himself in a sitting position, with his hands tied to a corral fence post. He struggled to rise, but groaned at the searing pain in his right shoulder. Higgins shook the water from his eyes and focused on a young man sitting on his haunches, a bucket at his side. In his right hand was a large club that he lightly tapped against the palm of his other hand.

Clint's face showed the disdain he felt for his prisoner. He craned his neck and said, "Looks like I mighta broken your shoulder with this little club."

"What, what the hell is all this?" Higgins growled, but there was fear in his voice. "Who the hell are you? You a gov'ment man? Hell, I ain't had a still fer years."

Higgins grimaced, showing rotten, tobacco-stained teeth. His mouth had thin, cracked lips that dropped almost into a drool, and his leathery skin was smudged with dirt. His clothes reeked of vomit, urine, and feces. But it was the alcohol on the man's breath that made Clint's stomach turn.

He fought the impulse to back away, finally snorting out the the foul odors that assaulted his nostrils. "Where's Hanna?" He demanded, tapping the club lightly on the ground.

Higgins scowled and grumbled, "I, I don't know no..."

Clint snapped the club forward and whacked the broken shoulder. Higgins screamed and writhed in pain until Clint threw more water on him. Now, Higgins's eyes bugged out in terror when the club hovered above his shoulder. "Aiy!" Higgins squealed. "Don't hit me no more! I'll, I'll tell ya anything ya wanna know."

Clint leaned forward menacingly, and Higgins leaned backwards. The words rushed out of Clint's mouth. "Where's Hanna? I want to know where she is."

Higgins grimaced and spoke haltingly, "I, I had her doin' chores for me for a coupla months. Then she run off."

"You're lying."

"No I ain't! She just up and—" Higgins stopped in mid-sentence and his eyes widened as Clint unfolded a long slim blade from his pocket knife and carefully tested it with his thumb.

Higgins gulped and wailed, "What're ya gonna do with that there knife? I already told ya what ya wanna know."

Clint kneeled and moved closer. Higgins, bad shoulder forgotten, pressed hard against the wobbly fence post, his eyes glued to the knife. Clint placed his hand on Higgins's right shoulder, causing the man to whimper. His voice was low, threatening, "It was my intention to cut your balls off and let you slowly bleed to death."

"Ah! Ahh!" Higgins cried out. He dug in his heels and tried to push away.

Clint's voice was impatient, furious. "Now you listen to me, and listen good. I want to know where Hanna is. If you tell me the truth right here and now, I won't cut you. But if you try to lie again, I'll cut you slowly, and you'll wish a thousand times while I'm doing it that you were dead."

Higgins began to blubber and beg. Clint stood and stepped back. "Now, one last time. Where is Hanna?"

The words gushed from Higgins's mouth in frightened spurts, "The guy, Curly…He takes my shine up ta Butte…He got ta eyein' the girl a couple months ago…Says he might c'n get me good money fer her. Says them rich copper mine bosses like their girls young. Says they'll pay twenty dollars fer a girl ain't been used up yet. Said we'd split the money."

Higgins stopped and grimaced. "Maybe ya kin loosen these here ropes on my hands. This busted shoulder's killin' me."

175

Clint laid the club on the bulge where the broken bone was pushing against the skin and barked, "Talk!"

Higgins' eyes widened and he blurted, "I sent the girl up ta Butte...three weeks ago with Curly. He brung back a ten dollar bill."

"So Hanna is in Butte. Where?"

"They got her and a couple other young girls hid up on the top floor at the Dumas."

"What's that?"

"A whorehouse."

Clint stood in front of Higgins, unsure what he should do next. It had been his intention all along to kill John Higgins. But now, staring at this disgusting, filthy man, he wavered. He'd been responsible for too many dead men in his life already. Then his eyes dropped to Higgins's groin. He had no intention of putting his hands close to those filthy pants to cut him.

"You're lucky," Clint said as he carefully closed the blade on the pocket knife. "I believe you." Higgins heaved a loud sigh and his shoulders sagged. Clint took two steps backward, and the fear left Higgins's eyes. Then Clint took a long step forward, gathering momentum, and kicked Higgins in the groin with all his might.

He berated himself as he hurried down the trail. Why hadn't he gone after Hanna when he'd escaped from Gustav Schmidt? It would have been so easy. Knock Higgins over the head and take her. Now she was off somewhere, sold like a slave. He thought back to his days in Denver, the degradation and violence the prostitutes had been subjected to—and Lil's swollen, toothless face. How could he have gone on a yearlong drunk while Hanna was being subjected to who-knows-what in that shack?

He retrieved his hidden bag and hurried back down the dirt road to the rail yard, waiting impatiently in a clump of brush for a northbound freight. When a train finally lumbered by a half-hour later, Clint lunged into the first open boxcar. He had to get to Butte, fast!

# CHAPTER 13

The freight train, to Clint's dismay, twice detoured onto sidings to wait for other trains to pass. At the depot in Rocker, the train stopped to unhook eight empty grain cars, further increasing his anxiety. It then sat idling while another train pulled in and took the empty cars north to the grain-rich Hi-line country of central Montana.

These were routine daily railroad activities, but for Clint they were maddening delays in his hurried journey to get to Butte, especially since the town was just eleven miles away. He even thought about walking and running the rest of the way, but the day was warm, and the boxcar's inner dusk stayed comfortably cool. A sudden lurch brought a loud "whoop!" of impatient joy from Clint as the boxcar slowly began its grinding steel-on-steel journey.

He guessed Butte to be just another small cow town like Dillon, but as the train drew near, Clint stared in awe at a large, vibrant city set precariously on a gigantic hill. At the very pinnacle of the hill sat a megalithic wooden structure. Clint had seen such wooden structures before in the West. They were called mining derricks, but never had he seen one as gigantic at this one. Below the derrick were hundreds of tiny houses clinging to the side of the giant hill, and over to the left were massive stone building in what looked like the center of the city.

The train had barely slowed at the depot on the south end of town when Clint jumped off. He pitched forward, slicing a deep gouge in the heel of his left hand. He sucked the blood from the cut and spat it onto the ground while he frantically searched along the tracks, finally locating three heavy iron washers.

He rushed up to a conductor who was chatting with two porters in front of the depot and asked impatiently, "Sir, could you give me directions to the Dumas Hotel?"

The conductor eyed Clint with amusement. "What you looking for at the Dumas, young fella?" The conductor and porters laughed, and the man further teased, "At your age, you oughta be able to find enough free stuff."

The two porters exchanged knowing grins with the conductor, but Clint would not be dissuaded and replied, "I have medical supplies to deliver there."

"Well now, you should have said you was on a mission of mercy," the conductor said, winking at his buddies, and pointed up the giant hill. "It's up there. Follow Montana Street. Ya can't miss it, on the left."

"Thanks," Clint called as he ran, hopping over rails. "Better save some of that medicine for yourself if you're gonna visit the Dumas!" the conductor laughingly called.

ooooo

Montana Street's paved brick ran straight up the hill as far as Clint could see. The steep grade punished his churning leg muscles, and his lungs screamed for more oxygen from the thin, mile-high air.

Halfway up, he wobbled to the curb and sat heavily, feeling light-headed and holding his side. When the pain eased and his head cleared, he walked for another half mile, until Montana Street ran into a maze of busy intersections. He hurried from one building to the next, searching for the Dumas, then turned left onto Park Street and wandered among huge stone and brick buildings. Clint took a few minutes to stare in wonder at the stunning array of modern architecture. Even back in New York, he had never seen such grand buildings.

What Clint didn't know was that the mining town of Butte, located just below the backbone of the Continental Divide, was referred to as the "richest hill on earth." The mighty Anaconda Copper Company had greedily filled its coffers to overflowing with hundreds of millions of dollars in profits from the copper mines. In addition, stockholders, merchants, and company-owned businesses had become fabulously rich, but like most rich people, they didn't know what to do with the sudden glut of money. It had become fashionable in Butte for these wealthy men to erect opulent buildings as monuments to themselves.

A building on the corner of Park and First Street was a replica of a French Second Empire mansion, while the building next to it was a monolithic structure of graceful semi-circular arched windows recessed in rough-hewn granite, and the building next to that one had Moorish tiles with ornate ceramic and copper facing. Anyone who roamed through Butte's uptown business district was struck, not only by its grandeur, but also by the realization that there was a lot of money on this hill.

But not everyone involved shared in this wealth. The miners, laboring under horrific conditions in death-trap tunnels two miles below the earth's crust, saw very little of these profits. However, these hard working men did bring a part of the mines home with them, hacking and coughing up greenish gobs of rock dust through the night. Though their sputum lacked the glistening black sheen of the anthracite coal miners of Pennsylvania, the results were every bit as lethal, with miner's asthma eventually killing forty percent of them. And when the Depression hit, it was the miners' wages and jobs that were the first to be cut back.

It created a seething anger, and a sense of outrage, among many of the men, but those who spoke out either died under mysterious circumstances or were banned from the mines. Periodic outbreaks of violence and strikes had been quickly and brutally subdued by company henchmen, or by local and federal authorities who were lying in bed with the Anaconda Copper Company and its eastern financial backers, the Rockefellers.

This was the vibrant, bustling, troubled town of Butte that Clint wandered through late that afternoon in the summer of 1931. He finally snapped out of his reverie and asked directions from a lad of about fourteen who was selling newspapers on the corner. The boy, dressed in rumpled knickers and a tattered wool touring cap, flashed haughty eyes at the young face in front of him, but after appraising Clint's broad shoulders and tight-muscled forearms, he stepped back and self-consciously pointed a thumb down State Street. "It's on Mercury Street. Three blocks down, take a left."

The squarish, three-story brick building was separated from the other clustered structures by vacant lots on either side, with a large, scattered alley complex behind. A huge, scowling bald man guarded the front door, nodding silently at the well-dressed men—some hurrying to and from their shiny motorcars to avoid being seen. He gruffly dismissed those dressed in the clothes of the working man with a jerk of his thumb towards the back.

No way was Clint going to get inside the Dumas through that front door. He wandered around back and was surprised to see about twenty prostitutes in various stages of undress touting their wares in the long alley that was hidden from the public by the backs of other buildings. Somewhat facetiously, it was called Venus Alley. Most of the girls who worked the alley were loners, though a few worked for pimps. They plied their trade in filthy clapboard shacks, called cribs, built onto the rear of the brick buildings. Conditions were filthy and venereal disease was common. The men who wandered through Venus Alley comprised the lower class, as evidenced by their shabby clothes and drunken behavior. Some men, fresh off their shift in the mines, still wore their mud spattered work clothes.

The Dumas also had a back door, where a different flesh trade flourished. Older prostitutes, no longer in demand by the well-dressed men who entered through the front door, could still ply their trade by luring working men into rooms on the bottom floor in the back of the Dumas.

A middle-aged woman—heavyset, with a round ruddy face and graying black hair—stomped out the back door and plopped her ample butt onto a stump, disconsolately puffing on a pipe. She stared off into space, oblivious to the lewd, suggestive behavior of a pair of nearby prostitutes who were trying to entice two leering miners inside. Clint walked up to the woman on the stump and said, "How about a poke?"

The woman turned hard eyes on him and blew a plume of smoke into his face. "Ya got any money, sonny boy?"

Clint pressed his hand around the cloth of his pants pocket, showing the substantial round outline of the three railroad washers. "I've got six dollars in my pocket right now to spend on you, and my buddy's coming along with lots more."

The woman's eyes grew wide as she stared at the bulge, then softened and her scowl evaporated, replaced by a sultry smile. "So ya wanna poke a mature woman, do ya?" she purred and thrust out her huge bosom. "My name's Big Belle, and my specialty's young men just like yerself."

She struggled to her feet with a loud grunt and shoved her hand through his arm. "C'mon," she said, jerking him along. "I got a special place inside for us."

One of the other prostitutes saw Belle leading Clint toward the door and complained, "Hey! He looks too young. Mr. Cortland said they gotta be twenty-one."

"Shaddup!" Belle screeched and threatened the other woman with a cocked fist. "He is twenty-one, and I'm the one he wants." The two prostitutes, having experienced Belle's ire in the past, warily moved out of range as she dragged Clint through the door into a dim hallway. "Have your money ready," she warned.

Clint abruptly stopped and grabbed at his stomach. "I think I'm going to puke. I've been real sick lately."

Belle swore under her breath and pushed Clint toward a small door. "The john's in there. Hurry up."

Clint staggered into a tiny, foul-smelling room and called, "Watch out for my friend. He's right behind me. He's the one with all the money."

He put his ear to the door and listened to Belle's heavy footfalls thudding out the door. He slipped out of the john and moved swiftly along the hallway, but stopped at the first room, which had a small glass window in the door. He peeked inside and was jolted to see a miner, dried mud still caked to the back of his neck and legs, straining on top of a heavy-set woman with blue-tinted hair. For a few seconds he watched, mesmerized by the grunts and groans and loudly-screeching bed springs. In spite of the grotesque sight, he felt a surge of excitement in his loins.

Tearing his eyes away, he moved to the end of the hall and poked his head through a door into the main parlor. The girls and their clientele were much improved, as evidenced by the three men in suits who sat sipping champagne with three slim, scantily-clad young women. Clint waited until they were distracted, then eased the door open and crept up the stairway.

Twice, he had to hide in empty rooms on the second floor when boisterous men and women clamored through the hallway. The third floor hall had only four windowless doors. He turned the shiny brass knob on the first door and eased it open. The room was luxurious, but empty. A huge crystal chandelier hung from the ceiling and several plush red velvet chairs and couches were arranged around an ornate table.

The next room was also empty, except for a large poker table and roulette wheel. The third door opened into another lavishly furnished, but empty room. One door remained. A wave of giddy anticipation swept over him. This was going to be much easier than he'd expected. He grasped the knob and slowly turned it.

At first, he saw no one. Single beds lined one wall of the room, while the opposite wall held a long makeup table. Several stuffed chairs and a large sofa were arranged in the middle. A jolt of adrenalin surged through his body when he spotted a girl sitting on a wooden chair, wearing a simple white dress with thin fabric that exposed long, slim arms—staring out the window.

He closed the door behind him and spoke in a hushed voice, "Hanna? Is that you?"

The girl turned her pale face toward him. Dull eyes stared through drooping eyelids. She looked different, even strange, but without a doubt, it was Hanna.

He spoke in a loud, excited whisper, "Hanna, it's me, Clint Henley, from the Orphan Train!"

Her eyes blinked, and she opened her mouth, as if to speak. No words came out, but her face brightened, and a slight smile played upon her lips.

Clint stepped forward and repeated, "Hanna, it's me, Clint. Remember? I've come to get you out of..."

A blow to the back of his head sent him sprawling. Two men—one tall and blond, the other shorter with black hair— dragged him to his feet. A man with a barrel chest and long scar down his right cheek stood in front of Clint. His voice carried a hint of triumph, "Higgins sent word you'd be coming."

Clint's eyes widened at that comment and a smug grin spread across the man's face. "Yeh, that's right. Higgins. That was real stupid of you to leave him tied to a rotted-out fence post." The man scoffed and shook his head. "Higgins made it sound like you was Paul Bunyan or something. Hell, you're just a punk kid." The man glanced down, saw the long bulge in Clint's left pants pocket and quickly stepped forward, jamming a hand into the pocket and coming away with the knife. "You won't be needing this," he smirked, "since your chicken to use it anyway."

Clint kicked out, barely missing the man's groin, though the blow made him grunt in pain and stagger backwards. His face became a mask of malice as he snapped open the knife and snarled, "Nobody does that to Jimmy Hobbs and gets away with it. Now, I'm gonna do to you what you didn't have the guts to do to Higgins."

Hurried footsteps came from the hallway. Hobbs hesitated and looked past Clint. A tall man with slicked-back brown hair and dressed in a pin-striped suit, strode forward and barked, "Put that knife away, Hobbs!"

Hobbs lowered the knife and blinked. "What you want done with him, Mr. Cortland?"

"Use your head," Cortland snapped. "We don't want no blood and a dead body and a bunch of cops snooping around here. Just get him out of here and teach him a lesson."

Hobbs kept the point of the knife pressed against Clint's back while the two other men dragged him out the back door of the Dumas, explaining to the curious that they were carting off a trouble-making drunk. They threw him to the ground in an alley behind an old warehouse. As he rose to his knees, he grabbed a handful of dirt.

Clint staggered to his feet, his back pressed against the bricks. Hobbs rose to the balls of his feet, crouching in a fighter's stance with fists up. "Ok, punk. This here is what happens when you poke your nose where it don't belong." He advanced, cocking his right hand, but Clint blasted his face with the handful of dirt. Hobbs howled, turning away as he pawed at his eyes. Clint kicked out, but missed his groin. The two other men jumped in and pounded him to the ground with their fists, then kicked him again and again with their hard leather boots. It lasted only a minute, but the results were devastating.

Clint lay in a bloody heap, groaning. Hobbs grabbed his collar and pulled his face close. "This is just a warning. You come back

here again, and I'll cut your heart out." He punctuated that statement by giving Clint one last vicious kick.

A light rain brought him back to consciousness, though it
took him a few seconds to remember where he was and why he
was lying in that alley in the dark. He groaned and rolled over.
Oh, how he hurt! His whole body was on fire, and every breath
sent a searing pain ripping through his right side. He struggled
to his hands and knees and watched blood mixed with rainwater
drip from his nose onto the bricks. He gingerly felt his face and
found a large flap of skin hanging from his forehead. Blood now
seeped through his hair and ran into his eyes.

Slowly, gasping at the pain, he struggled to his feet by using
the brick wall as a ladder and staggered out of the alley, away
from the Dumas to Montana Street. Near exhaustion and fighting to stay conscious, Clint collapsed onto the sidewalk under a
street light and was ignored by the throngs of jeering passersby,
who thought he was just another drunk. Finally, a man dressed in
a denim jacket and floppy hat pulled low over his eyes stopped,
hovering uncertainly above him. "Help, ooh…please help me,"
came Clint's tortured plea.

The man glanced furtively ahead, then back, before bending
over and hurriedly jamming his hands into Clint's pockets. "Oh,
lordy," the stranger mumbled excitedly when his hand wrapped
around something heavy and round, but he scowled and grunted
in disgust as his eyes studied the three rusty washers in his palm.
"You cheap drunk," he fumed and threw the washers onto the
sidewalk before hurrying away.

Gravity and willpower saved his life. Gritting his teeth, he
blocked out the pain and pulled himself to his feet by climbing up the light post. He stumbled down Montana Street's steep
grade, occasionally falling, but each time regaining his feet and
continuing forward until he reached the rail yard.

Mustering every ounce of strength in his ravaged body, he
climbed into an empty boxcar on a westbound freight train,

where he lay moaning as blood seeped from his body onto the plank floor. His mind desperately sought sleep, but he fought the overpowering urge to close his eyes. It was critically important that he stay awake because he had to get off that train at the next stop.

# CHAPTER 14

Rolling thunder and her cough had kept her awake late into the night. Ann Crenshaw was finally drifting off to sleep when she heard a faint tapping. Thinking it to be rain pelting against the window, she rolled away from it, coughed, and tried to ignore it, but the noise became louder, more insistent.

Suddenly, she went rigid, ears straining. She'd heard something. She rose on one elbow and gasped when a bolt of lightning illuminated a human form outside the window. She scrambled out of bed and fled, but hesitated at the door. That sound—a voice, familiar, muffled, wavering.

She took a furtive step toward the window, but jumped back when her name again floated back through the glass. Now, she could hear clearly: "Ann, help me. I'm hurt!" And then she recognized the voice.

She lunged forward, unlocked the window and threw it open. Every part of her being, except her eyes, recognized the man to be Clint. She almost fainted at the sight of the swollen, tortured face matted with dried blood and dirt. "Oh God, Clint," she gasped and grabbed his shoulders to keep him from falling. "What's happened to you?"

Clint groaned, "I, I need help. There's someone in trouble. I have to help her."

Ann hesitated, but shook that troubling thought from her head and helped Clint grab the window sill. "Hold on to this while I get my dad."

"No!" Clint's voice rose. "I don't want—" But Ann had already darted from the room. As loud voices and hurried footfalls drew closer, Clint lowered his head, moaned softly, and sank to the ground.

ooooo

His eyes blinked open, and he recognized Doc Hastings hovering over him. Hastings checked his pupils and laid back the dressing on his forehead. He felt Clint's cheekbones for fractures then commented, "Looks like you got worked over pretty good."

Clint's eyes blinked rapidly, as he recalled the events of the night before. "I've got to get back and help Hanna," he wheezed and struggled to rise. "I've...oooh!" A sharp pain ripped through his midsection.

"Hold on there!" Doc Hastings ordered as he held Clint down. "You've got two cracked ribs, and they're gonna hurt like hell until I can get them wrapped. Now lie still until I get some heavy gauze."

Clint lay sucking in tiny breaths. Every time he breathed deeply, it felt like a knife was slicing into his ribcage. Doc Hastings hurried back into the room and helped him to a sitting position. He poured a reddish liquid into a large spoon and put it to Clint's lips. "Here, take this. It'll make the pain go away. Now don't talk, and take shallow breaths while I wrap your ribs."

Five minutes later, Doc Hastings stepped back and announced, "There. Now you should be able to breath without pain."

"Thanks, Doc. Now I have to get going."

"No you're not. You're going to stay put for a week while those ribs heal. The Crenshaws are going to put you up at their place until you mend."

"You don't understand," Clint wheezed, shaking his head in frustration.

Doc Hastings cast an annoyed look upon his patient. "What I do understand is that you've shown up twice around here on your deathbed. You ever think that maybe you're not living right?"

"It's not what you think, Doc," Clint protested.

There was a loud knock, followed by Ann's voice, "Can we come in?" Clint looked up, then frowned. Beside her at the doorway stood Henry Crenshaw. Smiling, she came to his side and gently placed a hand on his forehead. "You look so much better."

A hard look came to his face as he stared at Henry Crenshaw—the man who'd thrown him out of the house the last time they'd spoken. Crenshaw turned to Doc Hastings and asked, "He ready to be taken home, Doc?"

Doc Hastings nodded and said, "He's got some cracked ribs and lots of cuts and bruises, but it's nothing that a week of bed rest won't cure."

Henry walked over and placed his huge hands under Clint's armpits, helping him to his feet. "Easy does it now, son," he said. "Just let me hold you up as you walk."

Clint shrugged away from his grip and replied tersely, "I don't need your help." Ann stepped between them, and Clint allowed her to help him out the door.

Doc Hastings raised his eyebrows and shrugged. "Guy's always showing up half-dead. Makes a man wonder."

Henry shook his head and replied, "I made a mistake with the boy last time. This time I'll hold off judging him too quick."

Doc Hastings took his friend's mild rebuke in stride. "That's probably a good idea," he commented dryly, "but do find out what got him into this latest fix before you adopt him."

As Henry started for the door, Hastings raised his hand in caution and added, "One more thing, Henry. You'd be wise to quit thinking of him as a boy. He's as big as a man and stronger than most."

Doc Hastings doubted that Clint would stay put long enough to mend, so he'd slipped a healthy dose of laudanum into the pain medicine. By the time they arrived at the ranch, Clint could barely keep his eyes open, and as soon as his head hit the pillow on the old cot in the storeroom he passed out.

He awoke to find Ann sponging his forehead. "How long have I been asleep?" Clint asked groggily.

Ann glanced at his eyes then focused on the sponge in her hand. "About twelve hours."

Anxiety rose within him at the thought of Hanna back at the Dumas Hotel, and he struggled to rise. "I've, I've got to get going."

"No!" Ann burst out and put her hands on his shoulders. "Doc Hastings says you need to rest for at least a week."

Clint lay back and took a closer look at Ann. Something was different about her. For one thing, she wasn't smiling. Those happy, dancing eyes were now solemn, with dark circles underneath. She also looked much thinner than he'd remembered. Paler, too, and she coughed a lot.

Ann's eyes sought his. She spoke in a low, measured voice, "Clint, I want to ask you something, and I want you to be truthful with me."

Clint nodded slowly, wary of the coming question and the look on her face.

Ann look off, a troubled look on her face as she gathered her thoughts. She finally turned to him and asked in a low voice, "Is there someone else?"

Clint looked at her like she was crazy and blurted, "No!"

She blinked several times before stammering, "But…but what about this girl you're trying to rescue? When I found you at my bedroom window, you said you had to get back and save some girl."

Clint closed his eyes for a second and a weak smile creased his face. "Remember when I told you about my life before I came here?" Ann nodded. "Well, after roaming around the country, wasting my life and feeling sorry for myself, I decided to do exactly what you said I should do. I started tracking down that brother and sister, Jonathan and Hanna, and the girl Jenny, from the Orphan Train. "I found Hanna in Butte. She's being used as a child prostitute. I tried to rescue her, but some guys knew I was coming and worked me over. That's who I was talking about."

Ann covered her face and moaned, "Oh, I'm so ashamed of myself. You've been gone for a year. I didn't know where you were. I was jealous and scared that you'd found someone else." She collapsed onto his chest and hugged him fiercely. Clint stroked her hair, wincing, and gritting his teeth.

Ann leaned forward, intending to kiss his lips, but stopped and leaned back. "Mom won't be home for two more days. Mrs. McElroy just had a baby, so Mom's taking care of the other kids until Mrs. McElroy gets on her feet. We called her last night and told her about you being here. She's really excited to see you again. She feels so bad about everything that happened last time."

Ann's eyes widened and she exclaimed, "Oh, and I have to tell you about my Dad!"

Clint's voice was tight. "I know all I need to know about your dad."

"No, he found out—"

A loud knock on the door stopped Ann, and she turned to see her dad standing in the doorway. Henry Crenshaw, hat in hand, said, "Ann will you excuse us? I have to talk to this, uh, this young man."

Ann squeezed Clint's hand and gave him an encouraging smile before leaving. Henry sat on the bed and got right to the point. "We didn't exactly part on the best of company last time you were here." Clint eyed the man coldly.

Henry cleared his throat and said, "After you left, Doc Hastings came by. He'd treated that guy you kicked, and he found out it was the same guy who'd...uh...uh...done that bad stuff to you on the train." Clint turned his head toward the window to hide his shame.

Henry Crenshaw rubbed his mouth and continued, "I don't blame you for doing what you did. If it was me, I don't know as I'da done anything different."

He exhaled loudly and waited until Clint's eyes returned to him. Henry Crenshaw's voice was low, grave, "I was wrong jumping on you like that without asking your side of the story. Truth is, I was more worried about you running off with my daughter. That's what all the stuff with Pastor Talbot was about. I was trying to find an orphanage that'd take you in just so I could save my daughter some pain."

Henry Crenshaw smirked and added bitterly, "But it looks like there ain't no way I can do that now."

Clint's eyes narrowed. "What do you mean?"

Henry Crenshaw gulped loudly, fighting back tears, and whispered, "My Annie has tuberculosis. We just found out."

Clint sucked in a loud breath, grimaced, and raised up on his elbows. "She'll be all right, won't she?"

Henry slowly shook his head and replied glumly, "Doc Hastings don't know. There's places called sanitariums that they send TB patients to. Some come back cured, some don't."

Clint fell back and said, "So that's why she coughs all the time."

Henry nodded grimly. "We ain't giving up hope, though. I'm prepared to do anything, and that includes selling this broken-down ranch to come up with the money to beat it."

Henry Crenshaw was silent for a few seconds while he gained his composure. He straightened his back and returned his gaze to Clint. "Now, we have to talk about you."

Clint stiffened. "What about me?"

"Well, for one thing, how'd you get beat up so bad? You're in my house. If there's something going on, I want to know about it. Is somebody after you?"

Henry Crenshaw's questions were a rough man's attempt to reach out and help, but with the bitter memory of their last confrontation still fresh in his mind, Clint folded his arms and replied coldly, "I got mugged by some guys in Butte. That's all there was to it."

Henry Crenshaw's shoulder's sagged, but he tried one last time. "You're sure there ain't nothing else you want to tell me?" Clint adamantly shook his head.

Ann appeared at the doorway with a tray of food, looking haggard, but smiling. "Time to eat, Clint."

Henry Crenshaw left the room still harboring a few nagging doubts about his new boarder. The feeling was mutual.

Ann helped Clint sit up and placed the tray on his lap. It held a large bowl of steaming chicken soup, two thick slices of fresh baked bread and a glass of milk. His belly grumbled, but he'd suddenly lost his appetite. His eyes tried to hide the anxiety he was feeling, but his voice rose when he asked, "Why didn't you tell me about your being sick?"

Her smile evaporated and she looked away. "Oh, that." She snatched a handkerchief from her pocket and coughed hoarsely into it. His eyes scoured the handkerchief for blood but saw none. Ann managed a weak smile and whispered breathlessly, "Doc Hastings says lots of people with TB get over it."

He extended his hand, and she took it. Clint gathered his thoughts for a second, then said, "You're the only good thing I have going for me in this life. Don't go dying on me. We made a deal before I left. Something about marriage, remember?" Ann blushed and nodded, smiling coyly.

Clint continued, "I need you to get better, so that when this Orphan Train business is done, we can get on with our lives together."

Ann coughed into her handkerchief, gasped for breath, then whispered, "I promise to get better."

Clint's demeanor turned somber. Ann noticed his mood change and asked, "What's the matter?"

Clint sighed and replied, "I need help to rescue Hanna." He dared not mention Hobb's death threat.

"Maybe my dad could help."

"No!" Clint blurted. "I don't want his help. He still doesn't trust me. Besides, there's nothing he could do about it. Prostitution is legal in Butte. I have to do this myself."

Ann shook her head, and her face showed concern when she said, "But you're hurt. There's nothing you can do until you're better."

Clint replied, "I have a friend in Chicago named Spike McKovitch. He's the biggest, meanest, toughest guy I've ever seen. He could whip every one of those guys that jumped me. I plan on leaving soon, ride the rails back to Chicago, and get Spike to come out here and help me."

Ann's brows furrowed and she gave him a wary look. "And just when are you planning to leave?"

"I was thinking about tomorrow morning, early."

"No!" She protested. "You're in no shape to travel. Doc Hastings said you need to rest for a week."

"My bed'll be a boxcar. I'm stiff and sore, but now that my ribs are taped, I don't feel too bad."

Frustration and fear gripped her, and she cried, "Clint, you could have died!"

"But I didn't die," he countered. "And while I'm on the mend, I might as well go back and see if Spike will help me. Besides, there's a guy back there who can help me find the whereabouts of Jonathan and Jenny."

They argued back and forth, with Ann occasionally pacing the floor while Clint, his appetite restored, slurped the soup while explaining his plan over and over again. Finally, Ann stood with hands on hips, impatiently tapping her foot on the floor, and said,

"There's nothing I can do to talk you out of it, is there?" Clint slowly shook his head.

She spun and stalked out of the room. A few seconds later she returned and handed him a wrinkled envelope. "Here. If we're going to be partners, this is my part. You'll need something to tide you over back there."

The envelope contained four dollar bills and some change. Clint handed the envelope back and protested, "I can't take this."

"Oh yes you can, Clint Henley!" She retorted, folding her arms. "And I'll make some sandwiches for your trip."

But all the excitement was too much for her, and she began coughing, which ended with a long series of hoarse bellows. And this time, she hid the handkerchief from him.

# CHAPTER 15

*D*awn was a faint glow above the rocky spine of the Continental Divide when Clint slowly rolled out of the cot. His hand was on the doorknob of the front door when an urgent, whispered plea came. "Wait!" Ann floated across the kitchen to the ice box and brought him a paper bag. "Sandwiches," she whispered as she followed him outside.

He studied her in the moonlight. Her face, thin and pale, took on an angelic glow, the sheer cotton nightgown revealing tantalizing glimpses of her fresh, warm body. He reached for her, but she stepped back and threw up her hands. "No, Clint. It's best if we don't."

She saw the confused look in his eyes and explained in a hushed voice, "Doc Hastings said I shouldn't get too close to people for a while. I guess this thing's catchy." Clint nodded. He started to leave, but stopped and turned back. Voice cracking with emotion, he whispered, "I want you to know that I love you." And then he was gone.

ooooo

The train made good time traveling through the sparsely populated states of Montana, North Dakota and western Minnesota because the Northern Pacific Railroad had a direct rail line for hauling cattle to the processing plants in the Midwest. With the money Ann had given him, he was able to purchase food without the extra effort, and hazards, of scrounging or stealing. He made it to Minneapolis in just a day and a half, but from there the towns and train traffic increased dramatically.

So did the hobos. In the West, a large train might have one or two men riding the rails, and sometimes none. But when Clint's train started out of a depot in eastern Minnesota, two dozen men scurried across the tracks toward the empty boxcars—some going to a city to avoid starving, others coming from a city to avoid starving. Neither worked.

Twice, Clint took the wrong train and had to backtrack then he got lost among the spiderweb of train tracks near Chicago. At dawn he found himself in Elmhurst, eleven miles west of Chicago, and hopped an Illinois Central train loaded with livestock headed into the city.

When the train slowed, Clint pushed his way past seven other men at the door of the boxcar and looked out over the stockyards—a vast patchwork of corrals stretching as far as the eye could see. After he jumped off, the roar of the train engine was quickly replaced by the thunderous din of thousands of bellowing cows, screaming pigs and bleating sheep being held for transport to the large meat packing plants a few blocks away.

He worked his way through a maze of narrow lanes between corrals until he left the stockyards, hiking north along Ashland Avenue toward a distant line of buildings rising above the horizon. He stopped several times to ask directions from wandering men with haggard faces and hollow eyes, but they all spoke in foreign languages.

He was accustomed to the barnyard smell of animals, but now a sickening stench assaulted his nostrils—it's foul, singed-flesh odor reminding him of the charred cow carcass he'd found after a range fire had swept through the Bar S Ranch back in Denver. His eyes watered and he fought the urge to retch, finally covering his mouth and nose with his hat as he stumbled along.

Embarrassed by the grins and nods directed at him by other men, who seemed unaffected by the stink, Clint pulled the hat away from his face.

A tall man with a wide, crooked-toothed grin called to him, "That smell getting to ya, buddy?"

Clint wrinkled his nose and asked, "What is that stink?"

The man chuckled and pointed a long, bony finger toward the stockyards, then slowly swung his arm toward a nearby building where a grayish-black pall of smoke belched from a huge round brick chimney. "It's them cows and pigs after the packing plants get through cooking and burning their rotten carcasses."

"By the way," Clint asked. "Could you point me towards Maxwell Street?"

The man shook his head and replied, "Never heard of it. I been here only a couple of weeks, but it looks like I shoulda stayed in Cleveland, for all the work I can find." A hard look came to his face. "If you're looking for work, you'd be smart to get back on that train and head out. These packing houses won't hire real Americans. They bring all these Irish and Wops and Bohunks in to work for slave wages. Can't even speak English, most of 'em."

The man smirked and shook his head. "But the joke's on them. Hell, these ignorant foreigners, they let the company grind 'em up like sausage and then just get rid of 'em and hire more fresh ones. It's a hell of a mess, I tell ya."

The farther Clint walked, the more people he encountered, until every street and sidewalk was filled with swarms of yelling, laughing, cursing humanity, occasionally drowned out by the roar of gas engines and the clang of trolley cars. Above, a pall of sooty smoke belched from the tall chimneys of meat packing plants and hide refineries, settling unseen upon the streets and the people in them, turning both cobblestone and flesh a sooty gray.

He eventually arrived on the corner of Thirty-First and Halstad and asked directions from a man standing at a store front. The man pointed north and mentioned that Maxwell Street was just a ways farther. But it was not long before Clint was lost again. He wandered along rutted, unpaved streets in a residential district of tightly packed two-story wood frame buildings with no sidewalks and heaps of rotting garbage out front. Small children in rags sat splashing in brownish-green pools of vile smelling water that seeped to the surface between houses. Some children sat in the putrid water wailing, while others sat hollow-eyed with arms hanging listlessly at their sides.

Clint spotted a woman ahead and decided to ask her for directions. She sat at a kitchen table staring blankly at an eviction notice. The rest of her belongings were thrown into a pile in the dirt in front of a house with a For Rent sign on the front porch. He politely asked for directions, but the dazed woman did not acknowledge his presence.

It was near noon when he left the squalid residential area and entered an older section of the business district, where he encountered a long line of men packed tightly four abreast. Clint walked alongside the line for two blocks before he turned to a short, glum-faced man wearing a sweat-stained hat pulled low over deep-set eyes and asked, "Excuse me, sir. What's this line for?"

The man cast a nettled glance his way then glumly looked away without speaking. Farther up the street the line entered a rundown brick building that housed a soup kitchen, where about half the homeless men would be fed a slice of bread, a bowl of soup, and a tin cup of coffee. The rest would not eat that day.

At the corner of Eighteenth and Canal, he spotted an elderly, white-haired Negro selling vegetables. Jethro Tulley had been one of the first black men from his small town of Hattiesburg, Mississippi to come to Chicago in 1910 in response to an advertisement in the infamous black freedom newspaper, the Chicago Defender.

After the Chicago race riots of 1919, which killed dozens of blacks who had protested price gouging of Negroes by white tenement owners, black people were rarely seen this far from their slum homes in the Southtown section. Jethro Tulley, being well-known and benign in appearance and manner, was tolerated this close to the open markets in the heart of the city that the Irish, Jews, Bohunks, and Italians operated to squeeze a nickel or dime from those fortunate enough to have one.

Curious to speak to a real Negro, Clint walked up and purchased four carrots and two apples for three pennies. He tried not to stare, but he was mesmerized by the black sheen on the Negro's face and his crop of tight, curly white hair. He was further surprised to see that the man's open palms were almost as white as his. "Sir," Clint began, "I need some help with directions."

Jethro Tulley's head jerked back at the unfamiliar tag of "sir" by a white man. He studied Clint for a few seconds, then said in a deep voice, "I c'n tells you's not from aroun' here, son. Where's you lookin' to go?"

"Maxwell Street."

Tulley pursed his lips and whistled low. "You sure you wanna go dere, son? It be a rough place for a stranger. An from de looks a yo' face, you don't need no mo beatin' on." He adamantly shook his head and continued, "Whew! I don't even go dere. No Suh. Dey some peoples ova' dere lookin' jus' fo' pups like yoself. If'n dey knows you got a nickel in yo pocket, dey slit yo throat. Better you stays away from dere, boy."

Jethro Tulley wasn't sure what made the young man's look turn hard. Maybe he'd made a mistake calling this white man a boy. But there was no mistaking an edge in those eyes. "Are you going to tell me how to get there or not?" Clint asked impatiently. His question ended with his palm extended for a refund and the carrots and apples handed back.

Jethro Tulley hastily pointed a long black finger down the street and said, "Dis be Canal Street we on. You stays on dis Street fo' a long ways, mebbe a half mile. Maxwell Street be on de left. Dere be a street sign on it."

Clint took back the carrots and apples and called back as he hurried away, "Thanks!"

He heard Tulley's distant warning, "Y'all be careful down dere, son! Don't keep yo' money in yo' pants pockets. Dey see a bulge down dere, dey gonna take it!"

Clint had so far skirted those lonely street corners where groups of men might cause him trouble, but with each block closer to Maxwell Street, the neighborhoods and the people changed. He found himself walking past dilapidated tenement buildings with garbage scattered over the sidewalks. And he was now forced to walk past men who eyed him coldly.

Maxwell Street was paved bricks, but mostly undriveable because it had been turned into an open-air marketplace that crowded onto the street. Some of the booths were clean pavilions, but most consisted of shabby lean-tos or rough-planked hovels. At the Maxwell Street market, you could spend your money on anything from vegetables to clothes, to jewelry. The smart shopper never paid the asking price, relying on strident haggling with the shrewd merchant to lower the price.

A great press of human flesh undulated through the Maxwell Street marketplace—some buying, and some looking to pick a rich pocket, steal an apple, or a head of cabbage from a preoccupied merchant negotiating with a customer. Here and there he saw them: women with painted faces strolling by, their lips frozen in a permanent, hard smile, eyes hungrily greeting any man.

In front of a boarded-up storefront stood a fiery-haired, freckle-faced young man—not much older than Clint, but almost as big. He was dressed in stained baggy pants, a wrinkled tan cotton shirt and fedora pulled low over his face to ward off the damp breeze blowing from Lake Michigan. He jerked his hands out of his pockets when he saw Clint coming and quickly sized him up with darting, arrogant eyes.

Clint stopped in front of him and said with a smile, "Excuse me, sir, I was wondering if you might help me."

The punk's eyes dropped to Clint's pockets, but detected no bulge. "Beat it," he said, then shoved his hands back into his pockets and sullenly looked away.

"My name's Clint." He extended his hand. "I'm looking for a certain man."

The punk ignored the hand and warned, "Get lost, or your face is gonna look even worse than it does now."

Clint continued to offer his hand and said, "I got a couple of bucks in my shirt pocket." The punk's eyes snapped to the pocket. "I'm from Montana," Clint said, still smiling, and shrugged. "Back there, men usually shake hands before business."

The punk's eyes darted between the pocket and Clint's face. "Coupla bucks, huh?"

Clint gestured with his outstretched hand. The punk's face broke into a sly grin and he said, "Sure, why not?"

The punk grasped the offered hand and pumped it twice, but his eyes widened when Clint wouldn't release his hand. "Hey, what is this?" the punk's voice rose as Clint continued to squeeze.

"What the...Aaah!" the punk howled. White-hot pain shot through his hand as the bones crunched together, and he slowly sank to his knees.

Clint maintained his punishing grip and tersely asked, "You ready to help?" The punk nodded vigorously while staring open-mouthed at his mangled hand. "I'm looking for an old buddy of mine named Spike McKovitch. He said anybody on Maxwell Street would know him."

The punk gasped and shot back a tortured reply, "I, I seen him down at the end of the street. Down by the bus depot where all the girlies hang out. If ya see a little red wagon, he'll be sittin' in it. He..."

Clint eased his grip, and the punk groaned and jumped back, rubbing his hand while now glancing fearfully at the powerful stranger. Clint started walking briskly in that direction but stopped and pulled a nickel from his shirt pocket. "Here," he called back and flipped the coin. "Lunch is on me." The punk had to grab the nickel with his left hand.

He hurried past an increasing number of seedy-looking people: Men with tight mouths and narrowed eyes, and women in tight dresses with smiling faces and unsmiling eyes. Several times he received invitations from the prostitutes, which he ignored.

At the bus depot a swirling mass of humanity moved to and from the terminal. Clint jumped onto an empty wooden apple box and scanned the crowd for a red wagon. After several fruitless minutes of searching, he was about to jump down, when he caught a glimpse of a red wagon a hundred feet ahead. His heart pounded as he pushed his way toward the crowd, and his spirit soared as he heard that familiar voice rise about the din. Clint broke into a small opening and came face-to-face with Spike McKovitch.

Spike's eyes opened wide, and he threw out his arms. "Oh my god, Clint!"

Clint was stunned. He remembered Spike as a towering hulk of a boy on the verge of becoming a man. But now, Spike's shoulders and arms were noticeably smaller than his. He also had no legs. "Hello, Spike," Clint said, woodenly reaching down to shake Spike's extended hand. "Oh, man!" Spike exclaimed. "You sure have grown. And that handshake of yours. Whew!" But then a mischievous grin spread across his face when he added, "But it looks like you mighta forgot some of my advice about ducking. Knowin' you, I bet the other guy looks a lot worse."

He followed Clint's open-mouthed stare. "Oh these," he said with a shrug, pointing at the two stumps resting in the red wagon. "A couple weeks after I run away from the orphanage, some guys come along and threw me in front of a train." He chuckled and added, "But I got most of me off the tracks in time."

"I, I didn't know," Clint stammered, shaking his head. "I'm so sorry, Spike."

"Don't be," Spike said with a smile. "Truth is, I was a no-good punk back then, and I'da probably ended up dead."

Clint's eyes narrowed and a flush came to his cheeks. "Who did this to you, Spike?"

Spike deflected the question with a wave of his hand and said, "It don't matter. Let's just say the old Spike died on those railroad tracks."

Clint's nostril's flared, and a vein throbbed in his neck. "Stallings did this to you, didn't he?"

Spike resolutely shook his head. "Like I said, it don't matter, Clint. Truth is, it was a blessing. They took me in at the Salvation Army. You see, now that I've found Jesus, I don't need no legs. I just lean on him."

Clint glanced into the back of the wagon and spotted a big black Bible and two empty whiskey bottles. Spike followed his stare and shrugged. "The Bible gets me through the day, but sometimes I need the drink to get me through the night, especially when my stumps get sores on 'em."

"Remember Mugsy?" Clint's voice was low, tight.

Spike thought for a few seconds, then brightened. "Oh yeah! Cute little guy. How's he doin'?"

Clint shot back a furious reply, "Stallings threw him out the fifth floor of the book building." He fought back tears and added, "Stallings came back, after you and me left. He made Mugsy pay for our sins."

"Oh god," Spike moaned, squeezing his eyes shut while sadly shaking his head, but he recovered quickly and said, "Hey look, Clint. Stallings is gonna hafta pay for his sins, just like you and me."

Clint shook his head and countered, "Don't give me any of that Bible-thumping stuff, Spike. I've had a few experiences with some of your 'good' religious people."

Clarence shook his head vigorously and replied, "The Bible says that true religion is taking care of the widows and children in their distress. Forget all that other stuff, Clint. Forget all that bitterness." Then he brightened and changed the subject. "Hey, what brings you here?"

Considering his friend's condition, Clint saw no reason to explain his predicament back in Montana, so he merely stated, "Oh, I was just passing through, so I thought I'd stop by and say hello."

But Spike wasn't listening. His eyes were on a well-dressed middle-aged man a hundred feet away who had placed a consoling arm around a young girl's shoulder. The man flashed a dazzling smile at the girl and gestured toward a cherry-red Ford coupe parked along a side street. "Hey, Yustice!" Spike bellowed and smacked a stout stick onto the sidewalk. "You get the hell away from that girl!"

The man whirled, and a look of hate spread over his face. "You mind your own business, McKovitch," he yelled back, "or else!"

"Or else what, huh, tough guy?" Spike challenged as he furiously pushed the wagon forward with the stick.

The man stepped menacingly towards Spike, fist cocked, when a hand shot out from the crowd and grabbed his arm. Clint squeezed until uncertainty, then fear, came to the man's eyes. Clint leaned forward. His voice was low, but with barely contained fury. "You get out of here before I make you sorry you were ever born."

The man jerked free and stumbled backward, regarding Clint with alarm as he rubbed his arm. He turned and ran to the safety of the red coupe before turning back to point a threatening finger at Spike. "I ain't done with you, McKovitch!" As the car sped away, the man angrily yelled out the window, "You'll wish you died on those railroad tracks!"

Spike was already ministering to the frightened girl. He gave her a dime and pointed her towards the Salvation Army building two blocks away. As she hurried away, he yelled, "And don't talk to no strange men along the way!"

Clint commented dryly, "So this is what you do."

Spike spoke in a detached voiced as he watched the girl disappear into the crowd, "Like I said, true religion is taking care of the children in their distress."

Spike spun the wagon around to face Clint, a tortured look on his face. "You have no idea how bad it is here. I thought it was bad back at the orphanage. But here! You wouldn't believe what they do to these kids on the street. Especially these young girls fresh from the farm. As soon as they get off the bus, filth like Yustice jump 'em. He gets seven dollars for every young girl he turns over to the pimps, who starve 'em and dope 'em up then they put 'em out as whores until they're no good no more. Then they just get rid of 'em."

Spike's eyes widened. "Hey! How'd ya like ta stay and help me here? I remember how ya loved Mugsy. I know ya care about kids." He clapped his hands together and exclaimed, "Oh, what a pair we'll make! You hit 'em high, and I hit 'em low! Why, we could…"

"No!" Clint cut him off. "I don't want anything to do with this life." He shook his head and glanced away. "Look, I have to be moving on. It was great seeing you, Spike, but I gotta go."

Clint grabbed a hand, pumped it then walked briskly away. He'd almost made a clean getaway when Spike's voice rose above the multitude. "Clint!"

He turned to face his old friend. They stared in silence while a mass of humanity swirled around them. Finally, Spike sniffled and wiped tears from his eyes. "You'll come back and visit me once in a while, won't you?"

Clint's lower lip began to tremble, and he squeezed his eyes shut in a vain attempt to staunch the flow of tears. A ragged sob escaped from his throat, and when he opened his eyes, Spike had his arms extended. He ran forward, fell to knees, and hugged his friend's neck. Hot tears poured down his cheeks and mingled with the urine and the alcohol and the dried sweat. "I'll be back, Spike," he sobbed. "I promise."

ooooo

Clint had been waiting across the street from the Chicago Home Society building for almost four hours before employees began leaving at quitting time. He scrutinized each man, fearful that he would not recognize the face, but when John Hoffman came outside, a jolt of adrenalin ripped through Clint's body.

He hurried across the street, waited for a man and woman to pass, then silently approached the man whose back was turned while locking the door. He rammed his thumb into Hoffman's ribs and hissed, "Don't turn around! Unlock the door and step inside."

John Hoffman stiffened then began to tremble. Over the loud jingling of the keys against the lock, he nervously muttered, "There, there's no money inside, mister."

"Just do it!" came the warning.

Hoffman turned the knob and slowly opened the door. Clint pushed him inside and into a back room, found a light switch and turned it. "Turn around," he ordered when the lights blinked on.

John Hoffman stood before him—fearful, yet puzzled. "I told you there's no money here. No food, either. What do you want?"

Clint's eyes bored into Hoffman's. "You don't remember me, do you?" Hoffman studied him for a few seconds then slowly shook his head. "I'm Clint from the last Orphan Train you took out West a couple years ago."

A slow dawning of recognition come to Hoffman's face. He spread his arms and gave Clint a bewildered look. "What's all this about? If I remember correctly, we placed you with a fine German family."

Clint leaped forward and screamed in Hoffman's face, "You gave me to a monster!" While Hoffman stood openmouthed in shock, Clint pointed at a chair and ordered, "Now you sit down, while I tell you just how great a job you did."

As Clint related his nightmare with Gustav Schmidt, Hoffman's face drained of color. But it was the story of Hanna that sent tears streaming down the man's face. Finally, he buried his face in his hands and wept.

John Hoffman collected his emotions and wiped the tears from his eyes. "I know you think we're bad people, but there have been many happy endings, too. We have letters from lots of children who have found loving homes."

Clint angrily retorted, "Who gave you the right to just scatter little kids across the country? You people had no right to sacrifice the lives of some kids just so others could be happy."

John Hoffman closed his eyes, gulped, and nodded. "You're right. And that's the message we got back from the country and the government. That's why the Orphan Trains were shut down. Now, we have to check the background of anyone who wants to adopt a child."

Clint waved off the small talk. "I want something," he demanded, pounding a finger on the desk. "I want the names and places where the two other kids I rode with on that Orphan Train were placed. I promised them, I'd check on them. If they're happy where they're at, I'll leave them alone."

John Hoffman hesitated for a second then nodded. He opened a tablet and grabbed a pencil. "Give me their names."

"Jenny Briscoe and Jonathan Fortine."

Hoffman walked to a large open file and began pawing through it. He pulled one folder, then another. He opened each folder, studied it, then scribbled onto the note pad. "Here," he said, tearing the sheet of paper from the pad and handing it to Clint. "The name's of the people they're with and the town and state.

Clint glanced down. Jenny Briscoe was in some place called Sandpoint, Idaho. Jonathan was in Spokane, Washington. He folded the paper and stuffed it into his shirt pocket. "Thanks," he mumbled and turned to leave.

"Wait," Hoffman called. "Have you had dinner?"

"Naw," Clint replied self-consciously, "but I best be going."

John Hoffman leaped to his feet. "Let me buy you dinner. It's the least I can do. Besides, you can furnish a lot of information for me to take back to my organization."

Clint opened his mouth to decline the invitation but hesitated. A dark thought raced through his mind, and his face grew hard. "Yeah." His voice was low, tight. "Maybe I'll just stick around and take the late train out of town."

ooooo

A midnight rain began to fall at the Chicago Boys Orphanage. Inside, 127 boys slept fitfully on urine-stained cots and scratched the welts from bed bug bites. The rain quickly soaked the sidewalk in front of the book storage building, washing it clean in preparation for the sacrifice to come.

Suddenly, a large window on the fifth floor exploded as Ned Stallings hurtled, screaming, into the back void. The scream ended with a sickening thud, followed by a tinkling shower of glass shards.

While his life oozed away in a spreading crimson pool across the wet concrete, Stallings's soul continued downward. All the way to hell.

# CHAPTER 16

*S*turdy steel rails guided the Great Northern freight train through dense early morning fog lying thick upon the Southern Minnesota prairie country. In an empty boxcar near the end of the train, Clint sat with his knees up, head resting on his arms. Every inch of his body was weary, but he couldn't sleep. Guilt and sadness enveloped him for he'd done something last night that could not be reconciled. Self-defense was one thing; this was different. He closed his eyes and asked forgiveness from a God with whom he was still angry.

He lay on his side and fell into a fitful sleep. Out of the black void came a vision of the Chicago Boys Orphanage, appearing clean and bright, its gates wide open. Little boys laughed and frolicked across a well-manicured lawn. A boy with slick black hair stepped away from the others and stood in front of the book storage building. He turned and smiled, and his small hand came up in a tentative wave. Clint awoke with a start then lay back, savoring the vision.

He spent the next day and a half staring blankly out the open doors of boxcars, replaying over and over in his mind the events on a rainy Chicago night, and arguing with himself why his actions had been justified, and then why they were not. But in the end, he faced an irreconcilable, irrevocable conclusion: If there was a God and he was a just God, then someday Clint would pay for his sins.

At five o'clock in the morning, the train lurched to a stop in Great Falls, Montana. Clint rubbed the sleep from his eyes and hurried to the depot, where he found a large railroad map and train schedules on the wall. He checked the piece of paper that Hoffman had given him, then studied the map again. Sandpoint, Idaho was just a hundred and fifty miles west on this same rail line, with Spokane, Washington, about sixty miles south and west of Sandpoint. He could pick up Jenny and Jonathan and be back in Deer Lodge in a day.

But to do so would delay Hanna's rescue. He agonized over the decision, wavering back and forth about which direction to go. Should he pursue Jenny and Jonathan who may, or may not, need help? Or go after Hanna, whom he knew was in trouble?

In the end, the train schedule was the deciding factor. A freight was scheduled to leave for Sandpoint in five minutes. The train to Butte had just left, and the next scheduled train to that city would not be leaving for another nine hours. But there was more to his decision than the schedule. Without Spike to help, he really didn't have a plan for rescuing Hanna. As the westbound train left the rail yard, Clint rushed out of the depot and dove into a boxcar.

ooooo

It was a maddeningly slow trip. Five times the train stopped at small depots, finally arriving in Sandpoint just before noon.

Clint was struck by the sheer beauty of the town, with neat rows of houses nestled among towering Ponderosa pine and Douglas fir trees along the shore of a large lake. Even the air smelled fresh and sweet. Maybe, he wondered as he gazed out at the deep blue waters of the lake, people reflect the places where they live. But just in case, he slipped into a wooded area and came out with a three-foot club.

Standing on the sidewalk in front of the Lakeside Boarding House, he glanced at the piece of paper and checked the address one more time. Because it was a boarding house, he wasn't too worried about being seen. He eased the front door open and stepped into a great room that held a long dining table. He padded silently through the room, peeked into an empty kitchen, then noticed a large room off to the left. As he stepped into the entryway, he spotted a girl busily sewing. It took him a few seconds studying the girl to decide that it was indeed Jenny Briscoe he was looking at. She had grown into a beautiful young lady.

A pine plank squeaked under his foot. Jenny looked up in surprise, with only an occasional blink interrupting her statue-like pose. Then a glowing smile spread across her face. She placed the sewing project on her lap and spoke in a sweet voice, "I know you."

Clint stepped forward, grinning self-consciously, and said, "Hi, Jenny. It's me, Clint Henley."

Jenny put her hands to her cheeks and nodded. "From the Orphan Train."

He was surprised she remembered him. He'd expected to encounter the same simple-minded girl who had stared blankly out the train window for hours on end. "How are you doing?" he asked, stepping closer to examine her face for any signs of abuse. "I was just passing through, so I thought I'd stop in to see if you were all right. Are they treating you well here?"

Jenny's eyes opened wide and she clapped her hands. "Oh, yes! I have a wonderful momma now."

A woman's voice called from upstairs, "Jenny dear, is someone down there with you? Do we have a guest?"

Jenny took Clint's hand and called back, "Yes, Momma! Come meet my special friend who came to visit me!"

Heavy footfalls lumbered down the stairs. A heavyset woman with gray hair in a bun waddled into the room and stood smiling with hands on hips. "Well now," the woman said in a cheery voice, "who might this friend of yours be? I don't think I've ever seen him around town."

Jenny beamed as she spoke. "Momma, this here is Clint. He was my big brother on the Orphan Train. He protected me from the bad boys."

"Well, my name is Mrs. Simpkins. I own this boarding house that don't have no boarders." She laughed at her joke until her entire body jiggled.

Jenny wrapped both hands around Clint's and stared adoringly up at him. "You said you'd come and make sure I was happy, and you kept your promise."

Fighting desperately to blink back the tears, he bent over and hugged Jenny tightly and kissed her cheek. Jenny stood, perplexed, and wiped the tears from his cheeks. "Don't cry, Clint. I found the perfect momma."

"Good," Clint croaked. "I'm glad. You know, uh, I really have to be going now."

Mrs. Simpkins would have none of it and insisted, "Not without lunch, you're not!"

Clint sat at the kitchen table and devoured four pancakes, six eggs, and a half-pound of bacon while Jenny scurried in and out of the kitchen, proudly displaying dresses she'd sewn.

Mrs. Simpkins, eyeing the mottled bruises and gash on his forehead, asked in a quiet voice, "And how has it been for you, Mr. Clint?"

He stared at the plate and spoke in a voice barely above a whisper, "Not all the people out there are nice like you, Mrs. Simpkins."

ooooo

With three thick ham and cheese sandwiches and an apple stuffed into his canvas bag, Clint hurried back to the small depot and hid in the bushes until a Northern Pacific freight train pulled out heading south. Two hours later, the train slowed as it pulled into the stockyards a half mile east of Spokane. Clint followed the smell of wood smoke to the banks of the Spokane River, a hundred yards north of the stockyards, where he found a hobo camp with five men staring disconsolately into the flames of the smoky fire.

He sat on a log next to a stubble-faced older man. The man poked at the fire and asked, "Where'd you come from, son?"

"Just about everywhere," Clint sighed. "Minnesota, Chicago, Montana."

The man lobbed a chunk of wood into the fire. "Any work back there?"

"None."

The man shook his head. "None here, either."

Clint fidgeted for a few seconds before commenting, "It's warm out. Why do you have a fire burning?"

A man across the fire shared a knowing grin with his buddies and said, "Ole Jake might be bringing back a chicken."

The stubble-faced man next to Clint snorted and said with a wry grin, "That, or a load of buckshot up his butt." The men chuckled.

"Would you know," Clint asked, "how I'd find Pines Road. I got an uncle lives there."

The stubble-faced man jabbed a crooked finger to the east and said, "About three miles that way. Sprague Avenue runs along the tracks. Pines Road cuts across it running north and south. Stay off the tracks, though. The railroad bulls around here are mean."

Clint stood to leave, but hesitated. He pulled out the three sandwiches and apple and handed them to the wide-eyed men, along with the admonition, "Save the apple for Jake, just in case."

ooooo

He walked briskly along Sprague Avenue until he came to a faded wooden street sign above an intersection which read, Pines Road. He approached an older man dressed in a threadbare white shirt rolled up to the elbows, and baggy brown pants held up by frayed suspenders. "Excuse me, sir," Clint said, removing his hat. "Could you tell me where I might find a man named Elmo Harris? He lives on Pines Road."

The old man frowned and replied curtly, "You mean the pig farmer?"

"Yeah," Clint answered. "That's probably him."

The old man pointed north and said, "About a half mile thataway. You'll smell it long before you get to it." The man chuckled, then turned serious. "If you're going up there, make sure Elmo knows you're coming. He shot a guy last month trying to steal a pig. At least, that's what he claimed."

ooooo

The gravel road wound uphill between massive black basalt boulders and huge Ponderosa Pine trees. At the top of the hill, Clint's nose wrinkled at the first offensive whiff of the pig farm, and his ears detected the distant squealing of pigs. He left the road and dropped into a brush-choked gully that angled toward the farm. The hysterical screaming of the pigs increased as he moved along the gully. A powerful ammonia odor from pig urine made his eyes water, and the stench become so bad that he put his hat to his face and breathed through the felt.

The first pen held several large pigs wallowing through a putrid mire of pig crap and mud, with thousands of huge black flies hovering over them. Only the very tops of their backs were free of the black muck. The animals looked gaunt and dangerous as they darted back and forth, searching frantically for the source of the footfalls. Two large gray pigs bit viciously at each other. Clint selected a sturdy club about four feet long, just in case he had to use it against the pigs. He circled the pen and moved cautiously forward.

Ahead came the sounds of hysterical, angry squeals amid the frantic squishy pounding of hooves. He climbed the first rail of an empty pen and caught a glimpse of a person carrying a bucket about a hundred feet away. He ducked down and climbed through the rails in the pen, moving forward in a low crouch. He passed by a corral where about two dozen frenzied pigs fought to get at the contents of a feed trough only eight-feet long. The lucky ones gulped noisily at the slop, while other pigs squealed and tore at each other.

He peeked over the top rail and spotted a young man about fifty feet away, struggling toward another pen with a slop bucket. Clint's heart sank. I couldn't be Jonathan because this lad had a bad left shoulder, and as he walked, he dragged his right leg. The boy's mud-caked body and smeared face made it difficult for Clint to get a better look at him. The lad staggered and dropped the bucket, then dragged it the last few feet to the next feed trough. The pigs on the other side of the pen screamed and banged their snouts against the rotted wooden posts, causing the boy to jump back.

Clint ducked down. The boy stood upright and looked around before bending over the bucket. Clint peered between the rails, but could not see what the lad was doing. He raised up and peeked over the top rail. The boy was eating from the slop bucket.

A gagging sound escaped from Clint's throat. The boy whirled and spotted him. Eyes wide with fear met his. Clint vaulted over the pen. His heart beat wildly as he approached the boy. Take away the fear from those brown eyes, wipe the mud from his face, and he was looking at Jonathan.

Jonathan hastily wiped his mouth, took a step backwards and struggled to stand upright. They stood a foot apart, eyes locked. Clint smiled and spoke softly, "Jonathan, do you remember me?"

Jonathan's frowned, then his eyes grew wide and his mouth dropped open. He stuttered, "Cwi, Cwi…" He cleared his throat, stood erect and pronounced, "Cl, Cl-int."

Clint put out his arms, and Jonathan sagged into them. The boy clung tightly to him, sniffling at first then weeping openly. Clint squeezed his eyes shut and gritted his teeth, berating himself again for wasting so much time since the Orphan Train. He gently pried the boy to arm's length and said, "Jonathan, I've come to take you away to live with me."

Jonathan began to tremble. He smiled and self-consciously swiped at the tears. "I…I always knew you would. Because you said you would."

Clint brought his hand up to Jonathan's shoulder and ran a finger over the protruding bulge of the poorly healed collar bone. There was an edge in his voice when he asked, "How did this happen?"

Fear returned to Jonathan's eyes as he glanced furtively toward a rundown farmhouse up the hill. "Mist-er Elmo caught me eating out of the bucket."

"And your leg?"

Jonathan gestured toward the berserk pigs fighting to get at the slop bucket and said, "A big pig ate some of my l-leg when I s-lipped one day."

"Hey!" a voice bellowed from above. "Get your ass up here, right now!"

Jonathan's eyes widened. He clutched Clint's arm and warned, "That's Mistow Ewmo. He's, he's weal mean!"

Clint pulled Jonathan down and whispered, "You stay here, and don't move until I come for you." He ran along the fence to a muddy path that led uphill and hid behind a large bush. Seconds later, heavy footfalls squished down the trail. A huge, red-faced man with a big belly, dressed in denim coveralls and knee-high rubber boots, stomped past carrying a large stick. The man yelled,

"Boy, you get up here quick, or I'll throttle your ass good!" He punctuated his tirade by smacking the stick into the mud.

Fear mixed with outrage gripped Clint as he sneaked up behind the big man. The closer he got, the bigger the man grew. Elmo Harris caught a glimpse of movement behind him, and started to turn. Clint swung with all his might. The heavy club smashed down hard on the man's right shoulder. The club broke, leaving Clint holding little more than a stub of wood in his hands.

But so did Elmo Harris's shoulder. He bellowed in pain and sank to his knees, grabbing at the busted bone. Clint grabbed the man's thick neck and shoved his face into the putrid slime.

Elmo Harris struggled for a second, then froze when he felt the power in the hand squeezing his neck and began screaming hysterically. Clint put his face close to the man's ear and whispered furiously, "Now you know how that little boy felt." Clint stepped over the gagging man and hurried down to Jonathan. Amidst the cacophony of squealing pigs and Elmo Harris bellowing in pain, he scooped the trembling boy into his arms and started for the ravine.

Keeping to the pine woods, he carried Jonathan all the way to the Spokane River, where they stripped and scrubbed off the stink as best they could with river gravel. Clint washed and wrung out their clothes. He studied Jonathan's emaciated body, and he was struck further with a pang of guilt: While he'd grown bigger and stronger, it looked as if Jonathan had grown smaller. Jonathan's leg wound, with a large half-moon of calf muscle missing, was scabbed over and festering and his shoulder bone had healed awkwardly.

Rather than walk back to the stockyards, Clint decided that they should hop a freight at a nearby grain depot. He helped Jonathan hobble over the tracks, and they hid behind a grain silo. While they waited, he told the wide-eyed boy about Jenny. He then explained that Hanna was with some bad people, but that he would be rescuing her next. "I know you wi-ll, C-lint," Jonathan said bravely. "I al-ways knew you'd come back fo-r me."

Clint swallowed hard, smiled weakly, and turned away.

An eastbound freight pulled up to the silo and hooked onto six cars brimming with grain. Rather than chance a dangerous stumble as the train pulled out, Clint hoisted Jonathan into an empty boxcar before following him aboard.

Three other men sat in the rear of the rail car, but a quick search of their eyes told Clint that they were not dangerous. A middle-aged man with bright blue smiling eyes stepped forward and said, "The boy hungry? We ain't got much, but we can't let no young'uns go without."

Clint allowed Jonathan to take an apple and a piece of bread torn from a squashed loaf. As he watched Jonathan devour the food, it occurred to him that the boy must be starved. Why else would he have been eating from the slop bucket?

When the train stopped a half-hour later at a grain elevator near the town of Post Falls, just into Idaho, Clint helped Jonathan off and took him to a small restaurant, where he ordered a big breakfast for both of them. "You got the twenty cents?" the waitress asked, eyeing their damp, wrinkled clothes, but her eyes brightened when Clint produced the last dollar bill that Ann had given him. Clint watched with satisfaction as Jonathan's eyes widened when the waitress plopped a plate of steaming pancakes, eggs, and thick slice of ham in front of him.

Jonathan paused and poked at the ham. "This comes fr-rom pigs, don't it?" Clint nodded with a chuckle. The boy ate ravenously, washing it down with a large glass of milk. All but the ham.

While awaiting the next freight train, Clint explained to Jonathan that he was taking him to a ranch in Montana, where he would be left in good hands while Clint fetched his sister. Jonathan asked, "A-re they you-r new momma and papa?"

Clint shook his head. "No, the people who took me in were bad people, so I left. These people took me in later."

Jonathan searched Clint's face. "Wi-ll this be ou-r new home, Cl-lint?"

Clint ruffled the boy's mop of shaggy hair and replied with a grin, "I'm not sure. If not, we'll find someplace nice. I promise."

Jonathan's face beamed as he declared, "I know we wi-ll because you al-ways keep you-r pr-romises."

# CHAPTER 17

The late afternoon sun's golden rays warmed Ann Crenshaw as she sat on the front porch of the ranch house. Inside, she could hear her mother clanging pots and jars while she canned beets and carrots from their garden. Normally, she would be right in the middle of things in the kitchen, but in the last two days her condition had worsened. Now, she dared not exert herself or she'd cough herself into another faint, as she'd done earlier in the day just washing the canning jars.

Doc Hastings warned that the infection had taken over half of her lungs. She was forced to breath in shallow, wheezing gasps. When she tried to breathe deeply, her lungs refused to accept the extra oxygen, expelling it in a cough. The first blood had appeared the day Clint arrived. Now, there was blood in her handkerchief whenever she coughed. Strangely, it did not scare her. Her mind was on a young man far away.

Dust rose behind a motorcar on the gravel road a half mile away. At the turnoff to the Crenshaw Ranch, the car stopped, then sped away, leaving behind two distant figures. Ann watched as the tiny figures grew larger. She shielded her eyes from the sun and by squinting, could make out the images of a man and a boy. She guessed it was their neighbors, Mr. Hobson and his son, coming to ask for a few eggs or bread, as they'd been doing every week since the hard times had started.

Two hundred yards from the house, the sun shone on the front of the hikers. Ann sucked in a quick breath then coughed it out. "Stay calm," she warned herself. "You don't want a coughing fit now." She rose from the chair and slowly crossed the front yard to the gate. Clint waved when he saw her, then pointed and spoke to the boy limping alongside him. Ann waved back, her pulse quickening. She coughed again and prayed it would stop.

Clint strode forward and extended his arms, but Ann shook her head and protested, "No, Clint. I'm not supposed to get close to anyone."

He scoffed and enveloped her in his arms, rocking her frail body back and forth. "I don't care about no sickness." He took her hand and led her over to the boy. "This is Jonathan, Hanna's little brother."

"Hi there, Jonathan," she wheezed. "I'm Ann."

Jonathan's large almond eyes beamed. He nodded vigorously and said, "Hello. Cl-lint told me he was going to mar-ry you."

Clint burst out laughing and ruffled Jonathan's hair. Ann allowed herself a careful giggle, but it ended in a frown when she wondered if she would be around long enough for them to be together.

Julia Crenshaw came out to the porch and placed her hand above her eyes. "Who is it, Ann?" she called.

Ann turned to reply, but stopped. She dared not risk calling out, so she smiled at Jonathan and said in a low, labored voice, "Come meet my Mom."

Julia Crenshaw walked swiftly to Clint. She burst into tears and hugged him fiercely. "I'm so sorry for what happened last time you were here," she sobbed. "We're not supposed to be that way. We're supposed to be different."

Clint patted her shoulder and said, "Oh, that's okay, Mrs. Crenshaw. I wasn't exactly up-front about everything that went on. You were only protecting your family."

She stepped back and wiped tears from her face, then turned smiling to Jonathan. "And who is this young man?"

Clint said, "This is Jonathan, one of the children I came out West with on the Orphan Train."

Jonathan bobbed his head and said, "Hello, Momma Cr-renshaw."

Julia's eyes made a quick, motherly sweep of the boy—noting his drooping shoulder, the way he favored his right leg, and his emaciated body. She stepped forward and took the surprised boy into her arms and held him tightly. Her eyes squeezed shut, tears poured down her face. She slipped an arm around the flustered boy's shoulders and urged, "Let's go inside, Jonathan. I have a piece of apple pie and glass of milk just for you."

Clint turned to Ann and studied her features. She looked even more gaunt and haggard, but he smiled and asked, "How are you doing?"

Ann smiled back and shrugged, "Oh, I'm a little short of breath, but I'm okay."

Clint looked around. "Where's your father?"

"He took a load of cows to Missoula. He won't be back until tomorrow." Feeling faint, she suggested, "Let's get out of the sun."

As they climbed the steps to the porch, Clint mentioned, "I also found the other girl, Jenny."

Ann, near collapse, dropped into a chair and asked breathlessly, "Is she all right?"

Clint nodded with a smile. "She's fine. She got adopted by a real nice lady who has a boarding house in Sandpoint, Idaho."

"Oh, I'm so glad," Ann said and smiled wanly.

Clint stood, concerned evident in his voice. "Ann, I have to get to Butte quick and get Hanna out of the Dumas Hotel."

Though lightheaded, Ann placed a hand on Clint's arm and said, "It's too late to do anything today. There's no more trains after five o'clock. Stay here tonight, and you'll be rested and fresh for the morning."

Clint started to protest, but Ann reminded him, "Jonathan will need some reassurance. He's in a strange place. Stay tonight. It'll do all of us some good."

Clint reluctantly agreed. They stayed up late into the night, with Julia fussing over Jonathan, much to his delight. Ann and Clint held hands and enjoyed the quiet of the evening together. The long hours had taken a toll on Ann. She joked that she needed her beauty sleep and excused herself. Clint watched with concern the effort she made just to rise and walk into her bedroom. With Jonathan tucked into the bed in the storage room, Clint lay back on the sofa and wondered what tomorrow would bring. He shuddered at the grizzly memory of those fists and boots pummeling him in that dark alley behind the Dumas. His ribs felt a lot better, but he was in no shape to face those men again.

He tried to sleep, but the steady coughing coming from Ann's room kept him on edge. About midnight, Ann's bedroom door opened and she came to him. Without a word, he made room for her, and she slid beside him. As he held her close, his hand ran down her back and felt her ribcage. He shuddered, and for the second time in a week, turned to the God he'd disowned and prayed.

Finally, he slept. It was a light sleep but not fitful. Through the night, he was aware of Ann's ragged breathing and occasional cough, but her presence was an emotional tonic, for he'd not felt human warmth in a long time. Half asleep, yet conscious of the gray light of dawn through the kitchen window, Clint snuggled close to Ann, basking in her warmth, and it occurred to him that this must be one of the main reasons why men and women married. He gently rose from her sleeping form and tip-toed to the door. He took one last look back at Ann's face—serene in sleep, with a slight smile on her lips, and wondered with a shudder, if she would still be alive when he returned. If he returned.

While he waited at the depot, Clint slipped into a nearby creek bottom, where he fashioned a three-foot long club from a limb about two inches in diameter. If he was attacked again, he'd make sure a few of them paid dearly.

ooooo

The Burlington freight train pulled into the Butte rail yard at nine o'clock that morning. As Clint hiked up Montana Street, he was perplexed by the lack of vehicle and pedestrian traffic. It wasn't until he passed a newspaper boy and eyed the date that he realized it was Sunday. In Butte, booze and women might prevail among the miners for six and a half days per week, but Sunday morning was church time.

The Dumas was locked tight with only two cars parked out front. Clint slipped around the back to try a window, but they all had bars. Two bleary-eyed men stumbled down the alley and spotted Clint staring at the windows. "Hey buddy," one of the men laughed, "you'll have to hold onto it for a coupla hours! The Dumas don't open until two in the afternoon on Sunday."

Clint walked up to Park Street, found an open diner and ordered three pancakes. Before the suspicious waitress asked, he slapped a dime on the counter. While Clint wolfed down his breakfast, the door jingled open and a blue-uniformed policeman entered.

"Good morning, Officer Farrel," the waitress called, smiling, and waved a cup at him. "Top o' the morning to ya, Lucy," the policeman responded with a generous smile and tipped his hat. "Yes, I'll have a quick cup."

Officer Farrel sat at the other end of the counter and sipped his coffee. The waitress refilled his cup and asked with tongue in cheek, "So how's Venus Alley treating you? You're not falling for any of those girls down there, are you?"

Farrel's bellowing laughter shook the windows. "Not me!" he protested with a gleam in his eye. "I like the down-home girls, like yourself. Besides, there's lots more than love that's passed around by some of those girls down there."

"Quiet night, last night?"

Officer Farrel shrugged and commented, "Typical Saturday night. A half-dozen fights, two muggings and a suicide."

The waitress shook her head while scanning the empty diner and muttered, "If things don't pick up around here pretty soon, I might have to go down there and drum up some business myself."

"Well!" Farrel's voice boomed. "Then I would be spending a lot more time down there." The waitress's cheeks turned scarlet, but she giggled mischievously. Clint paid for his breakfast and left, but waited in the doorway of the next building for the policeman.

Officer Farrel's head snapped left. Narrowed eyes studied Clint for a few seconds before relaxing. The policeman sauntered toward him with a disarming smile, twirling his nightstick. "Can I help ya, lad?"

Clint's desperation erupted. "I need to talk to someone."

"What about?" Farrel asked and when Clint could not find the words to express his anxiety, the policeman placed a meaty hand on his shoulder and spoke in a grave voice, "You can tell me, son. I'm here to help."

Clint studied the man's rugged face and searched his deep green eyes. This, he decided, was a man he could trust. He began slowly, "Is it true prostitution's legal here in Butte?"

Officer Farrel's features clouded. He replied, "Ay, that it is."

"What about children?"

Farrel's eyes narrowed, and there was an ominous tremor in his voice when he demanded, "What do you mean, children?"

"They got young girls up on the top floor of the Dumas."

Farrel frowned, his tone skeptical. "I find that hard to believe, lad. These Butte miners work and play hard, but they don't go for little girls."

"It's not the miners," Clint said pointedly. "It's the mining company bosses that are doing it."

Officer Farrel's eyes studied him for a few seconds, then he asked in a low, measured voice, "And where did you hear this?"

"I have a friend who's being held up there against her will. I think they got her on some kind of dope."

"You've seen this with your own eyes?"

"Yes."

"And they did this to you?" Farrel asked, waving a finger in front of Clint's face." Clint nodded.

Officer Farrel slapped his night stick against his palm and looked off toward Mercury Street. "You did the right thing telling me about this, Lad. There are dangerous men down there. No telling what they'd do this time if you tried something."

"This girl's name is Hanna," Clint said, then added impatiently, "Can we go down right now and get her out of there?"

Officer Farrel took Clint's arm and said, "You're darn right we can. Let's go get your friend."

Clint was beside himself with joy as he walked alongside Officer Farrel. Why hadn't he thought of going to the police to begin with? He should have known that most grown men, and certainly the cops, would frown on using young girls in such a manner. As they approached Venus Alley, Officer Farrel glanced down at Clint's club and ordered, "Hand me that stick, boy. I can do just about anything I want to uphold the law, but you can't go swinging that thing around."

Clint was about to protest that there were four against two, but when he surveyed this powerful man who stood a head taller than himself, and carried a gun on his hip, he decided that Officer Farrel was right. He was the law.

The two drunks who'd spoken to Clint earlier were slouched on a bench behind the Dumas. Officer Farrel strode over and whacked the bench with Clint's club. "You men get along now!" He barked, punctuating the order with another loud whack of the club. The men spilled off the bench and hastily gathered their belongings.

With the two vagrants gone, Officer Farrel took Clint's arm, and said gruffly, "Come on, now. Let's go rescue your friend."

The policeman banged hard on the steel door with the club, then cast it onto the ground beside the door. A man's voice inside angrily called, "Whaddaya want?"

Officer Farrel barked, "It's me. Open up!"

It wasn't the metallic sound of bolts being thrown back that made Clint suddenly alert. Whoever was on the other side of the door had recognized Officer Farrel's voice! The door flew open. Hobbs stood there—surprise then rage clouding his face. "You again!" Hobbs fumed. Clint started to turn, but a huge arm wrapped around his neck. Clint struggled mightily, arms flailing, legs kicking—until his struggling became more and more feeble, and he went limp.

He was dimly aware of being dragged along the hallway and thrown roughly onto a bed in a dark room. His hands were pulled behind his back and tied to his legs, which had been drawn up behind him, then he was lashed to the bed and gagged. He feigned unconsciousness until the sounds of footfalls moved away, and the door was slammed shut and locked, leaving the room black, except for a sliver of light showing under the door.

His ears strained to hear the muffled voices outside the door. He recognized Officer Farrel's voice say, "Well, don't do nothing until after dark when there's lots of drunks roaming around. And do it on the other side of town, away from my beat. That suicide last night caught the chief's attention. Any more of that stuff and you'll mess your own bed."

Another voice said, "We'll make it look like an accident. Douse him with whiskey and throw him in front of a train, nice and clean." There was more muffled talk as the footfalls faded. He lay trembling in the dark, feeling the terror of knowing that certain death was only hours away. Now that he had something to live for, he didn't want to die. He pulled at the ropes with all his strength, until his wrists began to bleed. With his legs tied and pulled back up to his hands, he could barely budge. Twice, footfalls sounded past his door, and he froze, hoping they were not coming for him.

Then he got an idea. The footfalls had sounded lighter. Maybe they were coming from the prostitutes. If he could somehow alert a passing girl to his presence, maybe she'd open the door and untie him. He began rocking back and forth on the bed. With each shifting of his body, the rusty old bed springs creaked.

Soon, he heard someone walking down the hall. He began bouncing up and down on the bed, straining against the ropes that held him down, but the footfalls clomped past the room, and the steel door slammed a few seconds later. He lay breathing loudly through his nose, hopeful that this tactic would eventually catch someone's attention.

About ten minutes later, he heard more light footfalls coming. Clint began bouncing violently, causing the bedsprings to squeak and clang loudly. The footfalls stopped in front of the door, and a female voice said, "Hear that?" Clint bounced even harder and began making muffled grunts.

Hysterical laughter erupted outside the door, and a female voice said, "Whoever's in there is really going at it!"

Another voice called, "Ride 'em cowboy!" Both women laughed as they continued on.

They thought he was... Clint shook his head and moaned. He was in the one place in the whole world where squeaking bed-springs and muffled moans were normal behind closed doors. A part of him wanted to lie back and cry, but a voice erupted from deep within: *Think! There's always somepin' kin be done!* And then he remembered that it had been Spike McKovitch who'd spoken those words to him in the days before he'd escaped the orphanage. Spike had no legs, but somehow got around in a place like Chicago. Not only got around but made a difference!

A pent up fury built in him, and he savagely bucked at his tethers, which refused to give. But something happened. Clint lay gasping, racking his brain. And then it hit him—he'd heard the bed frame scrape over the floor when his body had lurched forward.

He threw himself forward. Nothing. He tried again, this time harder. Still nothing. He gritted his teeth and put every ounce of strength behind the next lunge. The bed scrapped across the floor, but just barely. Twice more, he violently lunged forward, but only once did the bed scrape across the floor. He rested for a few minutes then lunged wildly toward the door several times, feeling the bed move about half the time. Now, there was hope.

But after a half-hour, the crease of light under the door didn't seem to be any closer, and he wondered if the bed wasn't moving, then settling back into a groove worn into the floor. But after one particularly long and violent fit of lunges, he could tell that the light under the door was closer.

Clint lost count of the times he'd lunged and rested, but he knew it must have taken hours. Finally, the front of the bed clanked against the door. He rocked back and forth, causing the bed frame to clunk loudly against the door. Now, any passerby would hear a noise different from the familiar bed sounds being made in other rooms.

Footfalls thudded down the stairs above, followed by angry, muffled voices. The footfalls that shuffled toward the room were heavy, like a man's, but different. Should he wait for the lighter footfalls of one of the working girls? When the footfalls passed by the door, he rocked back and forth violently, banging the bed hard against the door. His heart beat furiously when the footfalls stopped. "Who's there?" a deep female voice called. "Who's in there?"

Clint emitted a loud, insistent moan then pounded the bed against the door. The footfalls shuffled away, and a tiny groan escaped from his throat. Then he stiffened. The footfalls were shuffling back, and a second later a key scraped against the door lock. The door opened only a few inches before it banged against the bed frame. Clint moaned frantically through his nose, hoping the girl would go for help to push the bed away from the door, but to his surprise, a powerful body on the other side of the door pushed the heavy bed backwards with a loud grunt.

Momentarily blinded by the sudden burst of light, Clint blinked until his eyes became accustomed to the light. But when he finally identified the figure looming in the doorway, a tortured moan escaped from his throat.

# CHAPTER 18

ig Belle put her hands on her hips and fumed, "So that's where they hid ya! I was wonderin' where ya went."

Clint pleaded with his eyes while frantically gesturing with his head, prompting Belle to say, "I guess ya need some breathin' room." She reached over and pulled the gag from his mouth. "Shut the door, quick!" Clint croaked.

Belle frowned, but closed the door. She surveyed his condition before muttering, "They sure got ya trussed up. What'n hell'd ya do ta make 'em so mad?"

"I'd be glad to tell you," Clint replied while swiveling his lower jaw, "but first, could you untie me?"

Belle pondered the request, then pulled up a dusty chair and declared, "I ain't in no hurry. Tell me your story, an' then I'll decide whether ta untie ya or turn off the light and lock the door."

Clint sucked in a deep breath and began. After listening for a few minutes, Belle leaned forward and pointedly asked, "You mean ta tell me that they're selling young girls up on the top floor?"

Clint nodded vigorously. "I've been up there and seen it myself. That's where I got all these bruises on my face. They caught me last time and almost beat me to death. And they're gonna be back any time now to finish what they started if you don't help me. And it won't be good for you if they find you here."

That got Belle's attention. She lurched out of the chair and started fumbling with the ropes, while grumbling, "All the time Cortland's tellin' me I'm gettin' too old ta work, and he's got little girls up there! How sick c'n ya get." She gave a hard tug and grunted, "There!"

Clint's arms jerked forward. He winced while rubbing his wrists then undid the ropes around his legs. He searched the room for a weapon but could find only a spindly leg from a broken chair. He'd need something stouter than that. He also needed Belle out of the doorway. "Belle," he advised, "you'd be wise to get out of here before they come back."

Belle plopped down on the chair in front of the door and, to Clint's horror, began to sniffle. "I ain't got nowhere ta go, and no money," she whimpered. "They just kicked me out. Six years workin' here every day, and they just dump me like yesterday's garbage. Forty years old and now nobody wants me."

Clint saw the tears glistening in her eyes. He stepped forward and patted her thick, rounded shoulder. "You're a good woman, Belle. You just did something that will save lives, and I'll always be thankful to you for it." He hesitated, then leaned down and kissed her cheek.

Belle's lower lip began to tremble and she wailed, "That's the first time I been kissed in years." She buried her face in her pudgy pink hands and began to weep. Clint rolled his eyes and stared anxiously at the door, but there was no way he could squeeze past Belle's prodigious form. He sighed heavily and put an arm around her. She responded by hugging him so fiercely he feared his ribs might crack again.

Near hysteria himself, Clint used every ounce of strength to pry Belle's heavy arms away. She swatted at the tears on her face and said, "Thanks. I needed that. Sometimes a girl just needs a good cry."

Clint bent down, trying to control the panic that increased by the second, and said, "I have to go now, Belle. To save my friend upstairs."

Belle nodded. "Go get 'em." She pushed herself up and Clint slipped past, poked his head into the hall, then hurried out the back door past two middle aged prostitutes and retrieved his club. Belle, now fully recovered, stood in the doorway of the room and whispered as he hurried past, "Be careful."

He stopped at the door to the front parlor and sucked in a deep breath. It was dusk already. Soon, Hobbs and his thugs would be coming for him. Clint guessed he had a half-hour to get Hanna out—plenty of time, if things went right.

ooooo

Outside the back door of the Dumas, the two prostitutes argued. The taller girl, Dana, shook her head and said, "We should stay out of it, I tell ya."

But Rita, her hair dyed fiery red to make her look younger, countered, "They said to watch out for that kid. There's two bucks in it for us if we tell. We might even get put up front again with the younger girls." Dana's reluctance dissipated at those words, and they both rushed inside to alert the boss. As they hurried down the hallway, Rita pulled Dana back and said, "Just remember, it was my idea, so I get to do all the talking." Up ahead a door cracked open.

ooooo

Clint poked his head into the parlor. Two girls were sitting on the laps of two men in suits, giggling while they teased their clients. He slipped forward and tiptoed up the first flight of stairs. But when he peeked into the hallway on the second floor, he pulled back. A man and a woman were leaning against the wall in an ardent embrace. As he stood at the top step, uncertain of his next move, the sound of giggling below came closer. The girls were bringing their clients upstairs! He leaped over the railing, and grasping a spoke, dangled out of sight behind the stairwell while the two couples, laughing and jostling, slowly climbed the stairway.

In a private room off the first floor, Hobbs peered out the window, then turned to the dark-haired man sitting across from him and said, "It's almost dark. Activity's picked up. Let's get rid of that kid."

A door opened below Clint's feet. He glanced down, and his eyes bugged out when Hobbs and the dark-haired guy stepped into the hall, but they quickly passed through the doorway leading to the back hallway. Clint vaulted onto the balcony and tore past the startled couples.

Hobbs snickered at the sound of squeaking bedsprings and frantic grunts while he unlocked the door. He turned the light switch and stared in disbelief, finally muttering, "What the..." Dana and Rita, eyes blinking, lay hogtied on the bed.

Up on the third floor, Clint slowly turned the doorknob and eased the door open. Six young girls sat on the chairs and sofa—a few mumbling to themselves, while others stared blankly ahead. He scanned their faces, but didn't see Hanna. As he stepped forward, a scraping sound came from behind, and he instinctively ducked. The lead-filled blackjack missed his head, but thudded against his shoulder, sending him sprawling.

He scampered away and turned to face his attacker. The blond-haired man who'd worked him over last time waved the blackjack menacingly above his head and taunted, "Ya didn't learn yer lesson last time, didja?"

Clint lunged for his club, but jumped back an instant before the blackjack whizzed by. The blond man stepped over the coffee table and grabbed the club. "This'll do just fine," he said with an air of triumph. "Now I won't hafta chase ya around the room."

Clint's eyes darted to the coffee table behind the man's knees. He charged forward, catching the surprised man in the midsection with his shoulder. The man pitched backwards over the table and landed hard, with Clint on top of him. But the man was an experienced street fighter and rammed a knee up, just missing Clint's groin.

Clint straddled his attacker and grabbed his wrists. Both men put every ounce of strength behind their bulging muscles. The blond man's arms slowly edged towards the floor. With a loud grunt he wrenched his right arm loose and swung the blackjack, but Clint's head shot forward and smacked the man's forehead. His eyes rolled to the top of his head, and the blackjack clattered onto the floor. Clint grabbed for it, but a voice behind him warned, "Don't move!"

Clint turned and stared into the bore of a large caliber pistol in Hobb's hand. "Tie him up, Roy," he ordered the dark-haired man. "And make sure ya cinch it good this time." Hobb's demeanor lightened and he said, "Look, kid, nobody's out ta hurt ya. Ya kin get outta this without a scratch. I got orders ta take ya down ta the rail yards and put ya on a train. You mind yer Ps an Qs and there won't be no rough stuff this time."

Clint knew it was a lie, but he allowed his body to go limp while his arms were yanked behind him. Holding his head, the blond man staggered to his feet and lunged at Clint, but Hobbs stopped him with an outstretched arm and said. "Leave the boy alone, Burns."

"He ain't no boy," Burns muttered, gingerly touching the egg-sized bump on his forehead. "He's dangerous, I tell ya."

Clint winced as the ropes were cinched tight around his already-raw wrists. Hobbs waved the pistol at him and said, "Come on, tough guy. We're going for a ride." As the men slowly descended the stairway past clients and giggling girls, Hobbs hid the pistol under his jacket, but kept the barrel rammed hard against Clint's back.

ooooo

The huge bald man saw them coming and jerked the front door open. Hobbs stopped at the door said, "We got everything under control here, Curly. Tell the boss we're gonna take care of the problem." Curly scowled and nodded as Hobbs pushed Clint outside. Hobbs looked around and said, "Roy, go get the car, and make it quick."

Clint's heart thumped furiously against his chest as the terrifying thought crept into his mind—it was finally over. Escape was impossible. Powerful hands held his arms tight, and there was a gun pressed against his back. So this was what it was like to die. He reminded himself to not cry when the end came.

Sensing Clint's fear, Hobbs smirked and said, "Well, kid, you're not so…" His words were cut off by the sudden pressure of a gun barrel jammed hard into his back. "Don't move," came the order from behind. "Drop the gun."

Hobbs' voice was low, measured, "Look, mister…"

"Do it, or I'll kill you where you stand!" Hobbs opened his hand and the gun clattered onto the sidewalk.

A black car roared up and skidded to a halt. Inside, Roy glanced at the cluster of men, and spotted the rifle. He threw open the door and jumped out. A rifle butt swung in a tight, vicious arc that caught him flush on the cheek. He dropped like a sack of potatoes.

Clint stared in open-mouthed shock at his rescuer. "You okay, son?" Henry Crenshaw asked as he kept a wary eye on the three hoodlums.

"I…uh…yes!" Clint stammered as he pulled away from Burns. "How…how…"

Henry Crenshaw explained, "Ann told me everything when I got back home. I've been looking everywhere trying to find you. I finally sat across from the back door of the Dumas. I saw you when you ran out and grabbed that stick."

"Look," Hobbs said with a smile, "we don't want no trouble. The kid was raisin' a ruckus. We was just gonna put him on a train and…"

"Liar!" Clint yelled. "I heard you talking to that cop. You were gonna throw me in front of that train."

A car screeched to a halt in the middle of the street, and the driver called out, "What's going on over there?"

While Henry Crenshaw was distracted, Hobbs slowly slipped a hand to his back pants pocket and pulled out a single shot .44 derringer. Clint saw the glint of steel in Hobbs' hand and delivered a tremendous kick to the man's groin. Hobbs screamed and collapsed, sending the derringer skittering across the sidewalk.

Henry Crenshaw glanced wide-eyed at the derringer then yelled at the driver, "Call the cops, quick!"

Clint rammed his shoulder into Burns's chest and ordered, "Untie me!" The man nervously jerked at the knots until Clint's hands pulled free. Hobbs was still writhing in agony when Clint grabbed his collar and dragged him to his knees. "Where's Hanna?" he demanded. "She wasn't with those other girls. Where is she?"

Hobbs groaned, "I, I don't know no Hanna." Clint slammed him onto the sidewalk and kicked at his groin again. Hobbs screamed, "I don't know no Hanna! I swear! I don't know nobody by that name."

Clint grabbed his hair and yelled, "She was the girl you bought from John Higgins. Where is she?"

Hobbs squeezed his eyes shut and shook his head, so Clint kick him again and again. "Stop!" Hobbs screamed. "It wasn't my fault!"

Clint grabbed a fistful of hair and yanked the blubbering man to his knees. "What wasn't your fault?"

As a siren wailed in the distance, Hobbs gasped, "She's…she's dead. She killed herself last night. Jumped out the top floor."

Clint stumbled backwards. "No," came his stunned reply. Then he turned his face to the heavens, raised his fists and bellowed, "*Nooo!*"

ooooo

Curly, pistol in hand at the front door, hesitated at the sound of the police sirens. The boss's instructions had been specific: Any sign of the cops, take the money out of the safe in the side room and get it out of the building. He lumbered into the side room and turned the switch, but the light didn't go on.

Curly shook his head at the inconvenience, but there was still enough light from the hallway to see the dial on the safe. He turned the dial left to six, right to twelve, left to eight. He yanked the door open and scooped up several stacks of five and ten dollar bills, plus a large stack of twenty's and a heavy bag of silver dollars.

He threw the money into a large metal cash box and started out of the room, but a shuffling noise in a dark corner to the right of the door stopped him. The last thing he saw was a pudgy pink fist.

ooooo

The police asked Clint and Henry Crenshaw to stay overnight in Butte to answer any further questions that might arise, and to identify the dead girl. They learned in the morning that the owner of the Dumas wasn't charged, though Officer Farrel was released from the police force. That was the extent of the prosecution. The saving grace was that the six young girls, found to be doped on opium, were taken in by nuns from the Catholic Church.

Clint was then taken to the morgue. When the cart was wheeled into the room, he became light-headed and stumbled. Henry Crenshaw slipped an arm around his waist and asked, "You sure you want to do this, son?"

Clint nodded and sucked in several ragged breaths. A somber-faced man in a white coat slipped the sheet from the corpse's head. Her face was chalk-white, but she didn't look dead—more like she was in peaceful sleep. He slowly became aware that the attendant was asking him a question. Nodding numbly, he whispered, "That's her. Her name is Hanna Fortine."

ooooo

On the drive back to Deer Lodge, an ashen-faced Clint Henley stared out the window of the old Model T Ford. Henry finally cleared his throat and said, "I'm sorry about Hanna, but son, what you did back there saved the lives of those other six little girls."

Clint remained silent. Henry glanced over and added with a frown, "You can't beat yourself for this. Those guys back there were responsible for the death of that girl. You did everything you could to save her."

Clint's voice was devoid of emotion. "It seems everything I touch dies. My father. My mother. My friends. Strangers."

"Oh, now wait a minute," Henry protested.

"No," Clint continued, "I don't mean to make everything turn out bad, but it seems to follow me wherever I go."

Henry Crenshaw turned off the county road onto his driveway and said, "Now you listen here, young man. Ann told me all about you. The way you got thrown into the meat grinder as a kid. Most kids woulda never made it past that orphanage, let alone that German monster. And the way you…"

Henry Crenshaw peered ahead, spotted Doc Hastings' motor car parked in front of the house and stomped on the gas pedal. The Ford skidded to a halt, and Henry Crenshaw jumped out and bounded up the steps.

Clint started to follow, but Jonathan came out the front door. Hello, Cl-lint," Jonathan said, his eyes bright, searching. "Where's Hanna?"

Clint gulped hard, fighting back tears. He put his arm around the boy's shoulder, and they walked over by the garden. Jonathan looked up and asked in an anxious voice, "Whew's Hanna?"

Clint fell to his knees, hugged the frail little body and sobbed, "I got there too late, Jonathan. Hanna's not coming home. She died. I'm so sorry."

Clint felt a small hand pat him on the top of the head. "That's okay, Cl-lint. Hanna is in heaven now."

Clint held the boy at arm's length and asked, "Who told you about Hanna being in heaven?"

Jonathan said enthusiastically, "My new momma, Mrs. Cr-renshaw. She says all God's chil-dren go to heaven."

Clint smiled through his tears. "And why do you call Mrs. Crenshaw your new Momma."

Jonathan beamed. "She said to!"

A grim-faced Doc Hastings met Clint on the porch and said, "Ann wants to see you."

Clint searched the man's eyes and asked, "How is she?"

Doc Hastings looked away and frowned. "Not good. Her lungs are filling up with water and blood. So far, I haven't been able to stop it."

He saw the alarm in Clint's eyes and raised his hands. "Now don't jump to conclusions. She's very sick, but there's still hope. There's new things they're finding out every day about tuberculosis."

Inside, Henry Crenshaw stood at the sink—head down, shoulders sagging—as Julia stood by his side with her arm around his waist. Clint padded across the floor to Ann's bedroom. When he opened the door, camphor oil assaulted his nostrils. He hesitated, fighting the urge to flee from that familiar stench of impending death. He sucked in a deep breath and stepped into the room. "Hi," he said in a low voice as he sat beside Ann and took her hand.

A slow smile came to her face, and she whispered, "My hero."

Clint shook his head and muttered, "Some hero."

Ann said, "My dad told me how you handled yourself back there. He was so proud of you." She ran her hand over his cheek. "I'm sorry about Hanna."

He lowered his eyes and nodded.

Ann smiled weakly. "My mom has taken quite a shine to Jonathan. She's already talking about adopting him. He's such a sweet boy." She threw her hand to her mouth and coughed hard into a rag, the supply of handkerchiefs having been expended.

Clint cautioned, "Maybe you shouldn't talk so much."

Ann waved away his concern as she gasped for breath. "We have to talk."

Clint smiled and said, "About us, I hope."

But Ann wasn't smiling. "You have to go back," she wheezed.

"Back where?"

"To your home in New York."

"No!" Clint erupted, jumping to his feet.

Ann sucked in several slow, labored breaths before completing her statement. "For your sister."

Clint shook both fists and hissed, "They disowned me! Not once, but twice."

"Not your sister," came Ann's measured reply.

He shook his head slowly, morosely. "You don't understand."

"Tell me." Ann's voice was barely above a whisper.

Clint paced the room, wringing his hands. Ann beckoned him back with outstretched arms. He sank into her embrace. "Tell me," came her weak request again.

Clint struggled to keep his emotions under control. He sucked in a ragged breath and said, "My mother's last request was for me to take care of my sister, and I didn't do it. I don't know what I'll find back there. It seems everything I touch dies."

Ann's breathless reply came, "I'm not going to die."

Clint almost believed her. He sat back and said, "I, I don't think I could handle it, after losing Hanna, to find my sister hurt or dead." He rubbed his eyes with his palms and repeated. "I just don't think I could handle it right now."

Ann struggled to bring a hand up to caress his face. "Go find your sister. You'll never forgive yourself if you don't at least try."

She turned away and began to cough, and this time Clint saw the blood. He stood, wide-eyed and trembling then ran to the door. "Doc Hastings! Come quick!"

# CHAPTER 19

Ultimately, it was Ann's illness that changed Clint's mind. Watching Doc Hastings hover over her convulsing body, he was gripped by the panicked urge to flee—to run far away from what the camphor oil told him. Even if it took him to another hell. He walked up to Julia and Henry Crenshaw and informed them, "I'm going back to New York to find my sister."

"But you've been through so much," Julia protested. "You should..."

"Ann wants me to."

Julia paused, then nodded and whisked by him. "I'll make some sandwiches."

While Julia hurried around the kitchen, Henry Crenshaw cleared his throat and said, "There's a place for you and your sister back here." Clint stared at the floor, eyebrows furrowed, and nodded. Julia shoved three hastily-made sandwiches into his hands. He kissed her cheek and went outside, where Jonathan sat forlornly on the porch swing.

Clint put his arm around the boy and explained about his sister, and Ann's request. He read Jonathan's searching eyes and assured him, "I'll be back, I promise."

Through his sadness, Jonathan managed a smile and said, "I know you will. You always keep you-r pr-romises."

He wrapped Jonathan in a big bear hug, kissed his cheek, and started down the porch steps. Doc Hastings stomped out of the house and called, "You're either the bravest young man in the world or the craziest." The doctor clamored down the steps. "Here, take this." He handed Clint six five-dollar bills. Clint opened his mouth to protest, but Doc Hastings grabbed Clint's hand and shoved the bills into it. "Hush now!" he ordered. "You can't hobo your sister back here. This'll put both of you in a train seat."

Doc Hastings jammed a hand into his pocket and brought out a folding knife. "Here, take this," he said while shoving the knife into Clint's shirt pocket. "God knows what you're gonna run into riding the rails all the way back to New York."

Clint walked swiftly from the Crenshaw house for a few minutes, then turned back for one last look, shielding his eyes from the sun as he squinted to identify the people on the porch. Julia Crenshaw sat on the swing with her arm around Jonathan, as Henry Crenshaw joined them.

ooooo

He'd learned a lot about railroads in the past three years. At the larger depots, he studied the train maps and schedules, making sure the train he hopped was going in the right direction. Only once did he make a mistake—when he took the famous City of New Orleans train as it left Chicago headed east, but the train soon veered south. He realized his error within a few minutes and got off at the first stop.

Still, there were no efficient cross-country rail routes east of Chicago, with most trains stopping a dozen or more times between destinations. He lost count of the times he had to jump from the trains as they pulled into depots. It had taken five very long days to cross the country. This time, when the train jolted to a halt in a rail yard full of gondola cars brimming with coal, he knew he was in Scranton, Pennsylvania.

At eleven o'clock on the morning of August 18, 1931, Clint's shoes kicked up dust as he walked down the dirt road on the outskirts of Windsor, New York. With a twinge of sadness, he thought back to the exuberance he'd felt as a child just a few years ago when the town had come into view.

Bitterness enveloped him now as he recalled the changes—the cruelty, the suffering, and the death—that had ravaged his life since then. A rage, deep and hot, rose from within, and he could think of nothing but vengeance. He grabbed a heavy oak limb, angrily broke it off at five feet, and tested it with three hard whacks against a tree trunk. It would do. This time, a boy would not be pounding on the door.

But there was no door to pound on. Clint stood open-mouthed in front of the empty house. Its door was missing, along with the front porch swing, the ornate leaded glass from the upper halves of the front windows and most of the boards from the front steps. The corrals were empty and the barn door wide open. The place looked as if it had not been lived in for years.

He climbed onto the porch and carefully stepped inside where the kitchen had once been. Only the old table and a single chair remained, left behind because both were stained by a dark, crusted liquid. Clint slowly walked through the house, noting a broken lamp in one room, bed springs left behind in another.

A sense of foreboding crept into his consciousness as he wandered through the gutted house. Where was everyone? Most importantly, where was Henrietta?

He jumped the sagging corral fence and walked across the pasture, overgrown now with lush grass because there were no cows to eat it down. He pounded hard on the front door of his neighbor's old farmhouse until dust puffed out of the cracks. "Hold on out there before ya break the door down!" came an angry reply from within. Charlie Dawkins threw open the door and stared at the young stranger. "You want something?" he asked warily.

Clint offered his hand and said, "Hello, Mr. Dawkins. I'm Clint, uh, Bartholomew Henley."

"Oh, the heck!" Dawkins exclaimed. "You was just a pup last time I seen ya. You sure have growed up, boy." Dawkins stepped back and said, "Come in, come in."

Clint stepped inside to find Mrs. Dawkins hastily wiping her hands in her apron. "Well, what a pleasant surprise," she said, smiling nervously, and pulled out a chair at the kitchen table between two wide-eyed children. She produced a steaming cup of coffee and began rummaging around. "I'll find something for you to eat."

Clint noticed that the children's bowls had very little in them, though they continued to scrape with their spoons at the fragments of grain that stuck to the sides. "No, thank you. I've already had breakfast."

Charlie Dawkins cleared his throat and asked, "What brings you back here, Bartholomew?"

Clint frowned and pointed out the window toward the vacant house. "What's all that about? Where's my family?"

Charlie Dawkins' face went grim, and he cast a troubled glance at his wife. "You don't know?"

"Know what?" There was an impatient tone in his voice.

Charlie Dawkins sighed heavily and said, "After you and your sister went back to England to live with your relatives, things got bad over there, what with the depression and all. Albert lost all his money in the stock market crash, and the bank repossessed the farm." Charlie Dawkins glanced out the window. "Your father killed himself just before they came to throw him off the place."

Clint nodded and was pensive for a moment, then asked, "And my sister?"

Mrs. Dawkins gave her husband a worried glance and stepped forward. "We were told she went back to England with you."

Clint shook his head, restraining the anger and anxiety he was feeling, and tersely replied, "I was sent to an orphanage in Chicago."

Mrs. Dawkins threw her hands to her mouth and gasped, "Mercy! We were told you and Henrietta went back to the old country."

Clint shook his head. "I don't know what happened to my sister, but I'm here to find out."

Mrs. Dawkins' eyes narrowed, and her voice dripped with disgust. "You might begin with that...that woman."

Clint knew who she meant. He took a deep breath to calm his emotions then asked, "Where is she?"

"She was a bad one, that one," Mrs. Dawkins said while crossing her arms. "We weren't welcome with her over there."

Charlie Dawkins scratched the stubble on his cheek and said, "Last I heard, Maura was hanging out with that no good Dick Woods at the North Branch Saloon outside Windsor."

Clint rose to his feet and said, "I'd best be going now." He turned at the door and stuffed a five dollar bill in Charlie Dawkins' pocket. Dawkins started to protest, but Clint opened the door and walked away. "God bless you!" came Mrs. Dawkins' distant reply.

Clint shook his head at his stupidity. Giving away a five dollar bill! He'd tucked away two ten-dollar bills after a clerk at a depot in Fargo had informed him that train fare for two from New York to Montana would be about twenty dollars. He'd been living sparsely on the trip east, spending every penny shrewdly. And now he'd just given away his next to last dollar. That left him with just one dollar and eighty-seven cents for food.

ooooo

The North Branch Saloon was located in a shabby two-story wood frame building with a false front that listed more every year as the timbers underneath rotted away. The second floor held rooms for rent—by the month, day or hour. No questions asked.

The saloon occupied half of the first floor, with a boarded-up barber shop and beauty parlor splitting the rest. A long, ornate oak bar ran the length of the saloon. In better times, it was hard to find elbow room at the bar. Now, it was empty. Through a side door was a small kitchen to serve the half dozen tables opposite the bar.

Clint peeked through a window and saw the bartender idly wiping glasses behind the bar, while two men sat disconsolately at a table playing cards. Clint recognized Dick Woods, a thin, ferret-faced man well-known as a card shark who fleeced businessmen traveling between New York City and the tri-cities of Binghamton, Endicott, and Johnson City. Woods threw down his cards and barked, "Maura, where's that sandwich!"

Clint's nostrils flared when Maura, looking disheveled and haggard, shuffled out of the kitchen and sent the plate and sandwich clattering across the table. "You watch your manners, woman!" Dick Woods warned. Maura threw him a withering glare and stomped back to the kitchen.

Clint moved around to the back door. A slight trembling came to his hands as he nervously opened the pocket knife. Turgid emotions of despair, rage, and impatience crept into his mind. What did he intend to do? Cut her throat? Beat her senseless? Make her hurt, like she'd hurt him?

As he pondered his next move, footfalls inside the building staggered toward the back door. He slipped behind a pile of firewood seconds before Maura struggled outside carrying a large pot, which she threw onto the ground, sending a greasy brown liquid oozing across the dirt. As she bent over to tip the pot upside down, a hand clamped onto her neck. "Aaigh!" she gurgled, intending to scream, but the powerful hand squeezed her windpipe.

A furious voice whispered into her ear, "You scream, and I'll snap your neck!"

She froze, and the hand eased somewhat, but still kept her bent over. "Where is Henrietta Henley?"

"I don't know!"

The hand squeezed the bones in her neck until they grated, sending a jolt of pain and fear through her. "Aargh!" she gasped when the hand eased a bit.

"You know!" came the accusation. "Tell me where she is or I'll snap your neck like a match stick!" To emphasize that point, the hand on her neck squeezed again for a second before relaxing.

"Aaigh! She ain't around here no more!"

"Where is she?"

"Owww! She's, she got sent to an orphanage."

"Where?"

"Ah, aagh! Syracuse!"

"Where in Syracuse?"

"Uh, ooh! The New York State Girls Home."

Clint jerked his hand back, as if discarding something unclean, and Maura pitched forward into the brown sludge. She rolled over in the slimy mess and rubbed her neck before daring to look at her antagonist. At first, she didn't recognize the man who slowly backed away from her, but when he turned, her eyes widened. She staggered to her feet and stumbled inside, intending to alert Dick Woods, but his voice boomed from the other room, "Hey! You dead back there? We need another sandwich!"

"Shuddup!" she screamed and hacked viciously at a loaf of bread.

ooooo

The train followed the banks of the Chenango River north to the hamlet of Greene, then followed a large stream through country Clint had never seen. Five hours later, he washed his hands and face in a creek that coursed through a woodlot bordering the New York State Girls Home and did his best to comb his shaggy hair with his fingers. He pounded the dust from his clothes and hoped he presented a clean-cut appearance.

A large black wrought-iron gate protested loudly when he pushed it open. The grounds were neat and clean, with tidy little flower beds here and there among billowing beech and oak trees. He walked up to a large brick building and climbed the stone steps. Inside the building was a large entryway. A sign above a room on the right read: "Office. All visitors must sign in."

Clint walked in and smiled at a dour-looking woman peering suspiciously at him over her reading glasses. "Yes?" It was more a challenge than a question.

He nervously rolled his felt hat in his hands and said, "I'm here to see my sister, Henrietta Henley."

"Do you have any identification?" the woman asked and folded her arms, waiting.

He blinked. Identification? A piece of paper that said who he was? Ignoring the knot in the pit of his stomach, he managed a weak smile and spread his arms. "Look, mam, I'm her brother. I came a long way to get here. All I want to do is see her and say hello. Then I'll leave."

The woman eyed him coldly and sniffed, "Without proper identification, I cannot release any information about our residents. Now, if you'll excuse me, I have work to do. Close the door when you leave."

Clint leaned forward and slammed a hand on the desk. The woman shrieked and jumped away from the desk. He sucked in a deep breath and raised both hands in a conciliatory gesture. "Look, lady, I know my sister is here. Just let me see her."

The woman pressed a button on the wall, and a buzzer sounded in the entryway. "That's the guard's alarm," she said in a loud, frightened voice. "You have ten seconds to get out of here, or I'll have the guard arrest you for threatening me."

The last thing he needed was trouble with the law. Clint slowly backed away and said, "I'm sorry, ma'am. I didn't mean to scare you. I'll leave." He hurried out of the building and ran into the woodlot, just in case the cops showed up.

He stopped at a small store he'd walked past earlier on his way to the Girls Home and spent thirteen cents on two tins of sardines and a package of crackers. He walked back to an overgrown homestead and sat under an ancient apple tree before devouring the sardines and crackers, plus a dozen wormy apples. And then he rested. It was going to be a long night.

His impatience grew until he could stand it no longer. Dusk had barely settled upon the Girls Home when he climbed over the stone wall and trotted across the lawn to the administration building. He'd noticed that the large window in the office was not locked. He stared in the gathering gloom at the window about seven feet above the ground. With any luck that shrew of a woman wouldn't bother to lock a window that far off the ground.

He found a garbage can behind the building and placed it under the window before carefully climbing onto the lid, wincing when the lid creaked loudly. The window had a ledge of sandstone almost a foot wide, and he had no trouble climbing onto it. He placed his hands on the wood frame at the top of the lower window pane and pushed up. It didn't budge, so he pushed harder. Nothing. He pressed his nose to the glass and a small moan escaped from his throat. The window's thumb lock was turned closed.

He leaned his forehead against the glass and sighed. If he broke the window glass, someone would surely hear it and come running. He pressed his face to the glass and pushed up on the window frame. The lock held, but it jiggled a bit when the window settled back down.

He opened the pocket knife and slipped the blade up between the top wood frame of the lower window and the bottom wood frame of the stationary upper window. The knife blade caught the edge of the thumb lock and bit into the brass. He exerted pressure and the lock turned until the blade slipped off. Twice more, he was able to move the brass knob, until it had turned as far as possible from the sideways pressure of the knife.

But it still lacked a quarter inch of clearing the catch that held it. Beside himself with frustration, Clint grabbed the lower window and exerted every ounce of strength, window be damned! His arm muscles screamed in protest and began to violently tremble, causing the old window to rattle, which nudged the thumb lock a fraction of an inch more. The window flew open with a loud bang. He looked around to make sure no one had seen or heard him then climbed inside.

He pulled open the file drawer behind the desk, but it was too dark to read the files. Dreading his next move, he turned the knob beside the door. The globe in the ceiling sent a blinding light into his eyes. He hurried over and scanned through the open file drawer, but it ended with the name: Finley.

He slammed it shut and pulled open the next drawer. He found a file titled: Helman. The next file had to be...He bent forward and scrutinized the name: Holland. Where was Henley? He scanned through the names on either side, hoping the file might have been misplaced. Nothing.

Clint stepped back then tore open the third file draw, but it ended with a file titled: Zygnew. He rolled his head back and let out a loud sigh of frustration. There was no file in the cabinet for Henley.

Then a thought hit him. Maybe they used her first name. He pulled open the second drawer again but found no file titled: Henrietta. He even checked for a file titled: Hen. He closed the file draw, anxious to leave the office before someone noticed the light. He stopped. Something in his subconscious screamed at him to look again at the files under the letter H. Frowning, he pawed through them, hesitated, then grabbed a file labeled: Homes.

The file held eight pages—each holding the names of about twenty girls located in a home elsewhere. He leaned close, silently mouthing the names as his finger ran through page after page. Suddenly, his finger stopped and a great whoosh of air escaped from his lungs. He slapped the file shut and replaced it in the file cabinet before turning off the light and scrambling out the window.

ooooo

She hated her breasts. They weren't much bigger than mosquito bites, but they'd already gotten Henrietta Henley in trouble here at the Endicott-Johnson Shoe Factory where she worked with sixteen other girls from the Binghamton Girls Home in exchange for reject shoes. Why couldn't she be like her friend, Cindy, who was flat-chested and blessedly ignored?

She'd jumped at the chance last month to get away from the drudgery at the Girls Home in Syracuse, where she'd worked in the laundry room from dawn to dusk six days each week for the past two years. She even ate a little better at the Binghamton Girls Home, thanks to a few local women who sent over extra food. It would have been a good way to pass the next two years until she was released. But six months ago, she'd lost all her baby fat, and her breasts had begun to develop.

At first, she'd been flattered when Mr. Shakson, a short, rotund, balding floor supervisor, had chosen her to be the cleaning girl in his busy department where twenty-five women operated large cutting, sewing, and binding machines that produced ankle-high leather boots. Mr. Shakson was helpful and never yelled at her. He even gave her little presents—a stick of candy or a sandwich when no one was watching.

Then Mr. Shakson started pestering her. It had begun with innocent pats on the shoulder and compliments about her good work. It progressed to short hugs then long ones. At first, it confused her, since most grown-ups treated the girls like slaves.

Yesterday, while the other women were outside having lunch, Mr. Shakson put his arm around her and announced that he would like to train her on a shoe machine. She was thrilled to run the huge machine and watched, mesmerized, as the gleaming needle pushed the heavy cord effortlessly through the thick leather.

She hadn't been alarmed when his belly pressed against her back and his hands slipped around her waist as he instructed her to push this button then turn that dial. But his arms always seemed to rest against her breasts. At first, she nervously discounted what was happening as an accident, but as the workers entered the building after lunch, those pudgy hands had grabbed her breasts, squeezing them until they hurt.

As the morning wore on, she kept her head down, busying herself on the opposite side of the room, glancing away whenever Mr. Shakson passed by. The noon dinner bell clanged, and the girls rushed outside to catch some fresh air away from the heat of the machines and the pungent acid smell of freshly-tanned leather. Mr. Shakson stepped out of his office, took a quick look around, then called, "Come over here and wash the floor in my office, Henrietta."

She resignedly dropped to her knees in front of him and began scrubbing the floor as hard as she could. Mr. Shakson sat in a chair, peering at her over a sheet of paper. Sweat glistened on his forehead, and he licked his lips while his beady eyes devoured her. His chair had just begun squeaking its way toward her when a secretary hustled through the sewing room and rapped on Shakson's office glass. "Mr. Carlson wants you upstairs to go over the monthly totals."

Shakson replied irritably, "Can't it wait? I still have some figures to go over."

The woman shook her head. "He's got the other floor supervisors up there right now. He wants the monthly totals sent to Mr. Johnson by quitting time." Shakson sighed heavily, glanced wistfully at Hen, and waddled out the door behind the secretary.

Hen threw the wet rag onto the floor and aimlessly scrubbed. It was useless to complain. One of the other girls had accused her supervisor of slapping her, and she'd been sent back to Syracuse.

That wasn't going to happen to her. If Mr. Shakson grabbed her again, she'd run away.

She stiffened at the sound of a man's heavy footfalls thudding on the floor behind her. They advanced slowly, paused for a few seconds, then moved toward her. She tried to ignore whoever it was, but he stood right in front of her. The shoes caught her attention. Unlike the other bosses, who always wore new shoes furnished free from the company, these shoes were worn and dusty.

A soft voice said, "Hen." She froze. That voice! A surge of confusing emotions and fragmented memories flashed through her mind. Her heart beat furiously as she slowly raised her head. In front of her stood a powerfully-built young man in a floppy felt hat. He slowly stooped down, and a loving smile spread across his face. And then the queerest thing happened. A single tear ran down his cheek and splashed onto the floor.

A loud gasp escaped from her throat, and her hands flew up to her mouth. He reached a hand out to her. "Hen, it's me, Clint, uh, Bartholomew."

"Oh my god!" she blurted then fell into her brother's arms. He held his sister, gently rocking her back and forth. "How did you find me?" she sobbed.

Stroking her hair, he whispered, "It's a long story, Hen."

"Did Poppa send you for me?"

Before Clint could answer, he stiffened at the sound of footsteps trudging down the stairs outside the room. Clint pried Hen to arm's length, and there was an intensity in his eyes that startled her. "Right now, we've got to get out of here and on a train before somebody figures out you're missing and calls the cops." With that, he jerked Hen to her feet.

ooooo

Beads of sweat had formed on Shakson's brows and his breath came in short, ragged gasps. His entire body trembled in anticipation. He slowly opened the door, but frowned at the pail and scrub rag on the floor. His beady little pig eyes scoured the room then spied the back door cracked open. The ladies room. She was in the ladies room. He flounced into a chair and waited. And waited.

# CHAPTER 20

*A*fter the boredom and drudgery at the Girls Home, Henrietta stared out the window with a mixture of awe and excitement as the Black Diamond passenger train roared south toward Scranton.

Clint studied his sister. She was no longer a pudgy, little pig-tailed girl. She'd slimmed down, grown taller, and she was filling out. But it was her face that was most remarkable, with high, graceful cheekbones, pale skin, and a mouth seemingly on the verge of a smile at all times. She looked so much like their mother. And like Hanna.

Hen turned, surprised to see her brother staring at her, and asked, "Where are we going, Bar? Won't Poppa let us come back home?"

"Clint," he corrected her with a grin. "My new name is Clint. No, Hen, we're not going back to the farm. I'm taking you to our new home out in Montana."

Hen's jaw dropped, and her eyes opened wide. "Are there really cowboys and Indians out there?"

Clint chuckled and nodded. "Yes, there are still quite a few cowboys, and even some Indians." He became pensive for a moment then asked, "Hen, do you know anything about where I've been, or about Poppa and Maura?"

Hen shook her head and frowned. "After you left, Maura started treating me bad. Even badder than before." She paused and became pensive before continuing. "One night, I had the strangest dream. I dreamed you were downstairs calling me. I got out of bed and started down the stairs, but Maura grabbed me. She was real mad and threw me back in bed. Then Poppa took me to Binghamton and some lady took me to the Girls Home in Syracuse."

She turned her full attention to him. "How was it at that farm they sent you to?"

Clint scoffed, and his words had a bitter edge. "They didn't send me to no farm, Hen." And then he began to talk about the Chicago Boys Orphanage, his escape back to Windsor, how he'd called her name as they dragged him out of the house, and the dreaded return to the orphanage. And of the Orphan Train, the promises he'd made to the three children he'd befriended, how he'd been able to track them down, and that one of them had died.

Sadness flooded his face and his eyes brimmed with tears as he stared at the floor, but he forced a smile and then told her about Montana and the Crenshaw family, and the wonderful mother and father waiting for her, a special big sister named Ann, and a cute little brother named Jonathan.

He was quiet for a few seconds then added, "Its changed me, Hen. I don't have a lot of patience, anymore. And I've developed a bit of a temper."

She stared out the window and asked, "Whatever happened to him?"

Clint knew who she meant. "He's dead."

"And her?"

"She's not living such a great life right now."

Hen straightened her back, crossed her arms and replied firmly, "Good. She was mean."

That evening, Hen discovered what her brother meant about a temper when he erupted at a drunk who was harassing a handsome woman and her daughter across the aisle from them. Clint grabbed the shocked man by his collar and threw him into a backseat, where the man cringed as Clint stood raging over him.

ooooo

The trip had gone much faster than he'd expected. The passenger trains skipped many of those small depots where freights stopped. At eleven o'clock on the morning of their fourth day, the train was chugging south from Helena to Butte.

It had been ten days since he'd left the Crenshaw Ranch. A slow feeling of dread crept over him as the reality sank in—that sometime that evening, he would know. Either he would finally have peace, or he'd be thrown into an emotional tailspin from which he was sure he'd never recover. He squeezed his eyes shut in a vain attempt to drive from his mind that last horrible sight of Ann, coughing blood, with Doc Hastings hovering helplessly over her. And that was ten days ago.

Hen glanced at her brother and was startled to see him trembling, fists clenched, eyes squeezed shut. "What's wrong?" she asked, her voice rising in alarm.

Hen's voice jolted him back to the present. "Oh, uh, nothing's wrong. I was just having a bad dream."

He tried to keep up with Hen's chatter, but his anxiety increased, until he could barely pay enough attention to answer the plethora of questions coming from her.

As the train slowed for the Butte station, Clint was gripped by the impulse to jump off and hop another train and continue on, so he would never know for sure—and he would never have to endure the pain of the loss of a loved one again in his life.

But Hen, bouncing on the seat in her excitement, brought him back. He sighed heavily and said, "Well, Sis. This is as far as the passenger train takes us."

"Really? How do we get to the people on the ranch where we're going to live?"

Clint winked and offered a rueful grin. "Now, you'll see how I usually ride on trains."

Hen shrieked with girlish excitement as she dove, with dress blowing up around her waist, into the slow-moving boxcar. Clint dove in right behind her and quickly pulled her dress down while scanning the dark corners of the car. "We should've hoboed all the way across the country!" she shouted exuberantly, while staring out at the Montana Landscape. Clint grunted, sharing none of her enthusiasm. It had been dangerous enough for him riding the rails alone, let alone with a girl.

The house was just a speck on the horizon when they began walking from the tracks, but it grew—far too fast for him. He slowed down, hoping to delay the inevitable.

Adrenalin scorched through his body, making him light-headed and unresponsive to Hen's prattling. Already, they were at the turnoff from the county road, and now he could see the front door of the farmhouse. It was dinner time. Everyone would be at the table and he would quickly know.

And then he was at the gate, walking faster now with Hen struggling to keep up. His breath came in short gasps, and the color drained from his face as he bounded up the steps and burst through the door.

Julia and Henry Crenshaw were seated across from each other, with Jonathan between them. There were no other plates on the table. He glanced past them to Ann's bedroom. The door was open, the bed empty.

He tried to speak, but only a small wounded groan escaped from his throat. He slowly backed away and would have fled if the strong hands of Henry Crenshaw had not grabbed him.

"No!" he heard Julia Crenshaw call out. "No, Clint. It's not what you think!"

And then Julia was in front of him, grabbing his shirt and laughing. "She's alive!" Julia shrieked. "Ann's alive!"

Clint stood dumbfounded, struggling to understand what he was hearing. It took all three of them grabbing at him and yelling the good news over and over again before it began to sink in. He looked from Julia to Henry, to Jonathan. Shaking his head in wonderment, he stammered, "She's...she's alive?"

"Yes!" Henry Crenshaw's voice boomed joyously while roughly shaking Clint's shoulders. "She's at the Galen State Tuberculosis Hospital just an hour away!"

Julia gushed, "And they think she'll get better." She stepped forward and took Clint's face in her hands. "Clint, she's going to live!"

ooooo

The ward was quiet at midnight, except for the coughing. Ann sat in bed, propped up by four pillows. Since she'd been restricted in her physical activity, she'd become a bookworm—at first, devouring books to escape the boredom, but then relishing the emotional trip a book would take her on.

Now, she shook her head to ward off sleep as the lives of Tom Sawyer and Huckleberry Finn unfolded on the yellowed pages before her. A door down the hall squeaked open. Even as soft footfalls padded her way, her eyes refused to leave the book. Probably the ward nurse, Mrs. Labbey, with her nightly admonishment about staying up too late. With a sigh of resignation, she closed the book and looked up.

As the imposing form of a young man stepped from the shadows, the book fell from her hands and she gasped, "Oooh."

"I'm back," he whispered as she reached out to him.

# CHAPTER 21

*A*nn Crenshaw came home four months later, pale and gaunt, but smiling again and with no cough. The tuberculosis virus had been arrested, though half her lung capacity was lost to scar tissue. Her release was a bit sooner than normal, but it was the only way hospital officials could rid themselves of her boyfriend, who came for a visit and refused to leave.

Ann gained back some weight, though she never regained her robust farm girl physique. Her pale complexion and tall, slim physique made her look, in Clint's opinion, as beautiful as one of those models in a Sears Roebuck catalog. However, the tuberculosis had robbed her of the stamina required for ranch life, and she was forced to watch in embarrassment while Julia and Hen did the hard work.

Ann returned to high school, having acquired a hunger for book learning while bed-ridden at the hospital. Clint felt too old to be going to school, though he occasionally checked in on Tommy Brookings.

Clint also checked in on Gustav Schmidt. One rainy spring afternoon, he stalked, grim-faced, up the timbered draw leading to the sawmill, a club in one hand and a can of coal oil in the other. The place was empty. He stood in the midst of the homestead and studied the skeletal frames of the once-tidy cottage and sawmill. People had scavenged all the windows, doors, siding, steps—just about anything that could be packed away. With

Gustav Schmidt gone, the place was just a quiet timbered draw slowly moldering back to nature. Clint discarded the club and coal oil and walked away.

Hen and Jonathan became inseparable as playmates. When not in school, they could be seen tearing through the cottonwood trees in the creek bottom, whooping and hollering as they played cowboys and Indians, or cops and robbers. Clint was a bit unnerved to see his sister, entering early womanhood, running madly through the trees playing children's games, but Julia reminded him that both Jonathan and Hen had been robbed of their childhood and were just catching up.

To Clint's relief, Hen and Jonathan soon outgrew their childish behavior, but that was replaced by a more troubling concern. Hen and Jonathan had "discovered" each other and were as inseparable as he and Ann had been. With a touch of amusement, Ann sat Clint down at the kitchen table one evening when they were alone and reminded him that Hen and Jonathan were not brother and sister, that their early lives had created a special bond between them, and that he should maybe stay out of it and avoid the mistakes her dad had made with them.

It was during this period that Clint began to exhibit peculiar tendencies, such as stealing children. At least that's what the red-faced sheriff accused him of after the police car skidded to a halt at the Crenshaw house. Yes, Clint admitted, he'd taken the two children from the tarpaper shack south of town. He walked into the barn and returned with a filthy, frightened eight-year-old boy and his six-year-old sister. Clint admonished the sheriff for allowing their well-known drunkard parents to leave the boy and girl alone and hungry for days at a time.

Such quirks earned Clint the reputation around Deer Lodge of being slightly off his rocker, though folks generally held him in affection because of his resolve that, no matter how bad the Depression got, the children would be fed. Ann steadfastly justified his actions, for she knew why he was driven to come home in the middle of the night holding the hand of an abused child, and she loved him all the more for it.

A month after Ann graduated from high school, she and Clint were married. They moved into a small house in Deer Lodge, and Clint took a job as a guard at the prison, while Ann worked part time in the cafeteria. A year later a daughter, named Elizabeth, was born.

It should have been a time of happiness for them, but Ann detected an uneasiness in Clint. Several times she found him gently cradling his baby daughter while staring wistfully out the window. One evening, Ann stood in front of him and asked, "Are you happy with me?"

Clint knew why she was asking, but answered, "Yes, I am."

"Then why are you so sad?"

Through the evening and into the night, they talked. He told her about Spike McKovitch's work saving children in Chicago—the invitation that Spike had made to him, of the sins he'd committed that dogged his thoughts, and of his desire to do something to make things right.

Two days later, Ann put baby Liz down for the night and stood beside Clint as he sat at the kitchen table. "I want to go to Chicago."

Clint looked up, startled, and protested, "Look, Ann, I was just frustrated with this crazy Depression the other night. It's got a lot of people antsy. I was just blowing off steam."

"No, I really want to go."

Clint studied her face. "Why?"

Ann sat next to him and sighed heavily as she took his hand. "I can't keep up with the work at the prison cafeteria anymore. I'm always tired and out of breath."

Clint remained unconvinced. "You're doing this for me, aren't you?"

Ann gathered her thoughts for a few seconds, then replied, "I'm doing this for us. I can't do physical work anymore, but I

don't want to sit around and do nothing for the rest of my life.
I've been reading about Chicago. It's got a great university. I'd like
to go to college there."

Ann and Clint Henley saved their money and kept their peace
until Jonathan and Hen graduated high school and were married.
Then they broke the news that they were moving to Chicago.

ooooo

Clint Henley's atonement began on a sultry July night in 1937
when a cherry red Ford coupe idled to the curb on the corner
of Maxwell and Halstad. George Yustice watched through the
windshield as two frightened young girls walked toward him on
the sidewalk. When the girls drew even with the coupe, Yustice
leaned across the seat and called, "Hey girls, ya wanna…"

The windshield exploded in a shower of broken glass. "What
the…" The words died in his throat. In front of the coupe stood a
powerfully built young man, an axe handle in one hand, a berserk
look in his eyes.

Yes, everyone agrees that it all began that night, though they
differ on a few minor details. The optimists claimed that Yustice
was so frightened he left town that night, while pessimists
retorted that he probably ended up in a vat at a nearby render-
ing plant.

Their first two years in Chicago were Ann and Clint Henley's
best. Ann loved the open air markets of Maxwell Street. She began
working for John Hoffman at the Chicago Orphans Society,
while attending classes at the University of Chicago at night.

Clint and Spike McKovitch cleaned up Maxwell Street and
vicinity. Some pimps grudgingly moved their operations elsewhere, others were strongly persuaded. A few, like George Yustice,
disappeared. Rarely did the police investigate. The result was a
safe street complex for the homeless and runaways to seek refuge
from predation; where food, clothing, and lodging were provided

from donations that John Hoffman obtained from churches and a variety of benevolent organizations.

During the winter of their fourth year, an influenza epidemic hit Chicago. Both Ann and Lizzy caught it. Lizzy recovered. Ann's lungs, scarred from tuberculosis, developed pneumonia. On a cold, blustery day in February 1941, Ann Henley passed away with Clint at her side.

When he emerged from the room, pale and stunned, his only words were, "I killed her." No matter how much his friends, including Julia and Henry Crenshaw, tried to mollify him, Clint Henley was convinced that his beloved wife had been taken from him by God because of something he'd done on a dark rainy night many years ago.

It was little Lizzy who kept him from sinking into a morass of alcohol while the pain was still fresh. And it was Lizzy who began tailing him to Maxwell Street. Stern reprimands, even a spanking, could not dissuade her. He reluctantly gave in and allowed it. And in so doing, Clint and Spike gained a valuable asset, for it was young Lizzy who could quickly gain the trust of a frightened boy or girl who'd been preyed upon by every grown-up they'd known.

With Ann gone, Clint chose celibacy and dedicated his life to the children of the Chicago streets, and to Lizzy. Or so he thought. One day he and Lizzy, now thirteen, were driving along Halstad Street in an old Nash someone had given him. Suddenly, Clint slammed on the brakes and jumped out of the car. Knowing her dad was capable of anything when he got that look in his eye, Lizzy ran after him.

On a street corner stood the object of his ire. A red-haired prostitute Clint knew only by the name of Kitty leaned against a lamp post explaining the rules of the street to a frightened young girl not much older than Liz. "You!" Clint exploded, sending Kitty stumbling backwards at his menacing approach. "You should be ashamed of yourself! You're sentencing this child to death!"

As Lizzy led the frightened girl away, Kitty recovered enough to protest, "Slick Eddie won't be happy about this."

Clint spun around, charged back to her and barked, "You tell Slick Eddie if he don't like it, he can come to Maxwell Street any time and look up Clint Henley." Clint's eyes narrowed to slits. "But you make sure Slick Eddie understands that he won't be coming back."

He turned to walk away but stopped. He wasn't finished having his say. "And you!" he fumed and wagged a finger in her face. "You should be ashamed of yourself. After all you've been through, to bring a little girl down here. You should be ashamed."

Kitty hurried away and told Slick Eddie what had happened. He showed his appreciation by slapping her hard across the face. Kitty continued working as a prostitute, but Clint's outburst had struck her heart, and she spent sleepless nights wrestling with her demons.

A week later, Clint and Spike were talking with John Hoffman about a new "safe house" for runaway children planned next door to his office, when a woman interrupted them. It was Kate Wilson, aka Kitty. Her words were barely above a whisper. "I want to help." She steeled herself for the verbal assault, but none followed.

Kate and Liz hit it off well. Though no one could replace Ann in her life, Kate became a big sister and friend to Liz. It was a welcome relief for Clint, who had difficulty attending to the things young girls like to do. More and more, though, Kate and Clint were seen together.

Of course, Slick Eddie showed up a couple of times on Maxwell Street, driving a white Cadillac and looking for Kate. The first time, the Cadillac left without a windshield. The second time, the car was stored in a lot, windshield intact, until Slick Eddie was released from the hospital.

In 1951, the state of Illinois passed the Child Welfare Law, and the City of Chicago, with John Hoffman at the helm, began to implement a legal system to insure the protection of children. Still, some fell through the cracks. When that happened, Spike and Clint took over. They used an intricate network of lookouts and spies to alert them when authorities were helpless to protect a child.

Though Spike and Clint were inseparable most of the time, occasional incidents grew from their frustrations to protect young people from the skyrocketing rise of crime in Chicago. Like the day when Clint, holding the lifeless body of a twelve-year-old girl in his arms, angrily confronted Spike at the corner of Halstad and Maxwell.

Somehow, they'd missed her. Sick with grief and helpless rage, Clint struck out at his friend. "Where is your God now!" he railed. "What kind of God would allow something like this to happen? If your God is so great, why isn't he down here helping these kids?"

Outraged by the sight of the lifeless girl lolling in Clint's arms and the blasphemy of his friend, Spike screamed back, "He is down here, you idiot!"

"Where?" Clint demanded. "Where is this wonderful God you're always talking about?"

Spike, tears streaming down his face, chest heaving, pointed a crooked finger at the man holding the lifeless child and spoke in a hoarse whisper, "He's right there."

The words stunned Clint; they penetrated his heart, his soul. He sank to his knees and began to weep. Spike pulled himself over and wrapped his arms around his friend and comforted him. It marked a turning point in Clint Henley's life, for Spike's words had sliced through a lifetime of bitterness and finally revealed to him how God worked.

In the spring of 1963, Spike McKovitch's stumps started to fester and bleed. He hid his condition until Clint spotted the blood in the bottom of the wagon. Spike initially allowed Clint to browbeat him into seeing a doctor. Later, he stubbornly refused medical treatment, for he'd grown tired of the pain everywhere he looked. He wanted to go home.

On a cold, drizzly night in late October of 1963, a night suitable only for angels, Clint held his friend in his arms on the corner of Maxwell and Halstad, for that is where Spike wanted to die. Clint wept, not for Spike, but for himself and the city of Chicago.

Spike suddenly bolted upright in his wagon, focused his eyes on the air and spoke with a little boy's eagerness, "Are you here for me?" Then his fevered body sagged into Clint's arms. From that day, Clint Henley prepared himself, spiritually, for he wanted to go where Spike had gone.

In the ensuing years, the knife wounds and bullet holes took their toll on Clint Henley. His once powerful presence became more stooped, and his stride more labored. That is, until he spotted a pink Cadillac cruising down Maxwell Street.

In the end, it was neither gun nor knife, or his sins, but the cold, damp winds blasting off Lake Michigan that drove him to his knees. Clint Henley lay in bed in a lonely hospital room with lungs hopelessly consumed with pneumonia. Liz, tears cascading down her cheeks, held a gnarled hand, while Kate wiped his feverish forehead with a damp cloth.

At times, Clint was conscious and whispered words of encouragement to Liz and Kate. Other times he fell into a stupor, repeating over and over, "Jesus, please forgive me. Jesus, please forgive me."

And then his labored breathing seemed to stop. But before Kate could check for a pulse, Clint Henley's eyes blinked open and he breathed deeply. He raised up on his elbows, eyes focused on the far side of the room, voice childlike with wonder. "Are you here for me?" And then he slowly sank back.

On the night of February 17, 1971, Clint Henley joined Ann and Mugsy, and Spike with two good legs, and Elizabeth Henley, and the little girl he'd held in his arms that rainy night. And yes, his Savior was waiting for him with open arms, for his sins had been washed away.

# EPILOGUE

The night after the funeral, Liz walked in a daze through the streets her father had roamed for more than thirty years. She was unable, unwilling to accept his death. She could still feel his last breath—a long, ragged sigh—on her cheek. In her despair, she thought back to those last hours at the hospital. It should have been a quiet, peaceful time when father and daughter spent their last hours on earth together.

Instead, the scene in the hospital ward had been chaotic, disturbing. The hallway was packed with scores of strangers—people dressed in expensive suits and furs who'd flown in from faraway places, standing beside people in rags, hoping to kiss her father's hand, his cheek.

Already, she noticed, the perversion had begun to seep back into Maxwell Street. A white Cadillac purred past—mocking, insolent—without fear of a sudden windshield explosion. On street corners, shadowy figures stood, with furtive glances just in case the rumors about his death had been exaggerated.

She stumbled against a lamppost at the corner of Maxwell and Halstad. Trembling rippled through her body. She raised her face to heaven and sucked in a ragged breath. "We did nothing!" she screeched, shaking her fist at the black sky. She cupped her hands around her mouth. "Do you hear me, father? It was all for nothing! We solved nothing down here! We accomplished nothing!" She slowly sank to the dirty sidewalk and moaned, "You're dead and already they're back. Now what am I going to do by myself?" Her fury spent, she wept bitterly.

The understanding came later, as strangers spanning two generations came forward when they recognized her face, her name—each with a story of deprivation, then salvation, thanks to a man who smiled only at the children. Finally, she understood how God worked. And she began to prepare herself, spiritually, for she wanted to go where he had gone.

Though barely a hundred pounds, Liz Henley returned to Maxwell Street and fearlessly stood in the gap for the children, just as Spike and her father had done, for the apple had not fallen far from the tree. But sometimes after a bad day at the Juvenile Division of Social Casework, when the legal system had again failed to protect a child, Liz Henley would retreat to her office and wish it could be like the old days, when steel-hard muscle and hot blood wreaked justice with one vicious swing of a scarred old axe handle. And when just the sight of one man made the bad people tremble.

And God help the pimp or pusher who walked down Maxwell Street when her father was there.

273

CPSIA information can be obtained
at www.ICGtesting.com
Printed in the USA
LVOW01s1554150616

492731LV00018B/877/P

9 781633 065215